About Ed

About Ed

ROBERT GLÜCK

nyrb **New York Review Books** New York

This is a New York Review Book
published by The New York Review of Books
207 East 32nd Street, New York, NY 10016
www.nyrb.com

Inside covers: Ed Aulerich-Sugai, *Kohada Koheiji 3*, mixed media on paper, 1989

Library of Congress Cataloging-in-Publication Data
Names: Glück, Robert, 1947– author.
Title: About Ed / by Robert Glück.
Description: New York City : New York Review Books [2023]
Identifiers: LCCN 2023012401 (print) | LCCN 2023012402 (ebook) |
   ISBN 9781681377766 (paperback) | ISBN 9781681377773 (ebook)
Subjects: LCSH: Glück, Robert, 1947– —Relations with men. | Aulerich,
   Edward. | Authors, American—20th century—Biography. | Gay authors—
   United States—20th century—Biography. | Asian American artists—20th
   century—Biography. | Gay artists—United States—20th century—Biography. |
   AIDS (Disease)—Patients—United States—Biography. | LCGFT:
   Autobiographies.
Classification: LCC PS3557.L82 Z46 2023 (print) | LCC PS3557.L82 (ebook) |
   DDC 813/.54 [B]—dc23/eng/20230328
LC record available at https://lccn.loc.gov/2023012401
LC ebook record available at https://lccn.loc.gov/2023012402

ISBN 978-1-68137-776-6
Available as an electronic book; ISBN 978-1-68137-777-3

Printed in the United States of America on acid-free paper.

10 9 8 7 6 5 4 3 2 1

Contents

About Ed

Everyman

for George Stambolian

Mac

MARCH 1985

I WAS ALREADY twenty minutes late. I had *made* myself late, following the minute hand in a loose reverie while my breath fanned mint into my head. I was shaved and dressed, longing for some memory or plan. I rose from the twisted sheets and looked out. Mac's window was empty and so were the sidewalks on both sides of Clipper. Lily and I ran downstairs. We dashed to the corner and onto the median strip that divides Dolores. She sniffed the grass, then dropped into the gentle curtsy female dogs make when they piss. We crossed back at full speed; Mac stood on the sidewalk in front of my house. "C'mere, Bob." Lily ran ahead to greet him.

Mac was trembling. All winter he'd postponed going in for tests. "I'm going in but am I coming out?" He wet his lips and stared up Clipper at the rosy horizon. For a moment his face inhabited the light and the peaceful air. I consoled myself—Yes, yes, half an hour late, so what? Cars passed and continued up into the sunset where drivers lost definition and cars lurched and decided with lives of their own, but weak ones.

"Ed's sick too."

"That so?" Mac raised his hand to the back of his neck in sympathy, the gesture's small wind laden with witch hazel. When I say his face inhabited the sky, I scoop out space so my drama has its theater. Mac couldn't be distracted from the sky's larger court. Lily

3

sat in front of him, so alert she drew closer without changing position, big apricot ears tipped forward, beige tail broadly sweeping the sidewalk behind.

Mac lowered himself painfully to my porch step. For a long moment the sky without sun remained pure blue, then it subsided. "Aw, don't give me that you're too busy." Lily reseated herself directly in front of Mac, eyes beseeching, big tongue lolling. He absentmindedly drew dog biscuit after dog biscuit from a jacket pocket crammed with them. His joints were swollen so he lifted the biscuits lightly with two fingers. He held each one up; it drew Lily's eyes prayerfully. Half the cars had their headlights on.

Mac looked up with raised eyebrows and an open mouth as though I'd interrupted him with startling news. When I remained silent he said, "I'll tell you something, Bob. I went to the Castro Theatre last night and I did not even recognize myself in the mirror in the lobby till I moved." Now I was surprised, as though Mac occurred in the present for the first time. His sudden arrival pushed me backward. I became so tired I actually heard voices squabbling in my dream.

Mac emptied one pocket and started on the other. The biscuits were shaped like the cross section of a bone, the marrow a dark maroon. "I could see myself move," he added. "I'm not that far gone." Mac despised the drama that makes unique gestures, but he was wavering, losing his bearings. I wondered if he had ever recognized his body. It retained an applicable quality from his younger days. Short and nimble, it climbed a ladder to fix a window or paint the garage door white. Now it was a foreign vehicle, Saab or Toyota. Lily tenderly freed each biscuit from his fingers with the tips of her teeth, then chewed with head lowered and lips drawn back as though concentrating.

Mac was completely recognizable to me: his white hair and stiff part and shiny black shoes and his street and his biscuits. His sidewalk was still wet—he'd hosed it down. An old man with bright blue eyes. Lily wouldn't budge until she was certain his pockets were empty; she glanced back with disbelief when I prodded her. They united against me, the White Rabbit whose schedules and appointments diminish life. When the party was over Mac got to his feet and Lily climbed the first stair. It was as far as she could go on her own. I clasped my hands under her belly to lift her rump and we started up together. "Hey Bob, hope someone carries *my* hind end upstairs when I'm as old as your daughter."

I ran Lily up and threw a handful of kibble in her bowl. She disregarded it, her senses pitched upward in anticipation. She nudged the air toward the door with her snout to increase her chances. When I avoided her eye, her joy faded and she dropped into a corner. She brought her bushy tail around so she could smell her fur and declined to raise her eyes when I said goodbye.

"C'mere Bob, I got a shirt in my trunk for you."

"I'm in a hurry, Mac." But he was already on his way. I followed him into the dusk, pleading, "Why don't you wear it?"

He looked over his shoulder, not as far as my face. "Oh, I can't use it now."

He put the package in my hands. By the light in his trunk, I saw a blue dress shirt folded inside its cardboard-and-plastic box: "——— from Sears." He turned back to his trunk. "And these pajamas. Now wait a minute. You don't wear pajamas." We looked over at my bright window, then up at his dark one. I lowered my gaze to the spectator who cried in dismay, "I don't understand what you and Denny got going between you!" He actually waited for me to reply. I was gearing up when he continued, "You both leave the garbage cans on the street. You walk right by them. It's happened a dozen times. Let me tell you, that might be fine when there's no wind to speak of—I've seen lids roll clear down to Church when it's rainy and windy outside."

Mac closed his trunk, closing the subject of the garbage and my nakedness. He waved me on in disgust.

Mac had a waking dream that his body was hiding from him in the red lobby of the Castro. A few days later his wife, Nonie, told me Mac was in the hospital with cancer in both lungs. Still, I looked for him when I stepped outside. He'd sat on an aluminum tube chair on the sidewalk, weed killer in the cracks, uniting in himself our corner of the world. The garage behind him stood for economy and conservation; it smelled of paint and clean concrete. On the back wall he'd built a shelf for the orderly tool chest, a stack of yellow Pennzoil cans, and a green hose coiled around itself; on the floor, sand soaked up a blue-brown oil stain at its own pace. Elsewhere a city exploded and fire rained down, but here on hot days Lily sat with Mac in the shade of the overhead door, and neighbors stopped and talked as though his garage were the courthouse. I felt the romance of accord between a municipality and its citizens. The town square makes citizens, and they like to sit, consider, and mingle their stories with the present.

A few weeks before, Mac dialed me a wake-up call at eight. I rolled out of bed. "Thank you, Mac." I'd set the alarm for eight thirty; I think Mac was afraid I'd miss my eleven o'clock flight and blow his trip to the airport. What if you don't want someone to phone when the mail arrives, your tire is low, the police are ticketing, or garbage day comes? Mac provided such insistent Samaritanship that sometimes I felt exploited. We drove in his perfect blue Dodge, in its microclimate of witch hazel. It was Mac, not Nonie, who wore scent, who needed acknowledgment. Mac related a number of highway disasters witnessed by Nonie and himself. This was a strangely reassuring lullaby—his belief that the exact circumstances of death have value. We were driving down San Jose Avenue where it becomes a delicious canyon whose sides are retaining walls higher than the sketchy eucalyptus, the canyon bridged by walkways across the narrow sky with its bright clouds.

His landlord had just replaced the old double-hung wooden windows with ugly aluminum ones, and in the car Mac rejoiced. He praised them as unselfconsciously as a Greek chorus—thrift, conservation, he spoke from the darkness of those qualities. Then Mac asked, "Notice anything different?"

His face tipped back with sly expectation. Small men often seem flirtatious. I had an uncomfortable sexual moment. A black asphalt road curved upward, a light-gray concrete curb, a white metal railing, a few agapanthus, a few mock orange trees from bureaucracy's arboretum: the definition of nothing to see. I felt slightly hysterical to be considering it. "Mac, it's the San Bruno on-ramp to 280."

"They trimmed the trees. Things seem different, you don't know what it is—sure enough, they trimmed the trees." I'd say it was Mac's ability to tame the arbitrary by training on it the ecstasy of his surprise. He rescued Clipper Street—me with the others—by willing our lives into meaning, however incomplete. The corner market, the neighborhood *Progress*: the meagerness of these gods only displayed the intensity of his faith. I was not in his league.

On 280 we dropped into valleys of white fog and emerged in broad daylight. Mac needed some information to purvey back on Clipper. On the way I told him where I was going and when I would return, and about Denny's trip to Denver for his grandmother's birthday, Stanley's visit, and Lily's trip to the Russian River.

His comb raked dull blond furrows from his sharp part.

He sat on my steps when the sun left his side of the street. His big neck stood sore and naked.

Lily languished by the window as though she were calling his name. When he appeared in his window, she moaned.

He had a limp—he'd worked at the docks and had taken a bad fall. Ed sees an old man falling off a ladder because Mac was on one so often, but I think he fell from the deck of a freighter.

I asked him if he was in the union. "Aw, they were just trouble-makers."

He disliked the boyfriends of our women neighbors. "That Frank is a real Jew."

I lowered the trunk lid on my Toyota. "Mac, you know I'm Jewish." I found that hard to say. I was barred from the moment, no longer one with the day and the street. His insult was homegrown, but it also seemed exotic, like fascist demons in movies. Had Mac despised me all along? Had I provoked him?—by condescending from the vantage of class?—by forcing him to represent the past? Was he asking for more attention?

"Aw, that's not what I mean." He shrugged with exasperation. We saw each other as unwilling and limited. I'd thought of Mac as a master of ephemera, a novelist like me who worked outside the medium; he was bigoted, meddlesome, and loose-tongued, with a gossip's contempt for his neighbors. And me? I wanted my community romance intact. I wanted nothing new from Mac. *Good fences make good neighbors* could describe our inner lives. So Mac and Nonie make idle chitchat from racial insults over dinner in their yellow kitchen. I didn't want to witness the disjunction between Mac's speech, his actual life, and the romance I invented for us.

It took me a week to visit Mac in the hospital—a week in March 1985. During that time 70,000 people applied for 150 postal jobs, Reagan likened the U.S.-backed Contras in Nicaragua to our founding fathers, and six were drowned when a tugboat sank north of San Francisco. Pharmaceutical firms scrambled for the profits from the new AIDS blood test, the Dow surged 15.35 points to a record high, and an earthquake killed at least eighty-two on Chile's coast.

Iran bombed Baghdad, AIDS fears rose among embalmers, and an Iowa man won a restraining order to stop his ex-fiancée from having an abortion. Haitian Vodou priests doubted that Swiss pharmacists could make a zombie—"They have a long way to go." The woman had the abortion anyway and a gay man testified that a San Francisco policeman maced, kicked, and choked him, yelling "You deserve to die!" Fifteen people were killed by lightning in Zimbabwe, evidence of atrocities committed by the Contras took center stage in Congress, and Soviet President Chernenko died.

A Berkeley radio station interviewed Charles Manson, 93,000 midsize farms were going broke, and Gorbachev became president of the Soviet Union. Interferon stopped the AIDS virus in test tubes, and doctors who implanted a baboon's heart in Baby Fae overstated her chance for survival. Nonie said I would have to sneak past the nurses to visit Mac. I was creeping along a lime-green wall by the second nurses' station, averting my eyes, when I realized they didn't care at all. A Chinese nurse leaned against the counter, a jolly audience for the seated women who laughed with excitement and called, "Ireeeen … Ireeeeen …" They were some impediment Nonie had invented; without remorse, she had pretty much stopped going.

Mac's room was dim. I stopped in my tracks. Two nurses, young Chicanas, stood on either side of him. One cradled his head against her shoulder and moved a white cloth over his arm. The other gazed up at his IV with a solemn expression. I was shocked by his blunt nakedness, his smooth wiry body. His legs and thighs looked fresh. His hands lay open on either side of his luminous torso. His eyes were fixed, but when he caught sight of me he modestly averted them. I had not meant to see anything so personal, and I felt a pang of anxiety as the borders of our friendship shifted. I retreated to the hall.

One nurse asked, "Mr. McMillan, are you comfortable now?"

"I know where I'd be more comfortable."

"Just a little while longer."

The other nurse echoed, "Just a little while."

I drew a chair up to his bed. A knot or splinter on the inseam of my jeans irritated the skin of my inner thigh with every move. "You look good, Mac." I sided with the stupid philodendron in its bid for normalcy, undermined by stainless steel buttons, C and D, on the wall behind it. Mac was hooked up to an IV, only that—no tubes, blood, or respirator. He received no therapy, yet I treated him as though he were recovering. In the hall someone whistled inside the echo of his own whistling, someone with soft shoes walked down the corridor calling "Jackie, Jackie, Jackie . . ." The air was empty to breathe and papery, but crowded with dings of elevator arrivals, squeaks of carts and gurneys, deep coughing and clatter of dishes, doctors' names paged, names that could never be understood, summarizing the anxiety of illness. The lack of stimulation made me sleepy and hungry for sensation. When I closed my eyes a slice of pecan pie bled amber syrup on a Melmac plate.

Mac rose to the challenge: faced with the annihilation of particulars, he organized his part of the abyss. He pointed to the nurses' station across the hall. "See that gal, Bob, that's Maria, she's got a sister in Fresno who . . ." The trouble was not on my pants but on my leg, a pimple or rash or ingrown hair—I longed to go home and see what had appeared on my skin.

Mac was telling me about Maria's sister. His rambling story replaced the subject of his death. Mac believed in the value of Maria's sister's experience in Fresno because knowledge was an end in itself. His solidarity was consoling because it was faith in the value of everyone's life. Then again, maybe I was consoled by Mac's inability to locate a frantic loneliness in himself.

You go along and something's different. The second time I visited, it was apparent that Mac was dying. He had already started, his body was stuttering, losing integrity. I had seen this stuttering once before but had forgotten. I held his hand and he covered mine with his other, then held up all three hands to show how swollen his fingers were. I couldn't make out what he was saying. I could tell he was loaded by the way his irises dropped to the corners of his eyes when he rolled his head. There was a sense of dangerous speeding, time as space, like speeding over the ground as the airplane descends, when just a moment before in the air we seemed almost motionless.

Mac was out of time, whispering. Then with perfect composure he asked, "Bob, do you know my mother's number?" When I didn't reply he said, "Why don't you let me drive you home?" His blue eyes were bright with conspiracy; he cocked his head on the pillow.

"I'll come visit you again."

"Hope you find me here." He frowned at the ceiling and asked, "Is that your luggage?" When I turned to go he added, "Take care of yourself, Bob." The words gave me a little push. Mac always took care of everything. "Wait," he said. In time or space?

I doubt they did "everything they could." Mac didn't expect that kind of care. He followed the prescribed behavior with a conviction that resembled faith in an afterlife, which doesn't give much to the dying except to structure the experience of death. Mac's illness existed for the hospital, his death belonged to the nurses and doctors and the world beyond.

Mac's service was held at Reilly Company, a neighborhood mortuary at the bottom of Dolores, gone now. Two plump businessmen stood chatting in the sunlight on the corner with all the time in the world. The gray building was vaguely Italianate, with ponderous brackets and rusticated stucco. Small cypresses grew in stone tubs on either side of the grand portal. A man in a black-and-blue uniform stood inside the door; he was so fat and pigeon-toed that his arms swung around when he waded forward the few steps to point the way. The space for death was an old-fashioned parlor—framed mirrors, green drapes, a floral-tapestry sofa, two torchères with candles of electric bulbs, and a grandfather clock.

I entered the chapel just as Mac's service ended. It was a small gathering, although Mac knew a hundred neighbors, and his works of mercy took him to other parts of town. "Bob, c'mere," and we'd be hauling scrap wood for the potbellied stove of an ancient couple who lived on a hill in a tiny earthquake cabin. The chapel emptied; Nonie approached, hunched forward in grief. She cried "Oh Bob" and her small body fell against mine like a slight breeze. We had never touched. I felt tremendous latitude, that anything short of dying would be appropriate. I laughed as though we were meeting at a party. Nonie looked confused, then fell into other arms.

I was stopped short by Mac in his big casket. Now I felt like an intruder. Mac was always so prim; he never broke the social contract except by dying. His cheeks were apple red as though he were ashamed to be in that position.

Denny

"Look at this, sweetie." I showed him a forgotten document found while hunting for checks in my top desk drawer. It was an agenda we had drawn up for a Saturday night long ago. Our evenings were still filled with meetings—the left wing of SEIU, BAGL (Bay Area Gay Liberation), Enola Gay (nuclear proliferation). The agenda was written in pencil on typing paper soft with age; it proposed categories and subcategories, beginning "Item One: Warm-Up Kisses and Music a) Denny wants 20th C. b) Bob wants 18th C.," and ending "Item Twelve: Pillow Talk." "Look at all the things we used to do," I marveled. We read silently the amazing access blocked off for the duration. "I forgot we did them." We glimpsed a lost horizon.

"Oh Bob," Denny said, a modest virgin. He reorganized us on the sofa. He sat face forward, his limbs so slight they resembled a marionette's. I reclined with my feet on his lap and I considered his bony eloquent profile. On the carpet Lily slept deep in the blond nest of her body, dazed by extreme age and arthritis medicine. Denny sipped clear liquid that broke into metallic greenness on his tongue and juniper in his nostrils. He furrowed his square brow and cocked his head in an attitude of considering and raised his glass, an outsize triangle on a stem, a shape so simple it might have been neon above a bar. "Nectar of the gods, *mon ami.*"

I raised my glass to the martini maker. "The modernist cocktail."

We drank from that utopian wellspring and browsed through *Architectural Digest*. The cost of the magazine was an extravagance, but we considered entire homes that were stylish blunders or myths of habitation, tried them on like new hats. A glazed chintz, silver peonies drifting on grassy green—the brief entertainment of lifting a flower to your nose—would it be right for this room? We saw ourselves against a panorama, climbing to the true global village. The flagstone terraces, heavy pages, and paneled bedrooms were a voluptuous garden without soil, the only home we ever pictured sharing. The gin gave the future we assembled a certain credence.

Our game was so retro. Above our acted-out feelings—retro, neo, post, and pseudo—arched a rainbow of pleasure. Denny curbed my taste for the ornate. Our love was predicated on convivial sex, validation, the luxury of shared assumptions, and an impulse to corrupt by creating new desires in each other. I wanted a Pompeian frieze above the picture rail. I looked up prayerfully, but Denny cautioned, "Pure of line, Bob. Look at this." He showed me a transom window, a fan of glass above a paneled mahogany door. "Clarity above an obstacle."

"You know, I'm worried about Ed."

"What's wrong?" he asked.

"Intestinal things."

"Oh Bob, Ed always thinks he's sick."

"Ed says, 'The pain is under my fifth rib and feels orange,' and the doctor starts shouting."

"Is he worried about AIDS?"

"Ugh. He stopped long before we did. Isn't it strange that you and I gave up all the unsafe sex on our agenda, even though the viral horse would have already left our barn?"

"It's your cow and your barn door and your horse and your stable door. That's ideology for you, *mon ami*. When is Mac's funeral?"

"Last Thursday. The service wasn't announced and Nonie kept it to herself. It started at twelve on the dot and lasted till twelve fifteen. A third of the mourners missed it trying to park. I came in at the tail end and you know—there was Mac. He still looked interested." We sat with our drinks. I thought, No, it's Ed's awareness of death in the midst of life that aroused me and that made doctors recoil, negating them as it does. The sudden friendship with a corpse shocked me. Mac was a ledge to jump off. I hadn't meant to see anything so alien. Nothing nothing nothing is more unlikely—not hell or rising from the dead or bardo states or the Isles of the Blessed—nothing is more fantastic than for someone you love to stop, just stop, and be lowered into a hole and covered with concrete and actual dirt.

"Cremation's the revenge," Denny said, "but you don't have the sense the person died. All these memorials and no body. I miss Mac. I wish I'd visited him in the hospital."

"He died in three weeks. Lily still waits by his gate." Lily's ears tipped forward, though her eyes didn't open. Then she slowly climbed onto her legs.

Denny called, "Lily?"

I sang, "Hey baby, where you been all night? Your hair's all mussed up and your clothes don't fit you right." She licked her chops thickly and surveyed us without interest. Then she walked away and a moment later we heard lapping in the kitchen.

"It took Mary-Madeleine two years to die of lung cancer. Her daughters chose a beach north of Santa Cruz."

Denny leaned back, miming boredom.

"She was in a box wrapped in gold foil. The ashes were actually thick flakes and bone meal. I took a handful and walked down, trying to be free."

Mary-Madeleine was as new to her mid-seventies as I was to my mid-thirties; she had freely scattered unfinished poems, unraised children and their dads. "I threw her out to sea, but wind caught her ashes and threw them back in my face, and Mary-Madeleine went right up my nose and into my eyes. I was so blinded I had to kneel. I probably have some of her lodged inside my lungs."

"A walking urn," Denny said.

I keep a motto that Mary-Madeleine copied out for herself on a scrap of unruled notepaper: "Luck is when Opportunity meets Preparation." The *t*'s aren't crossed, but the script is bold and the sentence is circled in red. It describes an imaginary encounter; she had no Opportunity, and except for her death, she was never Prepared. I held my breath by a bank of wheelchairs outside her door, listening to her doctor. "We've done everything we can," "You waged a good fight," "It's time to just make you comfortable." Which meant, *Pump you full of morphine and let you die.* She said, "I see." See what?—a short man with huge eyebrows and chalky skin.

In the hall he took my elbow and said in a whisper, "Make sure she understands." He was discouraged: he'd been forced to renounce for a moment the lie that everyone gets well, that death is weak and complex, an unsuccessfully treated illness. I went from bystander to herald, carrying a coffin into the sickroom. Beige drapes with abstract leaf patterns held the daylight back. I sat next to her. Her head rolled and pain sort of pushed her tongue out of her mouth, basking in slow motion. I waited with my question until the spasm subsided, one expression on my face as though no time had passed.

"Mighty Mouse is on his way." She was referring to a little blue pill.

"Mary-Madeleine, do you understand what your doctor said?"

She replied wistfully, "I guess everyone has to die sometime." With that she divorced her rambling life from the medical marvels and aligned herself with the dying of the ages—with them she met her destiny. Had she pretended to herself for our sake that she was recovering? She must have felt a pang as her departing relatives took life with them, and relief for the same reason. The farce was over and her solitude was complete. Her large body began to dwindle; one dawn a month later, she faded away.

I think of Mary-Madeleine's death in contrast to the death of Kelly, a very sweet man, my dad's best friend. Kelly died when I was sixteen. He checked in to the hospital for nothing special, some tests, and quickly fell apart; he didn't want to live. My mom told me he died gasping for air, head rearing up, eyes bulging, mouth gaping. She said it was heartless of the staff to let Eleanor see him like that, but now I see him that way and always will. He struggles for breath, the terror of suffocation, a surprise forever protracted, rising. While Mary-Madeleine subsides, her vital signs lose tension. She falls through veils of morphine to a second sleep. Kelly's spasm lasts through eternity like the end of a story where he gains or loses every-thing. After his funeral, stepping down from the porch, the tendons standing out from his neck became the elastic band in Eleanor's undies. It snapped; the bright red panties sagged into view below

18

the widow's weeds. The priest thought her laughter was convulsed sorrow.

On this stage I have constructed for my soliloquy, I *can't speak* about my death or bid you look in my grave. As for ordering my tomb, over the two dates put an image of men fucking—to show what made me happy. Do the following stories belong here? They don't "come to mind" but intrude. The first is more resonant but simple to tell. It's just the pleasure my mother took in four eggs she brought 350 miles to my house. "See, it has a blue shell." She held out the egg for me to look at, though not to hold. "Bob, look at this." She was submitting a new piece of evidence, asking me to reconsider, but the problem was beyond articulation. Her elegant face tipped back, a conclusive gesture, and for a moment she occupied the sixty-eight years of her life. It was a moment, breathless and possible. Sheer awareness of my own life made me tired. Dressing and undressing the body, treating its illnesses, feeding it, cleaning it, overwhelming it with orgasms *and so on*. I asked for her best maternal advice. She replied without hesitation as though she'd been waiting for the question. "You are alone and you have only yourself to depend on, emotionally and financially." Thanks Mom, I thought. The body you gave me has to go all that way *on its own.* My cousin's black hen laid the eggs. They did have a blue cast, and thick, sturdy shells, and my mother took urgent pride in the rich orange of their yolks.

Kathleen said of her husband, "Art's a lucky man." I asked what made him lucky—what is luck in general? She said, "His parents are both alive." Art was fifty-seven. Kathleen is not simple; she didn't mean his parents were pure joy, but that Art is still a child, his body still given to him. My mom's advice was chilling because she eliminated her own presence from my life. She gave her son exactly what he asked for, a survival kit. I should have asked for comfort.

Last week my dad told me this story. Forty years ago on Buckeye Road a traffic cop beckons him into an intersection where another cop tags him. At traffic court there are thirty people, all tagged at the same place. Judge O'Connell is a lush and a wild card. He raises a pistol and points it around the courtroom. Everyone jumps and ducks for cover. He explains that a car driven by a drunk is as dangerous as his loaded gun. Defendants plead guilty, except for my dad, who pleads "guilty with reservations." The judge calls him into chambers. My dad says, "O'Connell, don't you wonder why thirty people got tickets at one intersection? Doesn't that seem a little strange to you?"

The judge thinks a moment and says, "Why don't you call me Your Honor?"

My dad was sitting in a mission chair in the bay window of my living room. He lowered his face, the fierce eyebrows and heavy pouches I seem to be inheriting. He studied the legal situation. A vase of yellow-and-lavender stock emitted obvious perfume. I was suddenly aware of the southern sky behind him, not cloudy but flat gray, and that I had acknowledged the day by wearing an old green cardigan.

My father replied as though I'd asked the question. "O'Connell, I'm supposed to be judged by my peers. If I call you Your Honor, you'd have to call me Your Highness." My dad triumphed over corruption and hypocrisy with the small weapon of language, a weapon that guarantees happy endings—that is, endings where truth is completely expressed. "Anyway," my father confided, as though turning away from the judge, "O'Connell wasn't so full of honor. Chuck knew him. Chuck was my helper on the truck. Chuck was a nonperson: no driver's license, no social security number. No draft card. For ten bucks he beat O'Connell in some flophouse. His Honor used to shout 'Not in the head, anywhere but the head.'"

"So Chuck was gay?" I felt a restless mirth verging on anger. What was my dad saying with this fragment from the mid-fifties? Was he helplessly following the path of association?—as his son is doing in this chapter?

He looked surprised, annoyed. "Naw, they met outside some bar. Chuck was a drunk—ten dollars was a lot of money in those days." A man without identity was my father's helper and Judge O'Connell's helper, too, and both Chuck and my dad beat the authority out of the judge. With authority there are always spectators, with spectators always mirth.

I am intrigued by the specificity of my dad's memory, though he lacks the sheer disinterestedness and solidarity of Mac. My dad thinks it's easy for me to visit O'Connell's court with him; he doesn't realize how easy it is for me to visit O'Connell's hotel room. The child without home or name beats the father with his own paternal staff, lust turning their roles upside down. Antique Authority sheds his robes to become the baby Naked Lust. When there's a child in the family there's always a lesson to learn. Today's lesson is: Pleasure has performed its miracle—the lucky child will never die. Chuck is handsome as sin, sandy-brown hair, drowsy eyes, a few freckles, the narrow chest and gleaming skin of the prodigal son. Don't spare the rod. Sweet must of the red floral carpet, dusty venetian blinds covering an air well, pine furniture.

On his knees, torso across the bed, the child-martyr inhales the sour breath of old chenille while the torturer proceeds with lazy goodwill, not angry or fierce. Devils and angels debate on either side of the mattress, the debate of the urge for more life against the urge to break life's tension. "Congratulations to your soul," one of them says officially. "Welcome to some heaven of love." Another replies, "Not a very permanent heaven, this love affair," and as if to confirm this another voice says, "Back on the bus, everyone." Deliverance for the camera—memory constructed of film loops and pages from grainy porn magazines. The judge's moaning replaces *his* memory. Chuck rises to the occasion: he beats the judge with joyous destructive energy. It's like an old daguerreotype, the Golden Age always disappearing into mirror.

The beating sets the judge in his own soft body, but his intensity stands for the thrill Chuck might be feeling. DO NOT DISTURB hangs from the doorknob. The judge will base his orgasm on his mental reconstruction of pleasure in a patch of silky skin on Chuck's erection. I admit I'm attracted to their reassuring failure, their aura of the already-known. It's easy to back away from the two men. They shrink as the screen diminishes and descends, their actions cartoonish, hyper, the young man writhing, the judge throwing a tantrum, a frantic child.

When I was young the uncanny took the form of Abraham Lincoln. Writing this story takes me back to Lincoln's part in my childhood. A magazine spread shaped my fear: *Life* I think, on his disinterment—in the nineteenth century? Is that possible? The article described fingernails grown long and the handkerchief-covering-nose smell, and the disconcerting fact that the corpse was well preserved rather than a decent skeleton. In the grave he continued to be Lincoln. With his Frankenstein height and his long narrow hands, Lincoln embodied a bleak solemnity that made his benign gestures especially intolerable. There was some kindness to a little girl; he wrote to her after he had been murdered. He spooked me in photos where even the light is frayed and rotten—the wound at the back of his head, his bogeyman clothes, the intolerable resemblance of his body in the coffin to his photos and statues, a face from a waxworks whose expression is wax.

I confused Lincoln with a comic-book cover of Frankenstein bashing through a brick wall, and I feared for the safety and continuation of my being. Yes, I am lying in bed and the closet door stands half-open. I make out a few empty hangers and the shoulders and sleeves of my shirts, red and black, blue and white, forest green, white oxford cloth, allies whose value derives from their fidelity to me. A dark wind from the closet pushes the door, touches my face. First the dreary fear, then the lanky monster gives it shape. His body pitches forward, his eyes are dead, his huge arm is wildly foreshortened. Any feeling is an acceptable distraction from my bewilderment—even terror, even nostalgia for the tolling bell. In the bathroom he crashes through the wall of white brick tiles, a force nothing can stop that comes for me in its own time, but surely at night when I am fat, larval, without a reason to defend myself—what is there to defend?

This monster was further conflated with Muscle Man, a zombie casually invented by Denis, my older brother, and then forgotten by him, reanimation not worth considering, and it was in part his casual existence and the shabby materials of the story that frightened me, alerting me as they did to the random danger of becoming a living corpse. Intolerable, the dead who partake of life rather than the negation of all states. Muscle Man starts off as a kindly elementary school teacher who loves children (examples of fatherly love), but one bright rainy night his car skids off a cliff and crashes on rocks far below and explodes into flames, and all that's left for the doctors to put together are muscles, so he drinks only one drop of water a year and eats only one crumb of bread. He has no stomach but his muscles retain their vitality. I don't think he wears clothes but I am not free to look at his crotch. Physical commotion has a sexual dimension, the depth of perspective of the live body in the abyss, an impure reversed death. How can I appease Muscle Man's hectic spirit? He crashes through walls in his search for children—to do what? "Bob...Bob..." Why do the dead want my body? To relive their solitude?

I never got that far in the confusion of living and dead, and perhaps all this has little to do with the death of actual people. Dying is not the same as hiding. The lovers on my tomb are a bodily promise to keep the argument of my life open. My parents are a guarantee of possession, an incomplete document to read forward and backward endlessly. So it's no surprise that when I was a child, death was a matter of possession of the body. When my mother died, I put her in my wagon and wheeled her to our temple—they didn't want her. Then to my dad—he didn't want her. No one seemed to want her so I kept her for myself on my toy chest. I didn't tell the rabbi or my dad. I couldn't count on them to remain indifferent. If they *discussed* the dream or even reacted, my mother would be partly theirs and my dream taken as a challenge, and I did want to keep my mother with me.

Her skin begins to peel so I remove her clothes and place my toy on the hallway floor, on the green carpet, and smooth her skin back. I don't exactly see her body, it remains a blind spot, but my confusion distills a tremulous pleasure. Then I sit at my bedroom window. Instead of the despicable houses and front lawns, the landscape of my little soul has been replaced by a sweeping pastoral vista. I am conscious of the disjunction between the absolute visual stillness— intense blue through the firs, the meadow's gold sheen, the tremor of cattails by a fence—and the terrible rattle and cough of an old lawn mower somewhere down below.

Nonie

NONIE TRIES TO KEEP her weight up to eighty. She is entirely white and wrinkled, with fragile arms and legs and the pan face and nasal drawl of the Midwest. She is as reclusive as Mac was gregarious, though entirely united with him in keeping an eye on the street from the lookout of their third-floor corner apartment. On the rare occasions when Mac and Nonie appeared together, she stood slightly behind, adding solemn gestures to his conversation. Only after sunset did their curtains draw together, lit by the TV's quavering. Why make this portrait of Mac and Nonie? I'm trying to recover—what? Mourning is appropriate for separation, in this case divorce between Event and Feeling, the parting of the ways, the wound that leaks meaning. Mac died. Nonie mourns. They pass so quickly through story into metaphor and explanation. It's not much of a story, just cozy reruns with actors who do not portray people—incomplete expressions of destiny and nature—but the more recognizable character actors of yesteryear. Recognition is everything: Feeling agrees to be DESOLATE LONELINESS, glad that it has a part, however low, and at the same time it is TOWERING INDIGNATION to be so rejected. "Bob, this is Nonie 'cross the street, your front door is open." "Bob, this is Nonie, your lights are on." I run downstairs and sure enough, my actual headlights glow feebly in the dusk. Any story underwrites its experience with the value of experience itself.

Any language wants to be total, pathless yearning. "Bob, do you eat tomatoes?" Mac packs them in a brown paper bag. When he steps out his door, he is aware of the day for the first time.

When he opens his eyes again he's aware of "the day" and the gem-encrusted gold sky without point of view above and around him. He waits to cross the street. I relish his energetic relation to the everyday as I do the daily horoscope, his confidence that unwittingly supports doubt and emptiness, yet always coincides with reality *on some level*. At my door Mac raises the tomatoes toward me in a fixed gesture of offering. Embarrassed by his own generosity (a stiff eloquence), he counters my thanks with a gruff order: "Now share those with Denny." His face tips back as though in combat. Realistic portraits began with death masks and praying tomb figures in the thirteenth century. The surprising weight of the paper bag suggests moral gravity. The tomatoes are silky, fragrant; an increment of black in their skin adds density to the bright red. The nephew's backyard in Stockton, the slow ripening in his dusty garden, the heavy flight of bees, the vines' somber scraggly life in the full sun.

Three weeks after Mac died, Nonie called me over. The weather was springlike, robust and still. It had rained at night; the sidewalk was damp, the air was clear and calm, the sky held a few gray clouds traveling fast and low. Nonie opened her door a crack and backed away, leaving the rest to me. She stood in a blue quilted housecoat a few yards down the hall. She had a flu that first constricted her chest, then gave her sinus headaches, then descended again five inches to her chest. She led me into her yellow kitchen and offered me a brown-and-gray Harris Tweed sports coat, an electric razor pristine in its square plastic case, and a brown bag full of TV dinners. As a group they had the thwarted quality of dead people's things. I examined them for signs of loyalty to Mac.

"The sleeves are too long for me, Nonie."

"If you don't give it to a friend, I'll just throw it out."

"I shave with a blade."

"Couldn't Denny use it?"

"Why don't you eat this, Nonie?"

"It's Mac's food," she explained to a child, her voice trailing up the edge of exasperation. She sat down on one of the two kitchen chairs. Maybe she couldn't swallow what was his, but I bet she just didn't like it, it didn't suit her. So they didn't share food when they shared a meal? Why did she think it would suit me?—did she view the food as male? Fish almondine? Pizza chips filled with shrimp meat? I understood that she wanted me to take it all. I found a new owner for the shaver. Phyllis liked the jacket, and the exotic food remained stacked in my freezer.

I didn't know how to feel about Mac. I mean, I was lost. I had missed most of his funeral because I was watching the clock, frozen in my bed, held in check by loud voices I couldn't interrupt or understand. I located no memorial service for Mac inside myself. Meanwhile I was depressed and teary imagining that I was remembering Ed's death, though he had not been diagnosed; that is, I could register my fear only as an episode from the past. Was I practicing remembering Ed?— rehearsing mourning? Was it disloyal? Lily waited for Mac's amazing abundance, refusing to budge from his gate, nose pointing up his stairway. She responded to my calls with quick glances of reproach.

"Look up, Bob." Nonie's small white head appeared three stories above. The baggie, wrapped in a rubber band, dropped from a terrible height and stung my palms. So dog biscuits were still an item on Nonie's shopping list. I doled them out on the spot. Lily ate them intently, but there were not enough or they were not what she wanted because she returned to her station by Mac's gate. Had I underestimated her? Meanwhile, Mac's food remained stacked in the deepfreeze eternally, a testimonial as tidy and contained as his garage.

From April to September, Mac's death remained in my freezer: *skeleton, death's-head, hourglass*. The sad and spooky food—so fraught and at the same time so generic—was hard to see. It was Mac's monument, a pure, solitary burial. Then I became busy, really too busy to shop or cook. I examined the fish almondine. The cover showed the meal as it was and would be, like the face on a pharaoh's coffin that preserves life by means of an image. The first resting place was temporary. Just directions to cook in a microwave. The fixed air in its plastic bubble. Then break the sack: a balloon of savory fragrance floats past my face. (Hold your nose against the searching odor of a corpse: fan it away with the word "*evocative*.") The food was not bad at all, lacking individuality but tasty, the kind of fish we Americans like, without a suggestion of alien existence or regret for the sea. But Mac was able to confer distinctions. You could say that in my dinner his blue eyes opened. Every night I turned the monument into ritual by taking it inside me. I consumed distinctions where before I had seen none, just an expanse of bright utopian images to appeal to the stranger passing the frozen-food compartment. To make wild assertions: to say I prefer Stouffer's Pizza Chips to Birds Eye Pizza Wraps.

To eat Mac's food, which was anyone's food—a generic confrontation with salt, oil, too sweet, pumped up with flavor, empty and exciting, a little sensational. I was not anguished. Perhaps I ate with a greater awareness of the moment, a curiosity that floated on the moment, an expectation that deepened the silence (I say "silence," though the TV was on, was on, was on). That's how I mourned for Mac.

Ed
OCTOBER 14, 1987

ED ASKED ME to take him to get his HIV test results.

In 1975, at a gay couples' workshop, the group asked Ed what he wanted from me. Ed replied, "For Bob to be a home I can always return to." With his usual clarity he summed up our relationship in these few words. The group turned and asked what I thought of that.

"Yes, that's beautiful." It took years to understand their downcast faces. All day they'd guided me toward a healthy response: "Ed, you can't assume love, you can't have affairs, you can't ignore Bob."

I'm still glad Ed regards me as a haven and he is always welcome, though I'm finally suspicious of that model. My relationship with Denny also seemed necessary, as though he needed some kind of help. Is this true if both lovers believe it? Now I believe I was the one who needed help—of course!—and who greedily helped myself to it, help that was given without expectation.

Ed is a presence who returns. He became a gardener in the Conservatory of Flowers. He lives with Daniel in a meticulous Victorian cottage. Ed and Daniel earn plenty of money; they built Ed a studio to paint in. Daniel happens to occupy the first-lover position in Denny's past that Ed has in mine. Daniel and Ed met by chance in the Fuchsia Dell in Golden Gate Park.

Ed's father is white and his mother is Japanese. He was a translucent beauty when we lived together, his bones hollow as a bird's. He grew robust during his gardener years, but he retains a floating quality. I experienced isolation more keenly with Ed than I did alone—can this be true? With Ed, solitude deformed and aroused me, so love of life came to equal excited desperation. When we separated I took into myself some of his solitude—I don't think that's unusual. If Mac is the spirit of conservation, Ed is the dreamer, and you can't look squarely enough at his face to speak of possession. Ed's solitude retreats through thresholds to the unspeakable, yet I bring him into this story because he's capable of a talkative grief that can still be trusted. He's in real trouble. Terror makes him clumsy—he feels sickening animation in inert objects, a rudimentary pulse.

Slow pinwheels, looming walls. I judge myself and Bob judges me. The day is sunny, windy, a strong autumn wind. I wear gray jeans that seem extra tight, especially in the waist. I've lost so much weight that I don't wear my coat, it hangs, making me teeter. Walking from the car to Dr. Palmer's office, my spirit races ahead, only to wait for my body to catch up.

I must be hyperventilating because everything's in a slow spin, time seems its own. On *Star Trek* an advanced civilization is invisible to the *Enterprise* crew because they live at hyper-speed detectable only by shrill insect squeaks caused by moving so fast through the air. Spock accelerates to see them, but then the crew appears frozen.

I avoid Ed's face; I have no reply to the rigid features there. I touch his shoulder. He says the mirror stopped returning an image he recognizes. He tells himself, Everyone feels this way, everyone feels shattering fatigue, internal collapsing akin to grief. At night he arches, ascends, wakes up drenched. He drags himself out of bed to dry off, lays towels over the wet sheet in dreary terror. He keeps the night sweats secret from Daniel, sleeping inches away. Ed says, "Everyone gets night sweats sometimes."

How amazing, I think, his secrecy and this disclosure. Ed's not giving me his story, he's taking it from me. I lose consistency, I give Ed the theater of my mind and faith in his images. Faith is still a means of understanding. Mac taught me that. Ed restages his troubles so he can benefit from the promise made by life-as-it-is. In the fifteenth-century play, Everyman pleads with Discretion, "Look into my grave once piteously." Everyman wants to bring his death to life by giving it a biography, but Discretion rejects him. Everyman tries to place the image of his fate in Discretion's mind to create a moment of promise.

Bob says he'll be surprised if my tests come back negative. That enrages me, as if he wishes it. Part of me is resigned to being HIV positive, a great burden would be lifted. All the months—one and a half years of diarrhea, colitis, the abdominal cramping that passes from one side of my belly to the other, taking my breath away. The anal operation that finally cured the fistula that took me through two lances to drain the infection and how my body shape changed after that. The fear and the blood. If I'm positive, it will be over, in some odd way I'll be cured. I almost want it. I don't want anything to stop, but positive means medication, some action I can take. These are my thoughts as we walk down the long hall to Dr. Palmer's office.

We wait on a burnt-orange couch. Daniel arrives and we all sit facing the same direction, like on a bus. My years with Bob confer an element of safety on what we are about to do. He's my past, he'll walk me through this judgment and somehow things will still go on. Across the room a woman lowers her magazine and stares at the orange cushion on the chair next to her. Her eyes open too wide— she's calling someone's name—she's furious in her dream—huge quarrels dwarf our voices and the weak office music.

Daniel and I wait for Dr. Palmer in a small examining room. Sweat runs off my nose and forehead, my scalp is damp. The pile of a dingy rug spreads across the walls. Daniel rotates on the black stool. We hold hands. He looks numb. He has great love and warmth. I am overcome by loneliness. I lean back against the wall.

Normally Dr. Palmer meets my eyes but today he hides his face, turns to close the door. Daniel scoots back and rises to give the stool to the doctor. Dr. Palmer looks at me and I begin to cry. He's confused by an emotion other than gratitude. My feelings seem artificial. He sits erect, rambles on. The room disappears in the same dark gray. Crying is all that exists.

I am ludicrous, I am crying for nothing, because this is a mistake, my results are negative. I almost laugh, so I step out of myself like leaving a noisy room and turn back to the commotion. Dr. Palmer and Daniel look shocked, I'm *jeering* at them. In disbelief my mind races back and forth from my death to the exact moment of infection, which sex act, with who…

Ed shrinks the space of contraries till he can't move. I also want to know where he got the virus, as though we can settle this by withdrawing it from chance, as though danger can be organized and set aside. Is that what Everyman wanted from Discretion? I am also too tired to continue believing in chance. I want to find some tiny inherent reason for Ed to die—the sudden clamor at the beginning of a storm. Well, he *would* contract the virus.

My death floats before me in the small dark room. I cry as it gives me numbers, lab results. Death doesn't offer anything else, no hand-holding, no apologies, no plan. It knows me in smaller and smaller fractions till it doesn't know what to do. Now these feelings are me.

I stand and my knees give way. Daniel holds me as we walk. Roz the receptionist looks up as we pass, sadness and confusion on her face, and I think I may be overreacting.

Bob stands as we enter the waiting room. We look at each other and he knows. We embrace. He absorbs some of my fear. Bob says, "Now you can figure out what you're going to do." He speaks firmly. These words bring us back. Daniel and I are caught up, but these words locate us in time and space. We are three standing together.

Daniel drives me to Bob's. Daniel has to return to work

and I don't want to be alone. Bob takes me upstairs. As we sit down he says, "Eat," but it's a pointless act.

I make a comforting gesture—it contains the thrown-open hands of exasperation. I reject him for threatening to die—and leave me! Why doesn't he get on with it? I stop believing in his story, not just in the "outcome" but the basic tenet, the pitiful urge for more life. I take inside me the disloyal sound of typing. The conflict ceases to be real, I have to retell myself the facts of the epidemic, I can't believe this...

We sit across from each other. Bob says, "Read," and I agree that's my ammunition. Bob says, "Dump Dr. Palmer." He suggests calling his mother—the thought of Dorothy is reassuring. I call Daniel's doctor and say I have AIDS.

We leave for Dr. Owen's. Sitting on the exam table makes the room seem floorless. It's painful to focus my eyes. It's like I never left a doctor's office, where such a small part of life has meaning. I must be hyperventilating—the air is gray, tiny black veins crawl over the walls and I'm tumbling forward.

Dr. Owen holds me as I begin to cry. He lifts his hand to the back of my neck; for a second he believes I'm his child even though we're the same age. He apologizes for my bad news. He says, "Get on AZT as soon as possible and have the P24 antigen test, it's only been out a few weeks." He suggests Valium to calm me and with that I want it badly. I don't want to continue the same feelings. As he and Bob talk, I'm already backing away, the scene before me is animated but two-dimensional.

Bob drives me back to his house. My future is determined, a passenger in a car. Crying eases the pain so I keep crying. I'm shocked by bursts of adrenaline. The air is heavy with fog. The windshield magnifies me, larger than life. Bob's terrified of my fear, he's wearing his face. I cover my eyes as I cry as though shielding them from glare. I feel the world needs me. I won't get to do all the paintings I have ideas for. Bob tells me in a sharp voice that I'm not going to die. I regret having a low opinion of myself for so long. I caused this whole mess, if only...

Bob's so much in control. His life looks simple because it is going to go on. All he has to do or think about is drive the car, get us home, very simple.

Lily greets us at the top of the stairs, wagging and huffing, shining black eyes. I'll die before her. I sit down next to her and she methodically licks my face with her rough tongue.

I tell Ed I'm writing about Mac's dinners. Ed says, "Maybe they weren't Mac's food—they probably collected in his freezer because he hated them. Did you notice that Mac's hair went from white to dirty yellow, depending on when he bleached it?" He laughs, surprised by what he said, but he doesn't want to be distracted. His life is suspended— its small increments give way to the intolerable coincidence of mind and world. The questions that lead him forward toward small answers become one question. He slowly rotates over a wild stasis while I try to domesticate his terror with language.

Bob wants me to merge my self and my medical existence. He's telling me that people have made something normal here. "This is going to be like a job, Ed. Something that takes planning, lots of time." His voice is rising. I think, Let me grieve, let me indulge.

Things in Bob's house feel either old or new. The old is good because it's familiar, but the new dares me to live, as if I will age before it. I look at the huge cedar bed Bob and I constructed and see years stacked up in it. I stand in the hall judging things by degrees of safety.

Bob brings me a Valium and goes to run errands.

Ed in the bathroom, the reassuring heat from his crack when he wipes himself, as though he really is a factory burning calories. He considers his face, puffy and sallow. His hands rest on the sink and one foot is poised behind the other. He always felt he could escape as a woman or become someone else if a situation demanded it, maybe because his Japanese features already belong to "someone else." Now he's trapped in a prison that allows no leaching into otherness. He lies down on my bed, feels agreeably fragile, abandoned, aware of the action of his breath, its regularity—he's made of flesh and is witness to this fact. Grief gives way to marveling reverie. Ed drifts, then focuses, drifts, then focuses. He's on his side, looking absently at his hand, his eyes drifting and refreshing themselves on the image, each finger's expressive curl, distinct ecstatic wave, as a Bernini is hyper-flesh though marble. Each image is an increment of promise. A cat walks across the roof, making a sound of rain beginning. The Valium is delivering its calming message. Then the dark dart of a splinter beneath the skin on the side of his forefinger comes into focus, so he becomes aware of the small hurt that must have been there all along. How did he experience the pain until now? Redwood infects, he informs himself. It pops out rather easily. A red bead forms on the small wound. Ed feels a thrill of self-love when he sees his own blood. He brings the finger to his mouth, hesitates—afraid of infection? He considers his polluted blood with pride and fear. Mac's illness belonged to the world, even in the hospital he was weaving together a collective destiny, while Ed's illness for now is his own possession.

I wake feeling very relaxed. Daniel's on his way over and Bob's in the kitchen cooking and shuffling papers. The more alert I become, the more startled I feel. No matter how hard I run I move only an inch at a time. My nap is a border. I fell asleep leaving one realm behind and wake to a weight and substance the old never had. I was never so entirely my physical being.

I leave Daniel and Ed alone on the sofa. In all the efficient friendship there isn't much room for emotion. I interrupt them, brightly enough to include myself, but not enough to claim squatter's rights to their suffering.

We three eat dinner. We watch a comedy video—the actors numbed by the sadness of their effort. I doze off halfway through. It's late. We say goodbye. Daniel and I step down into the night. The door swings on its hinges, the wind, the wooden stairs. All my feelings from before seem limited.

Nonie's Map

I CALLED NONIE every few months to see if there was anything I could do. It was a gesture, but I was surprised by how little she needed. Mac had been the world; Nonie, a navy-blue bandanna over her head, dark glasses, black leather jacket, white face, beer on her breath, had sometimes darted to Twenty-Fourth Street to buy an aspirin.

I was lonely to the point of fear and I couldn't reconcile Denny's goodwill with his lack of intention. I called friends but no one answered. Finally, a friend who was jealous picked up and I listed my disappointments and grievances to cheer him up. While we talked I looked at Nonie's window for signs of life. Since Mac's death the blue curtains had been drawn. She continued to look out, but secretly, as her temperament dictated. When I put the phone down, it rang.

"Bob, this is Nonie 'cross the street. Can you fill a prescription for me?" I looked up in time to see her curtain fall back. "You know the Sunshine Shopping Center?" She was surprised I'd never heard of it.

"It's in Colma, Bob." Colma is two cities away—a city of stone-cutters and miles of suburban cemeteries, a city of the dead, where Mac was buried two and a half years before.

"Nonie, maybe it's time to change to one on Twenty-Fourth Street?" Nonie was silent till the question ceased to be real.

"Okay Nonie, but come ride with me so you can show me where it is."

"Oh Bob, I couldn't do that."

I regrouped. "Okay, make me a map. Make a map so I can find it without any trouble. A map a child could use."

I crossed the softened asphalt to collect the prescription and map in the hell of our autumn heat wave. Heat banked against the stucco wall of her building and blistered the paint. Faint laughter of school-girls. I climbed the stairs. The bolt turned before I could knock and after a moment I pushed the door open. The apartment emitted waves of Pine-Sol. No more witch hazel. The photos were gone, as well as Ed's painting of their old cat, Fancy. I felt a helpless loss of scale in this apartment stripped of personal markers—the fulfillment of a blunt loneliness. Nonie stood halfway down the hall. She looked weak. Despite the heat, she had remained in her quilted blue house-coat and fuzzy blue slippers since the funeral. The white buttons on her housecoat, the view of Clipper Street from her window.

The map was ready, folded on the yellow Formica in the generic kitchen. An envelope contained some money and the prescription. I looked at the map. It was just a jagged line with another line branching off. I couldn't read it at all. At the top of the second line she had printed "Sunshine Pharmacy." We stood gazing at it, then flatly at each other. She waited for it to sink in that I would really be going to Colma. When it did, I asked, "Nonie, on this map, where are we?" She pointed to the bottom of the first line. "So what is this turn?"

"It's where you turn." The map was drawn in quavering pencil on a torn square of lined paper.

"But where is it?" I was glimpsing Nonie's horizon. Her map had no scale. It was a crooked line to the Garden of Eden, a freeway through elastic space to the fountain where Life blazes—the sum total coiling slowly on itself, rising up as an obstacle, greeting the traveler with the sound of *s*.

Nonie grew impatient. "The Sunshine Pharmacy, before the last cemetery." To prove her point she took the pencil and capped the top line with an arrow pointing to "Sunshine."

Silence and change began a slow spin around us. "How do I know it's the right cemetery?" The problem was too simple to utter.

"You just go along the line, then you turn here," she said to a child for the last time.

Everyman

WHAT CAN I WRITE for Ed? The question puts faith on the café table with the mealy apple and chopped orange, meager allegory garden of decay and orderly renewal. Scale falls off the map: To die and return from the grave.

A prayer begins: Inside me a handful of valleys, a dozen winds impending as an old *Life* cover. Our junky Chevy zigzags up a mountain and the horizon grows blue and heavy as it's left behind. Climb out. Legs wobble. Chill air, moist as a peach. My senses fall toward yellow lights clustering on the shell. An inhabited landscape, forest and pasture. Again and again I revive the visible to give eyes and a sunset to a joyous readiness that does not abate, whose fulfillment is not in sight.

A longing that goes with Ed's longing—longing as precision, a gesture forward. Why force an oracle I hardly believe in to speak? Ed's pressed to his bed by the volume of voices he can't interrupt or understand. The shadows somehow noisy. He covers his face, lost bearings. Then, as though remembering the "moral," he lives forever, dies and revives, keeps returning. What is the *circumstance* of his death, the *agency* of renewal?

I rewrite so the pratfall lays Ed in green pastures. Bees are bees or crosses of the dead. I dream for Ed, a commons producing images. Skin sore, tongue thick, sour. *The earth's surface.* I touch my face, pale worms swallow each other in the soil of my apartment.

I order sadness and fatigue like music. Parsifal melodic in his hymnal; singing, he's a note. In the next glade Ed's nose lifts to the scorched symbols. Terrified paper birds unfold in the blast. Burning isolation. From each red window Ed's outstretched arms. I'm safe in heaven, somehow. Like Saint Sebastian I raise my face, the cunning expression of Houdini.

Timelessness leads Ed by still waters in the travelogue. Loss spills over, filled too high with the water of opposites. I believe in the visible and the invisible but so what?—the former light as a toy, the latter a fallen tower in a steel engraving. Let me be battlements so chance can overwhelm me but long ago. "Something happened to me." Ed returns to himself; he climbs as stones crumble backward under his feet—the harsh path lit by torches and reaching music. Let death be noted in the guidebook.

The reader's expectation may be the faith to restore, the anticipation you enter and become. To answer your question answers every question; you move your arms and legs in the world's unfinished blue. Time sputters, catches like an outboard motor, the jolt toward yourself. Ed can never be done. He turns from side to side on the axis of his spine, radiant; sits forward, alert. Ed never sees or hears enough, he can't include himself, the next breath revises ardently.

"A formal feeling comes." Each leaf an image flung from the Tree. Ed safe, as image replaces image. His longing will be open (we dimly sense a god). HIV attacked what I meant to say (god as regression, god of interruption confirmed by lab results). Ed's longing has the tender physicality of a nursery, odor of talk and urine, like a nursery open to the future.

Let Ed sail past the coordinates. Let him be Sinbad, fast clouds over slow clouds. He tips forward to meet data that does not contain his image. Bark of a neighbor's dog—wind shifts, trumpet of deep distance. He returns from the hospital as dark transcendence in sunny seas.

God of deliberate fantasy, let Mac return. "C'mere Bob, you like the sky?" Mac cranes forward as he reels back from a city with traffic. "Up the hill an earthquake cabin, no heat, she can't move, pills on a wood shelf—he's—aw, don't give me that *I'm-too-busy*. Here's a fact I'm not using—"

Name the forces used in prayer or any magic. Ed's solitude, Mac's fact (a faith I almost believe in): Let Ed live forever, Cup on the Sill, Wind in the Flue. Let him live as the world unfolds into pages. Now I part my hands. Now I've said my prayer.

About Ed

Ed and the Movies
1989

H-MAN (fifties Japanese sci-fi about a clear green blob) slides up my kitchen wall and across the ceiling. It burns flesh and dissolves bone. It catches and envelops me. I wait in terror for the burning searing. A two-pronged irradiated fork appears in my hand. Whatever it touches survives H-MAN: walls, floor, utensils, me—safe from instant death, but radiation threatens our future. Recovery may not be recovery but the moment before the next attack. (HIV-MAN. The two-pronged fork: 2 AZT capsules every 4 hours.)

(Ed's dream, January 10, 1989)

Seven on a warm June evening. The glossy light is full, the shadows are mild. Little brown birds make weak metallic trills. I'm walking through Ed's garden to his front door. It's overgrown and orderly, the smell of damp earth and heavy roses. There are fronds and branches to duck under, red and green marble-sized apples growing out of their flowers on espaliered trees. Something in pots, and the brugmansia, night-scented trumpets, sweetly sinister. I climb the wooden steps. The porch light is on already. I'm empty-handed.

No, I hold the string of a white pastry box heavy with two lemon tarts and two chocolate éclairs that satisfy my greed under the pretense of fattening Ed up. He'll probably eat one bite. I feel sleepy and itchy as though some emotional demand will be made, and what

51

will I do then? I sense his death behind the door. I don't need to knock, he buzzed me in at the gate. The door swings open, he's very animated. *Would you rather see me lifeless?* his expression mocks. I hold up the pastry box and we moan with satisfaction. Death is too serious. I hug Ed and I want to say *I love you* but choke on the words as though I'm lying (I'm not).

I smell the Japanese half of Ed's childhood—soy and ginger. He intends to perfect a recipe for barbecue short ribs as he does for lemon Bundt cake and sushi rice. It's Tuesday, my night with Ed, an ongoing joke of self-interest. I contribute to Ed's welfare by eating complicated meals involving the stove, the oven, and the microwave that take Ed all day to prepare. The table is set, the food is a picture. Roasted pig—I start chewing before it is served, imagining fat. I can't get enough of the salty, burnt-sugar succulence. We dissect the flavors—more rice vinegar? ginger? Sophie, a small gray-and-brown tabby with a vexed expression, heedlessly scrolls against my shoes, burrows into my armpits, and vanishes.

Ed pokes at the meat with his chopsticks, takes a few bites of rice, praises himself for eating as much as he does. When we lived together, he could warm up to dinner with a jumbo bag of potato chips. His voice is strong but the air is seeping out of his posture. He's down to 120 and wears a disorganized expression. He brings me up to date on the daily horrors. He has neuropathy—the nerves along the soles of his feet strum like electric guitars. Some fungus looks like fur in his throat. He started a new med. Dr. Owen said if the new drug causes pain in his muscles it means they are disintegrating, so his body started pulling apart like taffy as the doctor spoke. Owen added that if Ed feels pain in his liver he should call him at once. Ed tossed and turned all night, a finger jabbing him there. I confess I don't pay much attention to these sagas, which are, like his blathering when we were together, tedious and appalling. I hear myself recite the stupid good advice I bestowed on Ed two years ago, my mother's voice in mine, calming, distancing. Ed's days are obviously precious but also lonely, threadbare, and twisted by fear.

What do I have to say? It's still the eighties: I feel so intensely the party is happening elsewhere that you could call my distraction a disease. That is, I feel like I'm reading a bad translation, knowing that a better one exists. Distance installs itself in me, from thrillingly difficult technical vocabularies to the ascendancy of the grid on, say, Calvin Klein sheets. Distance replaces the excesses and heartfelt essences of the seventies. Meanwhile, Ed sustains losses, giving up job, travel, movies—increased nakedness before death. He fights a hollowed-out feeling, hard to portray, not dramatic.

Last winter, flattened under the buzzing lights, Owen told Ed he had a few months left. Ed went home and planted 130 tulip bulbs. When he worked in Golden Gate Park, he would bonsai two hundred chrysanthemums for Easter. I'm bloated and wan. My life does not seem to apply and resists being shaped into anecdotes. Striving is vulgar. I've eaten too much fat. While Ed talks, I actually dream for a few seconds: I can't find my pen, and when I do it's on the kitchen table laid out between knife and spoon. Eating words and writing dinner. My dream sees me this way.

What am I leaving out? I remind myself to tape some conversations with Ed. Is that too gruesome? Half-asleep, I brew strawberry tea for Ed and black tea for myself in the blue-and-white spongeware mugs that belonged to Ed and me when we were together. I'm almost taking them down from my own cupboard. The clear flavor of the tea is so welcome that some of me goes into it. Ed opens a window—I'm surprised by his initiative because I expect nothing from anyone. He actually does eat his share of the pastry, which is a satisfaction. "You never cooked like this when we were together," I complain good-naturedly.

As though explaining, Ed says, "Remember Marty?"

"?"

"Who lived next door?"

"That greasy little beatnik who always wore the same sports coat?" I'm surprised Ed knows his name.

"We had sex. He'd just finished eating a can of sardines." Ed exhales to show the sardines swarming in Marty's breath.

I'm laughing and stung by this fourteen-year-old infidelity. Denny and I broke up three years ago. A year later I began seeing Loring. Loring lives in New York, but I experience my only moments of hope when I think of him. How to extinguish the useless surges? The action of the disease makes Ed's body attractive to me again. Is my love for him realer than I know? I attributed intention to his beauty because it had power over me. I remember the tenderness of snuggling in bed, soft cotton T-shirts and naked below—the cotton erotic, the hot and cold of train stations, a mix of directions. Ed replies with a look, *What do you see?* The face that detained me for so many years. Galaxies.

Why is Ed telling me about Marty? Ed was not confined to beauty and safety. I used him to experience risk, as I do in this story. The rough desire passed around at night by guys in a park or an alley. I'll bet Marty is where Ed discovered rimming. One morning he knew all about it—what a surprise *that* was. Pleasure hidden like treasure in that scary place. I covered my face in the simple justice of representation and my body made noises that meant it had instincts I'd never considered, like a school of salmon migrating up my butt.

These carnal updates from Ed and his primeval romps give our marriage a weird posthumous life. Since we are on the subject, I remind Ed of the evening fifteen years earlier when I cooked an elaborate birthday dinner for him. He turned up around midnight, explaining without remorse that he had been patiently guiding Sean into bed, a straight friend he was "liberating." "Having a reason doesn't mean anything," I cried. I blinked like a flustered professor and my body stuttered. Ed laughed in alarm and mimicked my frantic gesture. Then he offered, "You're just a victim of circumstance."

Ed laughs and says, "Well, weren't you?" He places a buttery crumb on his desiccated lip and translates the flavors into a panorama. I ask him if he's painting. "Every morning from my studio I see a nanny push a buggy up the hill. I think she's Nicaraguan. She looks really young. She puts the brake on the buggy, climbs a long set of stairs, unlocks the door, and then goes down for the baby. That buggy points right down the hill and it's held in place by a thin piece of aluminum. Every day I expect the baby to go flying down the street into traffic."

We share an expression of horror. Ed lives on a steep hill down which the buggy already careens. I say, "Someone has to tell that woman!"

Ed solemnly agrees. "One sentence could save that child's life."

"But Ed, why don't you tell her?" I feel a surge of relief—finally I can save someone's life. "All you have to do is walk across the street and tell her!"

It's so easy, but Ed has a question. "You think *I* should tell her?"

"Certainly, tomorrow morning."

Ed's head falls forward, his eyes pop, and his jaw drops in amazement. Once I thought that was gay body language, but then I learned it's Japanese.

"Do you know how *sick* I am?" He's thinking, Why should all of civilization rise to protect that stupid baby?

In self-defense I think, You are well enough to cook dinner, to paint, to dig in your garden. "You could do it. It's your responsibility—as a neighbor. Ed, you still go out all the time." I blanch at the word "still."

Ed's really angry. I'm a whirlwind in his head. The baby I can't save will not grant me permission to save some other life. His face is rigid and his mouth works on its own. "*I* am not responsible for that baby. Don't *I* have enough to worry about? *I* don't know that baby. *I* don't know those people. I am trying to stay *alive!*"

I grin in desolation. Ed is slightly revolting—I remember the absorbing spectacle of that jaw working against me, perpetual motion of amazing insult, the smashed furniture, the wonder I felt when his fury jumped a quantum level, beyond caring, heedless. His thin body or anything could be thrown onto the blaze. I know when I'm licked. Giving up is hard work. The baby must live or die without us. The buggy plummets and I lack the willpower to alter its course. I picture Ed by his window, the witness to this drama that inspires no call to action.

I watch TV to be somewhere else without exerting myself. Exertion is the only way to go somewhere else, so dissatisfaction builds up.

It's hard not to be bitter overall, as though I'd actually seen all those daytime talk shows. The entire message of TV is that life is not fair, more daydream than nightdream, yet the victim has his faults.

Not so with Ed. When we were together we watched TV with joy. In the early seventies, a cousin took pity on us and bought us a little black-and-white Zenith. We watched it through the night in Ed's studio. Ed painted and I kept him company. I am describing hours of perfect contentment. We liked Fred Astaire and musicals in general, but horror movies were even more histrionic. Ed and I felt delectation for these images of mayhem.

In Ed's bedroom, light is a translucent rectangle even though it's almost nine. The frosted glass arrests dappled shadows. Ed lies under the heavy indigo blanket, wasting; I lie on top, succulent. I'm happy to be lying down and I feel perfectly relaxed on Daniel's side of the bed. The disease leads some of us into a deeper engagement with the world. Denny became a science writer for *AIDS Treatment News*, and Loring joined Gran Fury. (At Bo Houston's funeral, his mother says, "Thank you so much," as though *I'd* done anything, and before I can stop myself, I say, "Thank *you*," as though *she'd* done anything.) An epidemic is like a mystery with heroes and villains, but I drift from my bedroom to Ed's bedroom, where light falls through frosted glass in a certain way. Above us the screen doles out images we love: the pre–World War II unknown lurches basso profundo through shadows and dry ice; the supersize zoo of spiders, locusts, snakes, ants, and lizards climbs out of the squashed air of the fifties desert. Ed and I love bad horror films for the lyricism of their failed effects. We must be among the few to have *twice* seen *Curucu, Beast of the Amazon*, a film that couldn't afford a visible monster or even gore. Branches twitch on the jungle trail, the mic slides into view, the victim screams off camera. Its very artificiality makes *Curucu* a convincing exploration of the afterlife, like a church service.

Tonight we watch a Mario Bava film in which moist decomposition replaces the genre's earlier effects, as though a horror of decay is more germane to the present. It's weird to be lying next to Ed, watching corpses rock back and forth in their own putrescence. The monster shows the world what she is: she throws open her robe with a triumphant expression to reveal a red chest cavity packed with roiling white maggots. Because of this image, I don't look Ed in the eye, as though I'd seen something too personal. What does he make of the skeletons with rags of flesh? I am the only one who can ask him this question, so I do. He rolls his head on the pillow and reminds me in a mild voice that he will be cremated, and that decay is not the same as death. He says, "My death is an emptiness that I can't fill." I am relieved, but why? We both know Ed will soon be reduced to ash. He's dying in stop-action like a good makeup job: the chaotic expression, the skeletal jeer, the pumpkin head wobbling with bonhomie on the broomstick neck, the pinched nose, the eyebrows pulled back, the eyes starved and hurt.

The monsters rise up while we sink into the pillows. But horror movies are actually comedies because death is reversible. Or it's a consummation: the one taken by the monster experiences the full extent of his death. In his last scream, the victim faces the monster and dredges horror to the limit. A sexual consummation: he groans from the deepest place where his body (the world) begins.

A False Step
MARCH 1990

I'm on my way to a health club. I run into Bob. I kept my health club a
secret from him for years. We walk up a muddy hill, shiny ochre—ivy
grows at an angle. Bob fills out the forms and goes in to steam but the
rules gyrate as I stare at the contract. The clerk won't look at me, the
price jumps. Bob comes out to find me but I'm invisible. I sign—partly
I'm giving in and partly I want it. I enter the multilevel gym. Luminous
gray fog swirls around familiar strangers. A man falls in the gloom—
he's sick, dying, DEAD. I look closer—*it's me!* I dial 911, "Help me please."
Then calm takes hold. Is dying the same as hiding?

(Ed's dream, November 15, 1988)

A MAN WATCHED me shower and followed me into the sauna.
The fragrance of hot cedar. He was short with large features, glossy
black curls, and a narrow waist fanning into cheeks as cantilevered as
the drawer of a file cabinet. He said, "I'm always watching the clock."

"The clock?" I looked around.

"The time."

"For work?"

"Work," he confirmed. He settled onto a bench below a small
yellow light and a temperature gauge. I wanted to interest him in
me, I began to see him as a destination.

"You work at night?"

59

He considered this. "The night shift." His voice was precise and deep. He spread his legs and his tip rested on the wooden slats. My skin prickled; we began to sweat.

I said, "I used to work at night. In New York. The night shift, unloading trucks at the Grand Central Station Post Office."

"Oh, and you went around New York during the day."

I wanted to interest him, but he was not being very interesting. Was talking in the sauna inappropriate, dumb-friendly? Three citizens filed in, smiles from the outside not yet faded, and draped themselves on the benches; in ten minutes they were dazed and suffering, their genitals poaching on white laps. I could not smell my own sweat, but I watched the shine on a drop that for some reason didn't evaporate. Sighing, the men hauled themselves up and left as one. The metal furnace clicked; the flame popped.

He did continue to look at me. Expectation translated into pressure. I sat in such a way as to attract myself, legs crossed at the ankles like a greyhound's, head tipped back, innocent intelligence, about thirty years old, though he would have seen a middle-aged man. I began again and told him I was a writer but that didn't get us very far. I told him I'd left New York but that was obvious. As though to defend myself, I told him about my bicoastal romance.

He said, "You always complain!" That was too accurate. He'd known me, what, thirteen minutes? Was he referring to something in his own life? I asked him what he did.

"I'm a nurse."

"Where do you work?"

"At Presbyterian."

"Oh, I have a friend who worked there...who just died." I couldn't remember my friend's name. I felt a jolt of fear.

"What's his name?"

"Terrance." Terrance returned as though entering the little room, his gestures, his plump face and enthusiasm, his roses, bleak lollipops in the overcast suburb.

"Terry"—he gave the ghost a nickname. "I didn't know him. In pharmacy?"

"Administration. He died quickly."

"My brother—"

"Is dying?"

As though correcting my grammar, "Has died."

"Your actual brother?"

"In a few months. He didn't want any medicine. His mind was strong enough."

"To cure him?"

"He had a belief system: the moment is all we have, why put a condom on it?" I am interested in people who believe the spirit has orientation. What I understood: his brother could project himself into an ectoplasmic medium through a calm that had direction like the eye of a sex hurricane, then spiritually freeze the medium and evaporate it until he was sort of freeze-dried as an essence. Like any fanatic, he needed to show the world what he had become: a glimpse of a sped-up shadow fucking hard.

The brother's system is a story for another time, but I was amazed when he mentioned Michel Foucault, a name wildly out of context, his brother's friend and mentor.

We were silent for a while. He added, "There's something beyond this."

His body seemed complete—the moons of his fingernails. I thought this talk of AIDS had shifted us hopelessly away from each other. I leaned against the wooden wall, my head tilted back as though relaxing into the empty heat, the arousing sedative, so he could look at me. I muted my own judgment of my soft body and let fear speed up my heart and pleasure flow in the skin on my chest, belly, and thighs. I would face him, we would be on our knees, impossible, face-to-face because of the emotion there, his legs spread, out of the way. I would feel perpetual whirring sweetness on a broiling day. We'd sweat freely, mightily awake.

Meanwhile we sat quietly with my old familiar cock and his, like a mood ring, a bag at one point, floppy, the connection to his body a hinge, then surprisingly blunt and meaty. I smelled hot wood and chlorine. My locker key was burning the skin on my thigh. Oil from countless backs stained a dark wainscot on the wall I leaned against. Michelangelo carved this man's foot. That is, its level of articulation created a dissonance—that perfection could hide. It made me feel helpless in a way that leads to sex.

Would touching him intimately equal eternal life? Lewd wonder. I would be allowed to separate his legs, dark shimmer. I push him over, then raise his torso so his ass unfolds, a place where everything is visible. Don't avert your eyes: it must be seen to be believed. He does not struggle against me, but against his own openness, jaw dropped, grunting as I slide in just a bit farther. I want to be inside. His rigorous beauty (tenderness and accuracy) is half of a difficult theorem. I want to prove that my life stands on the other side of the equal sign. The proof of this theorem is his orgasm.

My fantasy sort of replaced my man. To my surprise, he slid over onto the bench below mine and said, "Is this okay?—I couldn't tell." He barely touched me.

I barely touched him, touched his shoulder, we were folding into each other without contact, like the two halves of a tackle box. He smelled like sautéed mushrooms. I thought he was going to blow me. The human race fixed its eyes on that possibility. I blurted, "Would you like a date?" It was such a random thing to say that we both sat stumped for a minute. I tried to regain my footing—"That is, you're very handsome."

He said, "My heart is beating. It's so hot in here."

"Mine too. I'd like to sleep with you." Why didn't I say *have sex*?

"Sure," he offered, "that would be fun."

He looked a little caved in, teary. He raised his head. I tipped it farther back with a finger and brushed his lips with mine. His position emphasized his size. I could lift and hold him.

"Sweet," he said. Then, after a moment, "My name's Pete."

"What? Oh, Bob." But now my voice sounded strange, high and taut.

"I'll be here the same time for the next three days."

"The same time?" Weird voice.

"For the next three days." My ears were starting to burn. Rills of sweat ran off Pete's face and chest. He was getting up, but when I suggested we go out together, he was staying. First the heat aroused us, then it punched a hole in our arousal, though we both had semis. He stood up. The flesh on his lean body was intelligent and competent except for the mounds of his ass, which required tenderness, direction, and education. They gave blind access and needed to be organized. That's the penis orating as it disorganizes its—owner?

My hand slid down Pete's slick back. My lips brushed the most beautiful mouth in the world. I could have stayed, touched him, no problem, but I was urgent to go, to contain this rather than fall into it.

"'Bye Pete." Cold air and a rushing sound flowed in.

At my gym, the cruising is so intense it's like the hollow clanging in a factory. Pete and I sort of avoided each other, though I watched him shower and the two parts of myself that debate were in agreement. When he blew his nose it echoed. I laughed, possessing a little of him as though I'd gotten a private joke. Factory clangs, the odor of deodorant. He might be too much of a twink, I warned myself. I was attracted to beauty—it was lucky when they turned out to have character. I saw myself explaining that to Loring "over my shoulder" as Pete and I step into the future. I had presented myself as a boho, confident in the power of my simple heart, comfortable with failure. Someone who writes in cafés and thinks the muse is listening. In a way, HIV and the death of Pete's brother were the most neutral things we could discuss.

"Hello, hello? Gluckmann?"

"This is Robert Glück."

"Gluck? Gluck? Just a minute. Yes. That's right. Mr. Gluck, you are familiar with the Beth Shalom Elementary School, many Russian immigrant students? But with funds cut looking for fellow Jews to support?"

"No I—"

"You're Jewish? You are Jewish?"

"I can't give you anything—I give to AIDS and I'm—"

"To the Federation?"

"—on unemployment. Good luck and—"

"So next year?"

"No, I—"

"You're *not* Jewish?"

"A *fallen* Jew."

"You don't give?"

I squeezed the bud and fell asleep. Young men are held in a weedy corral. The flat full sun casts hard shadows. The men are sort of ancient Greek in that flesh glorifies itself with luxurious butts, each with its succulence and hot bitter kernel. We were kidnapped without force and transplanted to a Golden Age, to which we quickly adapt. When we arrived, electrodes were planted in the walls of our rectums, *in the nerves of voluptuousness*, my dream reporter explains. The electrodes emit gentle encouragement, as though a tab of mild acid were inserted there, but an ever-stronger thrill eventually replaces our memories, goals, and self-regard. On hands and knees in the dust, we fuck air with rapt expressions. With a cock in me my darkness is vaulted with pleasure and the blurred lights of ornate chandeliers. Eyes wide open, empty.

When I apologized to Pete, he said, "Those things happen sometimes," implicitly agreeing that I had been inappropriate. He softly punched my stomach. "Don't worry about it." But where did that leave us? Later he lingered in a rectangle of thin March sunlight in a corner—so I could walk over? He looked like Mickey Mouse with his simple face and legs that were muscled but basically sticks. Market Street out one window, a postcard, and winter pine boughs out the other, pen-and-ink.

"I'm trying to get my endurance up," he said.

"Up how?"

"Twenty minutes."

I really didn't know what he was talking about. His profile was more delicate than his full face. All around us, machines and limbs guided each other in semicircles while music welled up, imploring. "So would you like to get together—have coffee?"

"Sure."

"I can't do it today—Friday?"

"I'll put it on my calendar."

"At one o'clock?"

"'Bye, Bob."

Later I caught sight of him, a waif in street clothes, all muscles gone. How can perfection hide?

Late Tuesday night: moist air blurred the moon's edge. By the end of the day, I lived through the world. My eyes kept closing on their own. I wondered why I hadn't gone off with Pete the day we met, and why I didn't have sex with him on Monday. Would life improve if I hung faded cream wallpaper in my little bedroom? Was Pete just a floral motif? Although I was eager to see him, I had to remind myself that our Friday date existed. In the dark I looked forward to the morning *Chronicle*—to the Food and Home sections and to the horoscope—so intensely that I felt a welling up of love.

I woke up crying. Consequence flitted away like bats.

I was trembling when I went to the gym on Friday. My heart beat through my chest—why? I looked for Pete, estimating the damage. Was he avoiding me or just spacey? His disappearance appeared. When I was a baby sucking milk, stimulation equaled self-preservation. Now Pete's presence equaled self-preservation. Some part of me tried to "save" myself and I mentally summoned a guy I thought I had stopped liking. I watched the attraction assemble itself and take the form of my face between his thighs, etc. I started believing in those thighs and the unrest where they joined. His quick shallow orgasm furrowed his brow as though it were a math problem and gave him only ten seconds of respite. But his tension was more excitement to aim at Pete. A disco anthem came on. Sylvester, drag queen diva, sent me a message from beyond the grave—I made her feel mighty real. The monotonous beat was a wind pushing me, *You Are Happy You Are Happy You Are Happy*, till I felt exhausted and oppressed.

I moved through the gym, saying to myself what I would have said to Pete, and I went home and pinched my skin a little, trying to decide if I wanted pleasure in order to feel what I'd almost had. Failure reveals itself. Pete says, "That would be fun," but it doesn't amount to much, that is, huff, huff, spurt. It doesn't raise the dead. Pete's eyes roll, he's talking on the phone, "and then he asked me for a date!—*random*."

I'm shitting with satisfaction, fondly recalling the swordfish and mashed potatoes. I reach to flush and something snaps—disc? muscle? It jabs so that I'm winded and can't lift my arm. I crawl to the bedroom and lie groaning on the rug, having a bitter conversation in my head with Loring, and I can't get up, can't roll over, can't raise my arm, can't lift my head. I lift it with my other arm, but when it's in the air I wonder why it's there.

In *The Rapture*, a woman stands *forever* on a precipice—she put herself on this cliff and now she is stymied. Believing in God may be the happy ending, but what if He disgusts you, repels you? She refuses to go forward into his heaven (violence, death, separation). She refuses the old life—its grueling ignorance stands out like too much makeup. She can't accept and she can't reject. She can't move to a sheltered position, sheltered against the shame of self-knowledge. She rejects the supernatural and she has experienced too much to settle for the natural.

I read the first part of this story at a literary evening at Good Vibrations, a sex and vibrator store on Valencia Street. Afterward, William told me he recognized Pete from our gym. In fact he'd had sex with Pete. We outlined Pete's butt in the air, smacking our lips subnormally. Then William said, "He's very sweet," as though defending Pete against me. He added, "Pete has a lover," as though that explained everything. I processed the information that the relationship was "open" while trying to assess the difference between William and me from Pete's perspective. William and I had a fling many years ago, old, old news, somehow consoling.

The rest of the story takes place in my head, where Pete joins a central casting. I retain him to jack off with or to think about like a wish in which he is only the heft of his cock and some contorted expressions. I make him the deity of his brother's beliefs, a misshapen god with few attributes: the tilt backward without resistance, a mouth elongated by spasms. I spin the Gumby God, a pinwheel, stretch him out like taffy.

Pete passed me on the street and did not acknowledge me. I felt a moment of weird elation—I almost threw back my head and laughed. I desired him in a stale, self-conscious way. *Don't make me feel mighty real*: let me be a porn sketch of five thick lines by Joe Brainard, or the two on-screen whose flesh is powerful light. Do I want to—what—marry a man whose butt says *Have a nice day*? I wanted to put off our date, and his interest was strong for only a moment. His absence (the rigor of it) exposed my own inertia. Loneliness makes me a shadow, yet loneliness makes me too bloated and deformed to climb out of bed. I'd cry *save me* if there were something to save.

As if to confirm our lack of accord, I imagined settling into sex with Pete, then hearing the mailman's footsteps on the stairs and the small crash as mail falls through the slot onto the hallway floor. I am licking Pete's nipple, but I can *see* the thin blue airmail envelope from Kathy. I asked her for a favor that I later regretted, scolding myself so severely I brought tears to my eyes. Although I want to believe in sex with Pete, anticipation crashes through. I long to read Kathy's letter and I abandon him with mild regret and relief, as though we were having a boring conversation at a party. The story of my romance with Pete will be complete when I tell it to Ed and to Kathy.

A man who was not Pete and I were lying naked in my big wooden bed. This man said that romance leaves him cold. I'd desired him for years, long before he bulked up. I climbed aboard and wriggled and whispered his name in his ear—where did *that* come from? He tipped his head away—okay, no kissing, okay, no eye contact. I sort of forgot what to do. My orgasm was just that, a small calamity. Later he said, "I always wondered what it would be like to have sex with you." I didn't know how to protest.

He said, "They let me take naps at work."

"Because?"

"HIV, I guess."

A chemical fire traveled a high silvery note along my limbs for him and for myself. Fear made me shiver because heat retreated to my vital organs. A shift downward, a taste of saliva, and too much awareness of the space around our bodies. I remembered being cornered in the closet—the other children trying to pull the door open. I'm a desperate virgin. I'll die if they see me in my underwear. It would not have been a problem for another boy, and that was my shame, but I hung on to the doorknob for dear life. I was bewildered to find myself still in existence. How did you survive? I didn't, someone else was kept alive. Is it *enough* that I have memories? *Enough* for a personal truth? Let's forget about the shy little fag. It was an intermediate time. I started a novel, needed a job. My friends no longer seemed to like me. I treated them badly or ignored them, caught in the toils of job-dating-novel. I was not worth the effort.

A few solitary drinks lit a remote part of my mind. Little faggot activities: wearing my mom's housedress—the excruciation and pride when the milkman asked, "Who's that pretty girl?" After I learned to jack off, my memory improved—that is, once I became a man. Like all of us in the eighties, I walked around with multiple person- alities and repressed memories of satanic panic. They explained the present because emptiness and physical upheaval were more cruel, a pervasive fear whose expressions were anger and self-reproach. I reproached myself until my character crumbled to atoms. I here accuse my parents of ritual torture with electrodes; infanticide; can- nibalism; multiple rapes; mutilation with knives, wires, and fish- hooks (some requiring eighty stitches); sodomy with carrots, chicken parts, and a hose. Ants roamed all over my flat, not in rows as one expects but randomly, as though this was the magnetic center. My mother hung me upside down from a banister, a broomstick in my rectum, as she exhorted my brothers to beat me.

Although I wanted to believe, doubt crashed through. I wavered like an exorcised ghost. I might have disbelieved in character, but what if Pete didn't share that lack of faith? Then I would have to create a moment of revelation or madness in him, and that would have been our story. In *Black Sunday* the witch pulls her cloak aside to reveal the rotting cavern, the polluted Garden of Eden where death stands as norm.

The whole quote: "Desire reigns in an untamed state, as if the rigor of its rule had leveled all opposition, when Death dominates every psychological function and stands above it as its unique and devastating norm; then we recognize madness in its present form, madness as it is posited in the modern experience, as its *truth*." Michel Foucault

Notes for a Novel

I WALK INTO the orchid show with Ed. He says, "Few props." Like a play?—am I misreading this note? As soon as I see the tumultuous hall I know he won't last long. Ed walks like an old man though he is forty—HIV exposes his bones. The long disease duplicates quickly the attributes of age. After ten minutes on his feet, Ed vomits on some purple phalaenopsis. I get him out through a fire exit—he vomits into the bay. I find him a chair and he goes right to sleep, body caved in.

Once Ed understands that he will not have a long life, he starts working on himself, guided by banal authorities. Ed is not superficial though he may live superficially—what choice do we have? He inhabits banalities like an eccentric tenant, his innocence repurposing them. Louise Hay, *The AIDS Book: Creating a Positive Approach*. Magazine articles: "Positive Thinking as a Cure." "*Heal Your Life*: AIDS Is the Physical Manifestation of Lack of Love." A culture too stupid to know what it is asking tells Ed to perform an impossible task. "AIDS can be healed with love and forgiveness." Ed's family needs lots of forgiveness, except for Merri, his younger sister—*but they'll never get it from me*. They exploit his illness in carnivals of self-pity and ignorance, from forbidding contact with their children to erasing him as though he were already dead. Even in brutalizing fucked-up angry families, love devastates by making us participate. But death will hurt if Ed is not at peace, dissonance will violate the dissolving music of the self. During the long last moment between breath and electrical wave, peace is a painkiller and fear is the sign of false life. Is this the "good death" of the Middle Ages? Ed forgives the world for not loving him, for deserting him.

In 1989, Ed was in a show about HIV. Spalding Gray toured American cities, interviewing locals. Surely Ed was poised and diverting during the audition, but in front of the audience he sweated alarmingly and aired a frantic grief. His loneliness and terror undermined the living-with-AIDS anecdotes traded by the sex-positive cast like business cards of professional non-victims. Not having raucous sex equaled sorrow, trouble. "The MAI seems to be holding but my T cells keep dropping. Thursday hit hard with a hundred-and-three temperature, shakes and sweating. Friday my usual blood test showed the white count at thirteen hundred, so into the hospital I went with a bacterial infection . . ." Spalding Gray cut the exchange short as Ed disintegrated before our eyes.

Merri, Ed's sister, worked for the public utilities. In 1976, she happened on their dad's monthly energy bill—three thousand dollars. It turned out he owns hotels in downtown Tacoma. It turns out he's rich.

Ed on the phone: "My mother threatened me with a black rubber hose for chores, like vacuuming underneath the furniture every day. I broke her mother's lacquer plate. I threw the hose in the bushes in desperate fear. When she found out, she straightened a hanger, she wouldn't let go of my arm and whipped my back and thighs. She was a blur of screams. Blood oozed from the pain. My sister helped me take a bath—she cried."

Ed and I were hitchhiking in San Francisco one dark night. The driver asked if I'd just gotten out of prison. "Anyhow, you look like you did. Want to buy a key?" He meant a kilo of marijuana. I said no so he showed us his lame joke—a house key—and his partner showed us their gun. *They could kill us out of stupidity.* They took ninety dollars—our rent—drove us to an alley and made us walk into the dark. A few months later, the driver slouched against the brick wall of a blues club in Oakland—the only other white person. He grinned, sly-friendly, as though we shared a joke. I suppose we did, a lame one.

Ed and his dad with their dicks out in the cold air of the truck and later in the hunting blind. "Getting it ready," his dad says. The day is muffled, sounds blurt and expire. Electrons forget to spin, relation perishes, symbols and solar systems throw themselves onto the landfill.

"Merri and I finally went out to see Dad and Louise today because I couldn't reach him by phone. It was weird that I hadn't seen him yet. My dad shook my hand. We talked for a couple hours. They were really smashed. I was hoping they'd invite me back or set up a date since they're so hard to reach. When we left, I didn't want to touch either of them, so I just said goodbye. I guess they want to be left alone. He sold a fourteen-room complex today."

In 1971 Ed writes, "My goal right now is to support Bob so he can write poetry all day. He is so miserable, the least I can do is to make him happy." In 1974 he writes, "It's easier to love you when you're not here."

Ed's Tomb

ED IS THINKING about buying a niche at the Columbarium to house his ashes. I drive him out on a bright blue-and-white day so we can look the place over. I am preoccupied with the question of talking in the sauna. Ed is a genius at cruising. In the early seventies, I taught him to speak. Before that, he was known as Silent Ed. Every evening I asked him to report on his daylong journey. The story was interesting or boring. Standing in line at the bank took as long to relate as standing in line at the bank. Ed used his new skill to talk talk talk talk till he got his man in bed. We called it space garbage. He says my mistake with Pete is that I swamped the experience, that I tried to barter information instead of using language to lubricate my access to Pete's body, a higher form of utility. My sauna problem is a problem of self-mastery. My life's sole aim is to hide my own weakness from myself, but my weakness is the way into the world.

The ornate dome floats behind Pier 1 Imports on Geary Boulevard. The Columbarium was part of the huge godless Odd Fellows Cemetery. Most of it became tract housing in the forties. This neoclassical building housed the ashes of seven thousand San Franciscans through a century that included two big earthquakes. Ed and I find Masonic emblems and august family names on the oldest niches, so perhaps the Columbarium served the religion of business. I remember when it was a magnificent ruin. The niches have increased in value like all San Francisco real estate, and customers have the opportunity to control at least one aspect of death by making an intimate statement in public. This lovely wedding cake of a building houses the private gestures of the recently departed and the lilies and doves of the long gone.

We look up at the honeycomb of circular tiers, and Ed's final resting place starts spinning. He folds up, tasting ashes, but catches himself when he feels my hand on the back of his neck. As he bends forward, his ears are translucent. He sinks onto a folding chair and I brush his clammy temple with my lips.

In Japan in the seventeenth century, it was fashionable for a cultivated person to write a death poem, intended to be the author's last spoken syllables. Basho delivered his to sixty disciples: "On a journey, ill, / and over withered fields dreams / go wandering still." Taking words into death can turn death into a comedy because language is reversible; language undermines death's finality. Many of the newer niches at the Columbarium have that brand of humor—the hilarity of last words. Each niche is a tiny room covered by a glass pane "where dreams go wandering." Some seek the shelter of infancy, teddy bears and toy trucks. Others throw their obsessions (baseball, Elvis and his twin, gambling, the perfect martini) in the face of the very death that fueled those obsessions, the very obsessions deployed to hide from death.

In April, Ed and Daniel buy a niche and Ed makes his tomb. He invites me to see it before he installs it in the Columbarium. I walk through his garden—peach pastels and blue-gray shadows—and step down into his studio. Sophie steps down with me, a fly or bee in her mouth, the furious buzzing amplified by her delicate skull. She strolls around, eyes neutral, a drawl in her movements.

Ed's tomb sits on a small drafting table in the middle of the studio. Looking at it makes me dizzy. I don't think I'd have the forward momentum to plan my own tomb: Why not get dumped in the bay—or *whatever*?

The tomb is a diorama, a ground of polished viridian marble and a robin's-egg sky, across which drift solid white puffs with lavender-gray shadows. Ed's ashes go in a ceramic vase but he doesn't know how to seal it. I suggest a copper cap that would oxidize into blue-green. "Michael Brown could do it," I offer.

Ed tells me about the materials—long-lasting pigment and glue that fixes the canvas to a plexiglass liner so the cloth will not touch moist cement. I'm dubious. After you are dust, is there a difference between two hundred years and seven hundred years? Ed doesn't realize that nothing matters after you are dead, that you are no longer included. I think it shows a lack of imagination.

Ed has painted clouds for two decades; still, what does this sky say about him and his world? An emptiness without expectation, a panorama open in all dimensions. Is this the answer to the questions I ask myself?—What to do with the day and the wide blue sky? How to move in space both cramped and infinite? I recognize his isolation, an inorganic purity beyond striving. Ashes, stone, sky. The violence of dying flesh evaporates. What's left is the incorruptible skeleton of the world. I suppose the desire to be inorganic is life's plan B. When we were hippies on acid, I saw the universe fuck itself, bucking in dripping spasms, and I wanted to join in. Ed sat cross-legged, lost in perfection, captivated by crystals endlessly folding and unfolding on a white wall. Ed's niche says that nothing stands between him and the sky. Maybe it's a wish. The restraint of his installation interests me, a heaven characterized by lack of detail.

I resist Ed's tomb, but what is my aesthetic? A meticulous account of lightning striking. What faith does it support? My heaven contains even less than Ed's—as though there is nothing to pass on, nothing to propose, and no forum to say it in. Experience is so threadbare that sky effects are the only statements to make with confidence. Memorial art supposedly looks backward—old gardens and weathered cenotaphs—but actually it looks ahead, believing in a future audience and in the value of the world to come.

The idea that a future exists startles me and reorients me to the present. The waste and greed in the Reagan/Bush years creates a futureless mood. Can I link my life to experience beyond myself? The public sphere is so debased that saying anything true is a breach of etiquette. The profiteer says there is no tomorrow and then turns that cliché into the daily reality of his victims. My lack of belief in a future is a symptom of a massive and pervasive marginality. The recognition of a future is the beginning of a kind of sanity. Ed has an idea, however sketchy, of the whole. That is a powerful optimism, an enormously strong idea. A story that is a graveyard or a columbarium might open a "beyond" in more than one sense. Ed's tomb conveys an inside-out-ness, a grasp of time that makes me want to write my stories posthumously, image replacing image.

Nonie in Excelsis
JULY 1991

A KNOCK at the door. There stood Nonie's downstairs neighbor, hands folded and face lifted in pleasure. On second glance she was sixty or so and yes, beautiful. I was surprised; our relationship had been confined to waves and encouraging shouts. Even so I enjoyed her old-fashioned air, *continental*, her scarves and tailored jackets, and her tarnished silver voice. She'd been sent by Nonie, who had an errand for me to run.

Clipper Street was the Champs-Élysées when I strolled across it with this gracious woman, whose name I didn't know. I started up to Nonie's apartment, but my neighbor's hand on my elbow held me back. Nonie had moved to a smaller place on the first floor. Why? The old apartment was too large for her alone. When was that? Three years after Mac died. For a moment Nonie was still at a window high above me forever. I waved to her when I left my house. The curtain twitched—it was a safe bet she was watching from behind. I had depended on Nonie; now I understood that my life passed unobserved.

When I entered Nonie's apartment I was surprised again. Nonie had expanded. She was installed against a wall. I had to stare, sorting out the filigree of tubes, drips, and oxygen that surrounded her. She was breathless and even paler than she had been—how long ago? On her face too much thin white membrane was painfully exposed.

She cried in a proud whisper, "Guess what, Bob? I can't budge from here."

Nonie faced a TV that obviously had a life of its own. An Olympic diver was shaking out his celebrated arms and legs. I wanted him like I wanted anything and he sort of agreed to be mine if I resolved to diet and go to the gym. Above the TV, a window exactly framed my front door. I felt relief: Nonie was still keeping track of me. Her neighbor said, "Poor thing, isn't she brave?" We considered Nonie, glorious in a sky of pain, goddess of stasis. An ever-half-full glass of lager stood on a side table next to her. Nonie's neighbor enthused, "She never makes a complaint." Nonie beamed affirmation.

I envied her easy life, the far-flung lyricism of her glass of beer. Nonie was a jewel arrived at its setting, a fantasia on entropy. I also longed for immobility and sometimes even wished for a disease that would commit me to one room, one chair. I could taste the fat government check made out to ROBERT P. GLUCK.

I pulled up a chair. Nonie had a clear plastic mask over her nose to deliver richer oxygen, and it emptied the rest of the air. I said, "You know, you can call me anytime you like."

"I've had the same phone number since 1956," she breathed, as though I'd made a point and she were proving it. She sipped her lager and her wedding band slid down her chopstick finger and clinked against the glass. "We had a brown dog named Ranger—we could send him to the butcher on Twenty-Fourth Street." I thought Nonie was from the Midwest—she had that twang—but she grew up in Stockton and San Francisco.

"Do you miss Mac?"

My question was not as relevant as the passage of time. Nonie's pale eyebrows lifted in disbelief. "He died six years ago last April. Michelle wants to ride me out to his grave. Oh Bob, I couldn't take that." Nonie's neighbor—Michelle—shook her head no. She was delighted to be on the sofa, crossing her legs and touching her hair.

"Do you have an errand for me?" Life was pressing in too urgently against nothing, against a wild fatigue.

"That Albert," Nonie snapped. "I asked him three weeks ago. He lives two blocks away from it." So another trip to the Sunshine Pharmacy. Albert was my landlord. He and his family had lived in the house before they rented it to me. They became friends with Mac and Nonie, but the older couple's lips drew back from the taste of Albert's name: his blithe selfishness and the spectacle of his sins against order. Albert bought derelict properties like the house on Clipper, let them fall to ruin, and unloaded them when they outlived their usefulness. Mac and Nonie stewed as my windows fell out, the back stairs sank and chunked off, plates of rain-sodden plaster dropped from the bedroom ceiling. Mac had crossed the street to put groundwater-fouling poison in the weedy sidewalk cracks.

Nonie leaned out of the firmament and spat, "Albert may be an Arab, but to me he's a Jew." I went mentally cross-eyed for a moment. I could tell by the roundhouse punch in her voice that Nonie was drunk. Here at last was something authentic, a cultural tradition with roots. I felt elated by her hatred of difference. I wanted to congratulate her on her steadfast faith. Let evil be a weed that prospers in the next valley—rip it out, toss it in the trash, goodbye on garbage day.

Nonie, I wanted to cry, *everything is so much worse than you imagine!* Was enjoying her bigotry disrespectful?—I couldn't push down the laughter squirming in my chest. The dignity of tribal hatreds,

Nonie hieratic in her chair, her beliefs never deformed by a newspaper. I felt like flinging her around the room in a polka like the rag doll she was.

What identity did she support with so firm a grasp? Who were these people? I looked to Michelle for a moment of complicity, but apparently her goodwill did not admit conspiracy. She laughed with the sheer joy of the present, and I wondered if perhaps she was overmedicated. The present didn't look good to me. Michelle offered me tea or—worried expression—beer.

"Yes, beer." I wanted to participate. I broke my promise to the athlete on TV, forsaking without struggle our early-morning dives into the steaming lake, exertions of all kinds that keep us laughingly out of breath. Nonie and I could toast our passivity, our depressives' love of stasis.

Michelle brought me the beer on a tray, along with a glass and bottle opener. The toasty bitterness shaped my thirst. For some reason after a few sips I got a little drunk and a pressing image possessed me: The new husband stands naked in front of his bride, who is naked on their iron bed. They are entirely committed to their culture, and for a moment they know they are natural; they are only partly themselves because they are also a season, a culture, and a time of life. About his erection: I must remind myself how it works. It projects from his body—prong—and goes inside her and she wants that. With each thrust and smack her loose flesh ripples backward around her thigh bones. Her face radiates serene ecstasy. The young couple overwhelmed me. Boredom and beer, lowering my resistance, opened a door to their truth.

It would be fun to get drunk with Nonie, to find out something about her and to find out what she knew about me. I had never heard her speak three sentences together except to deride Albert. As though on cue, Nonie began: "Bob, Mac had a parrot. I hated that damn bird, but Mac loved her like a daughter. Polly had a foul mouth. We couldn't shut her up." Nonie paused a moment to let the problem sink in. Her respirator farted like a straw at the bottom of a glass. Michelle laughed to display her attractiveness. I could see the problem: Mac was rather prim.

"One day Mac got so mad at Polly that he threw her in a cupboard and you would not believe the din. He took the bird out but she was worse than before. Polly let loose a string of four-letter words that lasted fifteen minutes. Then Mac threw her in the freezer. 'That'll cool her off.' In a minute it got real quiet. Mac was afraid he'd harmed Polly, so he opened the door and that bird stepped out of the freezer and tiptoed up his arm as nice as a ballerina." Here Nonie became Polly, perching on her dead husband's shoulder. "*Mac, I know we've had some problems and I'm terribly sorry. I'll try to watch my language in the future . . .* By the way, what did the chicken in there do to get you so mad?"

Okay, that didn't happen. I couldn't control my imagination. In fact, Nonie told us about Ranger. "He was a good dog. We sent him to the butcher on Twenty-Fourth Street to get the liver. He loved my sister Annette—he waited outside her door. She played organ for the movies at the Pantages down on Market Street. She was the diva and the prima donna. She had the best furniture and kept her own room clean, period. She treated me like a pet, but my parents wouldn't let her marry her boyfriend because he was Catholic, so she took up with a musician. Ivor Carlson." Nonie whispered, still scandalized, "Annette became an alcoholic like our brother. She'd go to Oakland and do her carousing there. Things went from bad to worse in Oakland. They always do. Annette got sick and Ivor kept her in his cabin out in Walnut Creek. He was twice her age." Horses grazing on golden grass in the valley, the white road next to the brown river, cottonwoods, a bright dry outcropping at the top, the track of a narrow-gauge railroad, and coast live oaks against the blue. "Annette was sick in her heart or kidney and Ivor didn't get any help. They found both of them three months later." The sky bright blue and white, then rolling thunder and discrete blurs, smudges of rain down to the earth. "He left a note, she died and he was committing suicide. Her first boyfriend was a musician too." Nonie was still in mourning. "All that talent gone! If only we could pass it on! It was a wonder to behold."

Ed's First Sexual Experience

JUNE 1967

I GREW UP in Tacoma, Washington. I turned seventeen in May and I was so horny that everyone could see the need in me, I was made of glass, the need to be touched was an emergency, a frantic accident: 911FUCK. Cars slowed down, drivers could see it. My heart was thumping but I jumped in a car and we dropped acid and drove into the woods—the wilderness. Acid was an old friend coming on in the dark.

Jim was at least thirty and he did not say much. We walked into the forest—firs and huge feathery hemlock trees, the slight skittering of their needles—and he brought me to a halt in front of four stumps, except the stumps rose above our heads and supported a tree house. Vines twined up the stumps, looping before my eyes like the curlicues and exquisite filigrees that cover Sleeping Beauty's castle. Would I be going to sleep?—or was I sleeping and here's Prince Charming? The dark firs swayed and bowed down to us, we were going to have sex so we were the center.

I'm describing my first sexual experience. The woods surrounded us with multifaceted silence. The cabin made my nose itch. Jim lit a kerosene lamp. An atrocious clubfoot hung from the ceiling, its shiny eye glared at me. On a moldy mattress, Jim pulled my butt onto his mouth and that was weird. I mean, did he forget about my cock? And it was a week since I'd taken a shower. He spread my butt cheeks like parting the curtains before the diva's high C, so I guess he didn't mind and really that smell is part of nature, right? Then his tongue was squirming inside me, reshaping me from the inside. My anus was spinning clay on a potter's wheel and Jim was making vase shapes with his tongue. He said, "Shiva owns the place," and I thought, That seems right: throwing pots with his thousand hands. Jim's words were muffled by my butt and because he was huffing. The thousand arms of Death lifted our tree house to his fanged mouth and crunched like we were hard candy. That made me laugh and I said "Death" in greeting. Jim nodded so fast my ass felt like a snapping window shade in a cartoon.

He said, "Shirt is an ace." That was strange because we were naked and my shirt was balled up in the corner, a plaid flannel I got at Goodwill for free because there was a red stain on the back. I said, "Thank you," and that made Jim so happy. He said, "Shit on the race," and I had to agree—the whole rat race, you could have it. We were turned on, tuned out, whatever. He was bucking under me. He said, "Shickon my ace." Shickon my ace? That was code for something. Chatting away like this was a part of sex I had not foreseen, it was distracting. I thought sex would be like going to a library: when you have something to convey—*I love you very much* or *Will you be my boyfriend?*—you whisper it. Jim tipped his head out of my butt and bellowed, "SHIT ON MY FACE."

It took a second to realize what he wanted while a turd sprinted through my intestines and burst out like a dog responding to his master's voice. I jumped off the bogeyman's roaring shit-covered face and grabbed my clothes and ran into the forest, too scared to stop and put my sneakers on.

Haircut
JULY 1992

I pee red and black. I lie on my back, covered with quilts. A Japanese doctor runs his hands from my belly over my semi to my knees, pushing the paralyzing disease out my legs. I'm floating, afraid I'll break. Vidal Sassoon guides me through crowds and his business.

(Ed's dream, January 7, 1990)

YUSUF GIVES ME a little push toward the bed. We've been together for a year, but he is still in a hurry—it makes me laugh with excitement. He wants to be continually acknowledged, even waking me at night. I don't know what I am in his life. Possibly homosexuality itself. The phone startles me. Hearing Ed's voice is odd—I'd forgotten about him for a few days. Daniel looks after him, as he has for years, and that is always a relief. Ed's voice on the phone is strange because it's as familiar to me as the voice that speaks inside my head, as the feeling of my tongue inside my mouth. His voice is so embedded in me that it confuses inside and outside, like seeing the back of my head in a mirror. Then it becomes part of our old union.

Now Ed sounds as though I'm fighting back tears, rushing through memories and hopes. He says, "Lately, my body gives me moments of peace, moments of sweet decay, like a dead mouse in a trap." Then the world seems artificial and Ed's physical being is a minor part of a richer and more compelling adventure. "I think my body is showing me how to die. And sometimes a little girl jumps up and down on my bed. There's no sound, just the girl and her shadow."

Ed is diagnosed with lymphoma a few weeks later. The doctor gives him a week before treatment begins, as though that were the period allotted to accept his fate. Ed has never felt so alone: the spider delicately turns him in its eight arms, wrapping him in a web.

I am in Rome in June and July with Yusuf—sharing a high bed whose parts slide around on their own like the layers of an unstable sandwich. He studies in Queen Christina's library and I write the first draft of *Margery Kempe*. We live on the Vicolo della Penitenza, where prostitutes retired in the seventeenth century. Shutters bang all day long, canaries trill in cages as the sun comes around, the sky turns ultramarine, at dusk gnats and huge bugs with helicopter wings crowd the out-of-control garden light. Yusuf is a Moroccan bodybuilder postdoc in early modern at UC Berkeley. Oh Yusuf, he's like eating a peach over the sink. He is the beauty of Rome: the tenderness and excess in the paintings in the Galleria Borghese, the pouting muscles on naked stone bodies torqued with exertion and pleasure in the Piazza Navona. They express the glory of his flesh and the drama of arousal.

Ed writes, "It comes in a large transparent tube. Such a pretty candy-apple red. I picture it going into my bloodstream and slowly permeating the bone marrow. That wonderful red spills from one channel to the next, destroying every small tumor and cancer cell, turning them dark blue to black. Then the red fills the swollen tumors in my neck and face, making them glow. It doesn't stop there. I picture the growths in my groin, armpits, the bone marrow in my toes and feet, my fingers and arms, the massive hip bones, and each vertebra of my spine. I see the convolutions of bone in my face and my skull, everywhere candy-apple red."

Yusuf leaves a few weeks before I do. Sweltering empty days translate into *What should I do with my life? What should I do with my life?* translates into *Should I get up from my chair now? Now? Now?* Then I go out for dinner. Should I buy the meal I want—pizza baked in a wood oven—and spend the three thousand lire in my pocket, even though I know I will need more money tomorrow? Save enough to get to the airport, come what may? Eat at a restaurant I don't like just because it takes credit cards, or in a restaurant I am fond of but not dressed for and can't afford? Hot air ripples with an eerie pallor. The flat-footed voice of a child. I can't find tomatoes to cook pasta at home, so I hopelessly revisit the possible restaurants, transfixed by self-contempt.

I return to San Francisco on August 1. On the phone, Ed tells me he found half an eyebrow on his pillow. He is terrified of being disfigured by HIV, and now that's happening. The mirror stops returning an image he recognizes. Lightning is striking.

I have a brainstorm. "Ed, why don't you shave your head?—it's a popular look." There is a complex but legible silence: shock and then *you can persuade me.* I do. He has clippers, so Yusuf and I go over that night.

I can't look at Ed, he's molting and his face is swollen from the chemo. He is so low that I feel space warping around him and see the gathering shadows. We drag a chair into the kitchen and go to work. I feel the *zzzzzzzz* of the clippers, the delicacy of tipping Ed's head this way and that with my fingertips, my pangs of love. Heavy, dark clumps fall to the floor. Ed sees them with alarm. "Do you really think this is a good idea?" His expression says I can't be trusted. I remove the mirror because he looks dreadful, *naked before death.* When he was a child he plucked the hair from his scalp and face, follicle by follicle, a naked fledgling, and I suppose the finality of that childhood misery informs his present sorrow.

To confirm his mistrust, Ed asks Yusuf to take over. I sit and Yusuf works the clippers. He and Ed resemble an annunciation, two figures bending toward each other, intense interaction, miles of empty space between. The angel and deity share a contradictory stillness, time as hide-and-seek, as though they are vanishing down an arcade. Ed asks, knowing the answer, "Do I look okay?"

Yusuf cries, "Ed, you look so sexy!" I'm shocked and Ed looks up without bothering to act surprised. Doesn't he resent this obvious lie, seeing himself in the mirror that Yusuf holds? Ed tips forward without changing his expression and the tears flow. Yusuf says with complete conviction, as though he hadn't said it before, "Ed, you look so sexy!" He says it with joy, "Ed, you look so sexy!" Ed wears a questioning expression, and I can see that maybe he doesn't look so bad. Yusuf says, "You look so sexy," and I wonder if Yusuf is becoming demented. He says, "Ed, you look so sexy," and Ed brightens a little. Ed does not look so bad, the shape of his head is fine, his features sculptural. Yusuf is wearing out Ed's fear. Ed's ears protrude, but that's okay. Yusuf speaks with wonder and Ed begins to smile. *"Ed, you look so sexy."*

Then we see animated dinosaurs on TV, scaly and reptilian, and Yusuf says *they* look sexy. I wonder if Ed notices, but Yusuf's credibility stays high.

Middle Child
FEBRUARY 1993

CARL, HIS PARENTS, my parents, and Angie and Camille were having dinner together. I extended myself, the welcoming gesture of unfurling fingers. Angie was pregnant, I was the dad. Carl had been my student in a summer arts program in Santa Barbara—I'd defended my honor during office hours. He was bold and dashing in a way that made you go, Whoof! After he graduated, he moved back to the Bay Area, where he had grown up, and we began dating. I had the giddy pleasure of being Carl's trophy wife. His parents were amazingly supportive. In fact, they were even nicer than Carl, who could be a bully, acting dumb about it to maximize the power disparity—or to correct the disparity? "Think good thoughts," he'd say on the phone, and "I love you, babe." They took me along on a family vacation to Aspen, where we mountain biked.

I guess I arranged that dinner just to see what would happen. It was the novelist in me. My parents were visiting, so it was an opportunity for my mother to cook. We like to feed people. Our platters and bowls call out with voices of silver and porcelain, stoneware and glass.

Before dinner our guests' conversation scaled heights of avoidance—but of what? Sylvia, Carl's mother, asked questions about cacti in the friendliest way when she learned that my mother was the secretary of the Escondido Cactus and Succulent Society. Sylvia was graciously in charge. Finally she asked, "What was Bob like as a child?"

Others chimed in, "What was he like?"

We were in the midst of the food part of the evening, united in the light of my mother's cooking.

My parents sat awhile, considering. Camille pressed them: "What was he like?" In six months, she and Angie would be mothers of a baby with half my genetic array.

My mother said carefully, "He wasn't like our oldest—with Denis you never knew what would happen next."

My father seemed relieved, even proud. "It was always something."

"You mean Denis got into trouble?"

"He was never out of trouble. We were afraid he would burn down the house." My father and my older brother got off on the wrong foot, so to speak, because my father didn't want to share. Doesn't Oedipus's story begin with dad?—his unwillingness to share mom's love? Dad imagines that his son wants to kill him because he won't let himself imagine killing his son. My father's and brother's antagonism so obsessed and distracted them that in the end my mother was mine—at least I thought so.

"Denis would crawl out of bed and find the matches. When we hid them, he used the kitchen stove." If either parent had ever known me, the trauma of my older brother's childhood obliterated the memory. I fought an impulse to run out of my house before more could be not said.

Later, my guests made fretful observations: X was withheld, Y was aggressive. When Carl included on his list of grievances that I crack my foot when it's stiff, I knew our affair was over. He was going through a nonsexual period—at twenty-two?—and he would not promise to aim his revived urge at me. It had taken a while to learn to be attracted to him. His body seemed to need a narrator. Plowing into his mushy insides, I had to inform myself, This is Carl, defined as a foal's nostril, moist and fuzzy.

I suppose it doesn't matter, since Carl ran off with a Vatican priest a few months later. I had met Father Pierre Thomas with Yusuf in Rome. He was a baked apple with a pointed nose, an insatiable collector of writers and celebrities, a spiritual hero to some, who quizzed me on the names of the residents listed at the front door of my apartment building on Vicolo della Penitenza. As a gossip he was disappointing, telling us *who* he knew rather than *about* them: William Burroughs, Iris Murdoch, Gus Van Sant . . . I attended one of his Masses in Rome; he talked about kindness. I suppose it was a fitting end to an affair that was more Mozart than Wagner.

Pierre took Carl to New York, where they had Thanksgiving dinner at Joan Didion's, saw *Einstein on the Beach* with Allen Ginsberg, and spent a night at James Merrill's. Heady stuff for a twink. Pierre promised Carl a job at the UN and sent him thick envelopes of closely written letters on onion skin paper—did Carl read them? Later, Carl reported that these celebrities were a lot nicer to him than my friends had been, which I thought very likely but not to the celebrities' credit. Now my part of Carl's story is finished, the contact between our skins is broken.

The morning after our dinner, I pressed my mother. She had been my polestar, but she was at a loss. Finally she said I used to corner her in verbal games. When I complained that I was the stupidest kid in my class, she would assert that I was not. I'd say, "How can you know that? You are not in my class."

What do I remember of that remote and too-close fiction?—a beautiful giantess who stretches from my infancy to my old age. A certain dress, full-skirted. I demand that she twirl again and again, tearful with urgency, the dress billowing so she is Beauty from a tale. She lets me style her hair into flamboyant coiffures. Crushing boredom at school. I'm not compelled by a rich inner life, just lost in a fog. I can't be distracted, but from what? No wonder no one knew me. How is it possible for a child to be overwhelmed with exhaustion? Lack of meaning is exhausting. I want treasures, precious things, beauty, and she buys me bone china animals. She takes pride in her high school English achievements, her essay on "Alexander's Feast": "He raised a mortal to the skies; / She drew an angel down." Sometimes she launches into "To the tintinnabulation that so musically wells / From the bells, bells, bells, bells"—putting an elbow into it. The satisfaction of cleaning a room till it sings. Denis calls me the Housewife. I'm pleased, though I understand the insult. I want to be a good girl, but my fingerprints smudge the truth. After we read Byron's *Don Juan* together, my mother writes a poem using Byron's *ottave rima*. She waits by the sink, face averted, while I read it. I don't respond, unwilling, unable, reeling back from love. A bitter moment, pure. The drawings and paintings I do, I'm an artist. I paint a pink kitten in a brandy snifter, a self-portrait. The shadow-puppet theater. The backyard dramatics. The art projects I invent in place of homework. Then, reading.

I was dyslexic avant la lettre. From the start, I was illiterate with an illiterate's complex shuffling of appearances. Like homosexuality, illiteracy made me a better performer—that is, a better liar. The walls of books in my study create the impression of learnedness, and the fact that I have read most of them shows how far I will go to mask my inability. I have always worked like a maniac on a loose mosaic to create the illusion of literacy, the most preposterous extent of which is to write a book. For you this sentence may be drawn from a multitude that lead into the wide world. For me it is the dead end of what I am able to say, written at the crumbling edge of the cliff. Like an illiterate, I imitate conversance with "subject matter," fear of life, love of life. Inevitably I crash into the high wall of my ignorance, the overwhelming falsity of experience, as though I *misread* Ed's sickness and death. What remains is terror on a two-dimensional stage.

"No one is sure of the reality of his own contrition," wrote Martin Luther. No one is sure of the reality of his own loss, his own emptiness, his own grief. It's a double negative that does not make a positive, and how can that be? Not so many years ago, I wished to rescue my mother, to save her from the indignity of life with Dad and to have her for my own. Now we were trapped in isolation beyond our control.

My mother went on to relate advice Denis gave her—in his capacity as a therapist—to repair her own childhood. She said, "If you were not cared for as a child, it's not too late, you can go back and pick up the baby that you were and give it comfort and love." My mother teared up as she said this. We were in the cafeteria of the Academy of Sciences in Golden Gate Park, a vast echoing room with no darkness even

99

in the corners (it no longer exists), eating an It's-It and drinking coffee. We had seen the fish. My mother was charmed by the myriad forms of the world: an anemone, an animal that was an extravagant flower. Tears welling, her beautiful face tipped back. "It's *magnificent!*"

A revolution occurred in the way I valued my childhood. The good child is actually the unknown child. Attention exists only in conflict. I imagined I was a princess because I was never scolded. After a while, I held myself apart. I am afraid of falling into the past, and my parents offer an emptiness to justify my vertigo. Even when I was a boy I resented the way childhood shaped expectations. A hellish inner force drove other boys around playgrounds and parks, and this was supposed to prepare them. I never subscribed to that faith: to pursue the ball and believe the game. I could not imagine an adulthood I wanted, except that they could sit around and talk. Thinking about it, it's a false relief (like so much that comes from psychology) that my behavior has an antecedent, a structure that shapes the all-there-is of present being. Psychology charges in like unwanted cavalry to save a day that would be better lost. I'm surprised this affects me. I still care what happened seventy years ago to a child I barely recognize in the few blurry photos, docile and serious. I want my life and death to be inconsequential. When I die nothing will be lost, because nothing will have existed. I'm a morbidly good girl in the void, cleaning it of my presence.

The memory of childhood is full or empty, but memory itself is empty like any code that organizes matter or information. I associate the awareness of this particular emptiness both with the desire to hide it like a bad conscience and with the desire to be an artist so I can take revenge by showing how it tunnels through all experience, a madness that is the truth. I want to disappear and to be fiercely present. The writers who kill themselves are my colleagues. A rotting sill, a delirium of ants—I turn away as though pushed into a dream. If my experience had not been so empty, I'd need to empty it myself.

Notes for a Novel

ED ON THE PHONE: I slipped in a puddle on the porch and flew down the stairs. I landed on my back, full-force impact, my feet pointing away from the bottom step. Finally, after five years of illness, I could scream for help—"*Help!*" It felt so good to finally scream it. As if I'd waited for this moment through the MAI, the cancer—"*Help, Daniel!*"

Ed was often sick as a child and that helped him live with AIDS. He recognized sickness, imagined it. "Are there possible obstructions?—warts in the veins, polyps in the arteries?" Sickness amplified the mystery of his body. Hepatitis, 1973. Thyroid storm, 1976. From his journal: "Four men suck amyl nitrite overdose. An hour of cruise-talk with lonely night watchman, not yet twenty, blue-badged cap, orange curly hair. Bob jerk-off, teriyaki, aching scalp burning ring around crown of skull, exploding shoulder muscles, crying, sickening pain, vomit. Pick deeply into small finger, pleasure all over as I scrape fingernail between two layers of skin. Bathe, ecstatic numbing sensation behind eyes, quiet thudding. Roaring hail beating car roof, roar my own heart." Nurses allowed me to stay with Ed all night. I had no legal right. He was unconscious—his heart beat so fast that it would fail. At two in the morning, his doctor told me to call his next of kin. He left it to me to say, "You mean he's going to die?"

Ed's mother had remarried—incredibly, she was Mrs. Sweet. Mrs. Sweet declined to attend her son's probable death. I called our friends, I needed their presence. How toylike and dirty the city looked that night. The poets and artists sat in the lobby till Ed was out of danger.

In 1975, Ed's obsession smashed a head of lettuce against a wall. "Bob, in Dan's mind that lettuce was me." Dan's basement bedroom had clerestory windows at ground level. Ed continued seeing him after learning that five roommates watched them through those windows at Dan's invitation.

"The erotic is a lateral geology." *What does this mean?* "It's right that I should die but not my nipples." I make Ed laugh by describing a moron I penetrated—"Mountain Lion"—bucking, barking, chomping the pillow and shaking it like prey.

Kitchen chair high above his head, Ed smashes it against the floor—that chair is me. A revelation in his journal: I announce our relationship is over on February 17, 1978. I thought Ed left me. Did I put it into words? We lived together until November.

"I woke up in a Macy's utility closet, surrounded by cardboard boxes and aluminum props. I called Bob, and yes, most hospitals do look like utility rooms. But no, that was a nurse working on a computer and not a salesperson at a register. We laughed and joked while he talked me into the present and hospital walls became hospital walls, the bed became a place of rest and safety, and my bathroom was your typical hospital bathroom."

I don't understand: "Since words begin it, only language can absolve me." *What absolution?* "I don't want to sink in polluted fluids and thoughts without thought. I am only polished sentences from the height of…" "The need to bury time against the return of…" "The problem of not knowing how to feel—and the bathtub—" *With Reese? Kathy?* "If words were real, then the self could exist after death." ?????

1974: "Remains of a muggy day. Heat lightning—the whole sky flashes. I MISS YOUR COCK! I look out at the bay, the islands. The water is still and large. Trains shake the house, here comes one now. I cry hard in my dreams and when I wake each eye has a puddle of tears." Ed's letters: loving, observant, suffering—different from the feeling of Ed inside me? I watched the grass rise after his bare foot pressed it.

June 17, 1993: "I waited an hour in the funny hospital gown in the mint green corridor. And then another hour of closely timed X-rays of my bladder, urethra, and kidneys. Unknown doctors knew every detail of my life. And then five hours of blood transfusions. My platelet count is so low my bladder and kidneys are bleeding. My doctor asked if I can handle peeing crimson. It's so disheartening to see blood-red pee."

My mother's two versions of life: First, we are alone and have only ourselves to depend on, emotionally and financially. Second, we can go back to comfort and love our infant selves. Or are they different?

I drive through the desert with my parents. Bing Crosby croons "Deep in the Heart of Texas." My mom sings along with the next song, "Where the Blue of the Night (Meets the Gold of the Day)." I'm narrating a desolate mood. For them, it's a different story?

1993: "Denny, are you still a blue-sky person?"

"No, *mon ami*, not after ten years of AIDS."

October 1993

ED CALLS to let me know that twelve-year-old Polly Klaas was stolen from her bedroom by an intruder. It happened in Petaluma, a typical small town in California where kids play in the street till dark and front doors aren't locked. On the first of October, the man entered Polly's house, tied up her friends, and carried Polly into the night while her mother slept in the next room.

"Have you heard about Polly?" Well, yes, the abduction leads every newscast and her face covers every front page. Wholesome and beautiful: America's sweetheart. Ed says, "A few hours earlier, Polly and her friends were playing with white powder and black lipstick that made her look dead," as though that proved something. "Now there's a manhunt for a man in dark clothing and a long-sleeved shirt."

"On the hopeful side," he says, "Winona Ryder has become involved."

Bob and Ed
NOVEMBER 1993

David Bowie was shot into deep space in a narrow cylinder and the air bristles as I feel him returning. I see every mile as he hurtles across the sky, invisible in the graying twilight.

(Ed's dream, September 16, 1980)

I LIE DOWN on Ed's bed in the soft orderly room. Branches cast still shadows on the frosted-glass window. A bowl of mangoes in the kitchen emits powerfully. On his nightstand, plastic containers parse out the harsh pills in hourly doses. The medicines keep Ed going but degrade his blood as though it were a sewer for all the toxins in the world.

Ed wears a lavender ribbon on his lapel. He explains, "It's Polly's favorite color." He confides that workers in the basement discovered a huge crack in the foundation too extensive to repair in an ordinary way. "I don't trust them at all," he whispers with a raised eyebrow. "They insist that we move out for our own safety because the explosives could very well demolish the entire house."

"That's crazy, Ed. You can't let them do that."

Ed speaks with mild wonder. "We already went to the mayor's office and he was powerless." Ed shakes his head in disbelief. "This is our house and now we have to leave it and we don't know if we can ever return." Strange, the garden and house are perceptibly still, held aloft in the clear, flowerless autumn, without a sign of workers or machines.

One cold August night in 1970, after seeing Andy Warhol's *Trash* at the Cento Cedar, now closed, I shared the streetcar stop on Market with a young Asian. His face was delicate and dramatic, with lush lips. His heavy hair fell past his shoulders and he was absolutely thin. He wore a blue peacoat. He said, "I noticed you in the theater." His eyes were round when he asked, "Are there other movies like that?" He was so spaced-out I thought he might be simpleminded till he showed me his sketchbook and I could see his lyricism and intelligence. The N Judah lumbered to a halt. I climbed aboard. Late Sunday night, when would the next arrive? After a few blocks I jumped off and ran back.

Ed's lack of surprise was disconcerting. "I knew we would see each other soon." We had coffee at Zim's on Van Ness, now vanished. Eventually I gathered that Ed had hitchhiked to San Francisco from Tacoma a few weeks before. He'd lived out of garbage cans, then someone moved him into his flat on Eighteenth Street in the Castro. Ed was vague on the details—I surmised he was trading sex for food and shelter. Did his host think it was romance? I had just moved to San Francisco as well, crashing with friends of a cousin. Few people knew I was gay.

Ed visited me the following night. Ed was twenty and I was twenty-three. I put his cock in my mouth. That was strange, but Ed was appetizing, he smelled sweet and musky. Learning about each other meant learning about gay sex. I didn't go near his asshole—not even a thought. Ed's flesh was beyond value, my own flesh reeked of failure but was too precious to risk. Outside our door my cousin's alarmed friends whispered, "*Are they having sex?*"

Ed and I pushed and pressed and rubbed and beheld. *If my mind's touched, I'm totally touched.* "Like waves," he said. Ed's body: as skinny as the kid next door, with a high forehead, skinny neck, and small butt. My body made noises—it had agendas I'd never considered. We didn't know that our desire for each other included our longing for all men. *I concentrate I start small a small piece of his skin.* I didn't know that giving him pleasure meant exciting all creation. *I expand piece by piece and when I come I've created the universe.* In the morning, Ed told me every detail of his dream, the dream before that and the dream before that, retreating into the night. Not shreds, CinemaScope.

During the following decade we were rarely apart, we were Bob and Ed. The past gave way like cobwebs—outmoded customs, shadowy relatives whose dialect we shed word by word. Forgetting wasn't the result of entropy but of conservation. It cost less to forget heterosexuality than to maintain the leaky hydraulics of repression. That is, I had to forget myself to pursue my goals. Homos of my generation will understand. Ed and I were paranoid, driven, lonely, but our dominant feeling was relief that there was a world to enter, a human club to join, an adulthood that was recognizable, a cup, a friend, a dog.

Ed and I were lovers, that's the term we used in the seventies. Ed painted me in an ecstatic jungle of ferns. It was okay to be homosexual there. In that context. *My American body opalates under this sunlight of warmth.* Sex became the opposite of drudgery, of having no identity and no contact. Our bed was tenderness surrounded by hostility. What did the ferny jungle mean? So what? My poems and Ed's paintings are dated, but Ed's dreams speak the era—paranoia and spasms. The paranoia of having long hair in the early seventies—the intensity, the phases, Vidal Sassoon. We took LSD seeking explanation and guidance, like going to the Cosmic Visitors' Center. Ed had seen *2001: A Space Odyssey* eighteen times on acid.

Magazines, meetings, and demonstrations came later. Ed dyed his hair a deep inorganic cobalt, *Superman*. We weren't out to our parents. Later we became a voting bloc, a readership, a target audience. It took a year to try anal. *Ouch ouch ouch ouch!* I felt humiliated and invaded. We didn't think about it again for a year. Ed attended a workshop at GLIDE Memorial Church with his friend Sam. What was it called? "*Blah Blah Blah* the Body." An inventor presented a dildo that translated music into silent vibrations. He called for a volunteer. Sam went up and experienced Beethoven's "Ode to Joy" in his rectum while the class watched his italicized expression.

Every morning Ed told me his dreams. *I have the life of knowing you, me alone in the totality of my eyes.* He hardly spoke. "Do you like the sky?"—the question prefaced by hours of silence. Or perhaps "You can hear rain, but you can't hear snow," eyes clouded, insoluble. I asked him to describe what we were looking at, and he did with miraculous precision. He breathed through his eyes. Compared with him, I was an unsuccessful criminal, trying to steal the future from whatever I saw. What kind of witness could I be when my only subject, my only news, was the wound of frantic loneliness? To gain a point of view, I asked Ed to describe me and he said without pausing, "High-spirited and pessimistic." So I was a secret from myself but visible to Ed. It was the question I would ask my parents twenty years later.

Sometimes Ed spoke as though language isn't a barrier, as though words don't lie, just as he inhabited the contradictory perspectives of his dreams. He spoke without obligation. I understood from his reply that opposites exist in us without conflict. We were into Josef von Sternberg and Gustav Klimt—overall pattern that meant aching arousal. *When the flesh grows dusky and twists with sex and drugs we scream as much as it hurts.* *Aurelia* by Gérard de Nerval, impasses. Intimate distances, Georg Trakl. Puzzles attracted us because the language that could tell us what we were did not exist. *We keep the answers in our bodies but they make no sense.* *Hyperion* by Hölderlin, mazes to be lost in. We did not master these poems and stories, they led us into a state of wonder. I pushed up from the inside and pressed down on Ed's groin with my palm, mixing inside and outside. In the aroused twilight, slow convulsions, the advent of being *like a body torn into existence.* Ed moaned—sensation or idea? He seemed to know that most situations are hard to fathom because they are simpler than the consciousness that describes them. *Be sincere to Bob and Ed, we are the most beautiful type of all, the simpleminded fool.* Blowing him, I arched his torso as though kissing him passionately, turned upside down. Our orgasms made us hornier so we jacked off in the dark. Finally, rid of tension, we floated empty as box kites. I restore sex from earlier books to the point of origin. Ed kept a dream journal at my instigation. Our dreams were not puzzles to solve but a commons producing images that we harvested for paintings and poems. *A room appears as I enter it.*

"Well, sure I like the sky…" I was bored to the point of indignation. Behind boredom, I was wracked with joy. Not true? Felt to be true? The sky looked bored, stolidly overcast, glaring without detail. It was 1970. We stood in front of our stucco apartment building on dreary Masonic and Oak near the burnt-out Haight, a neighborhood utterly fallen. Our windowsills were level with the backyard where ferns filtered dreamy light into our rooms. We were safe inside. Did that retreat ever cease? Ed went farther than I, living in rooms like a cat. We heard gunshots at night (dregs of the Summer of Love) but cockroaches falling from the ceiling into our beds forced us out. In 1971 we moved to 3362A Sixteenth Street and in 1975 to 16 Clipper (across from Mac and Nonie) where I still live. I advised myself, Stay with him one more season. Two lonely people make a lonely couple. We didn't know how *not* to be lonely, what was required. We ate in silence at the restaurant, stunned by the expense. Ed found this note: "What is better, being lonely with Ed or lonely by myself?"

Ed and I were made for each other—loneliness so poor it couldn't afford words. The boredom of prison conjures arousal (Genet, Boredom=Sex) and there are other deprivations where the longing to exist takes the form of arousal. Our drastic childhoods—Ed's on an army base in Hawaii. Like Ed, I crawled shell-shocked to adulthood through the barbed wire of conventional warfare. Desire only a burden, only fetters, only isolating, only a bind. Sick with fear of my yearning flesh.

Ed at twenty: "A smelly old man fondled me on the bus today. He kept touching my cock and my thighs."

"Good grief, what did you do?"

"I showed him," Ed said, bristling with accuracy—"I didn't respond at all."

"Ed, remember about being more assertive?"

"I did what you told me. When I got up, I said, 'Thank you very much, and fuck you too.' The man followed me off the bus yelling and shaking his fist."

Surely most days were happier, calmer, and I am remembering the cargo I imported into our hippie paradise: I am a superior person who is harmed, etc. I cared less that Ed fucked so many than that I couldn't manage to. Ed lived the era, was committed to it; I only halfway. Nothing allayed my fear. Nothing touched his solitude. Does it surprise you that his silence was filled with words and music?— they didn't subtract from it. Ed was a hero, the songs applied to him. "There's a Starman waiting in the sky / He'd like to come and meet us / But he thinks he'd blow our minds." Being half-Japanese, he was often excluded from our community's self-description. Was our counterculture less racist than the mainstream? If you are precisely the image your community purveys, you attain the immortality of the vernacular. But Ed parlayed the exotic into glam rock androgyny: David Bowie. "You've got your mother in a whirl / She's not sure if you're a boy or a girl." A dance club turned Ed away. Stupefied, I blurted, "He's the handsomest man here!" The bouncer didn't reply and it took a minute to understand, *incredible*. Ed did not let me see his outrage but volunteered that the Club Baths had also turned him away. Racism in the gay community! We organized picket lines.

Ed sleepwalked into a full scholarship at the San Francisco Art Institute and painted heroic nudes rising-falling through clouds and sky. *The expressive body, naked and exploding, arches and twists in space.* Image-making and isolation describe my life with Ed. I spent whole seasons inside the creation of his paintings and sculptures, driving all over town to find the right watercolor paper, for example, and we lived inside the critique of his work. *With Ed I talk about Ed, his illnesses and his art, his boyhood a bracelet of scissors in the elementary fragrance of blocks and finger paint, and his fertility of dreams.* I went from not having a life to solving the problem of having one by giving it away. That is, I controlled the game by losing.

I wrote poems that sometimes appeared in small-press journals or in magazines that published anything by a homosexual or about homosexuality, from crude porn to learned essays. I beat back my isolation through writing. My poems sprang from a literary school that underwrote its psychedelic surrealism with strong emotion. At its height we "controlled" Intersection and a few smaller venues in San Francisco. Call our hippie bohemia Parachute Salon.

Am I still a member of this group? This was six or seven years before New Narrative, by comparison a household word. We were all white except Ed. They were all straight except Ed and me, though Tom made himself available. Courtly, he asked, "May I enter you?" He'd lost his front teeth in a bar fight, lending renown to his blow jobs. Like most young adults in the seventies, we had sex in almost any combination, a friend's interest or curiosity was enough. We viewed food stamps as a government subsidy. We were artists and everything we did was art, right? Ed attended my readings where I read grand love poems: *On acid I ask my dream for the definition of beauty—I see Ed's face against nebulas and exploding winds.* And later, poems on our disintegration: *You're beautiful I'm handsome fuck fuck fuck.*

Parachute Salon was ardent and toiling. I say without rancor that writing by functionaries without sincerity, or with only sincerity, stood a better chance. We were a group of friends living the counterculture dream. Most of us continue to write; as a literary school, history stood us up. Parachute Salon foundered over an anthology (classic!) as though we were poets in a Roberto Bolaño novel. We destroyed ourselves in schismatic fury and sank without a bubble. Then everyone moved away, as young people do. Our school's greatest moment was extraliterary, when Jeannie, Tom's mate, was carried out on a plank at one of our surrealist dinners, naked except for whipped cream. We devotees were not allowed to use our hands. We looked at beautiful her, stumped for a moment, when Steve cried, "Are there no Romans left?" and dove into her muff. Our dessert wriggled and moaned.

Twenty-three years after we met, Ed enters his dreams entirely—or do they overtake him? He talks, talks, talks in his quiet bedroom, stopping only to take a breath. It's like rowing. Twilight engulfs the shadows of branches on the frosted glass. Ed has the problem of describing life as life becomes the only thing left. Story runs shorter and shorter laps between Ed's body and Ed's being until we are looking at time. He takes my elbow as though I'm caught by a rushing current. Looking at time causes grief. This gabby child didn't exist in the first place: it was Silent Ed who remembered his dreams.

Ed chatters like a precocious eight-year-old, amiably, sadly. He wears the dazzled expression of someone who starves when food is everywhere. "The light is so beautiful here. We have to leave this house, I don't know why." Like Antigone, he bids farewell to the sweet light. "Yesterday Daniel started yelling about a crater—suddenly a crack appeared, a giant hole filled with bubbling water. Everything rumbled and the house shook horribly. I felt dizzy and weightless and I could hear Daniel's screams." The virus roils in his veins, brain lesions make him tipsy. "Winona is working just like anyone else at headquarters, calling people and putting up flyers, and she offered a two-hundred-thousand-dollar reward."

Ed is wandering, though the form that mostly takes is staying in bed. It's a period of tremendous activity. He generates images to suture an impossible wound. "I'm scared of the dormant garden and the sun so low. People die this time of year, responding to a natural cycle, and when I opened the attic door my dead body fell into my arms." He circles his cell, the condemned spinning out images of dissolution and harm—useless communication, pure communication. Ed's life is a flow of images, visual, then verbal—furious and sweet. What is the situation of an unrepressed unconscious? "We are a source," he tells me in a dream. "May your year be as clear as the glass in your hand," he says on his last New Year's Eve, raising his glass.

As Ed's dementia progresses, our households unmoor and drift away from the daily news. Kathy says, "You're not going to tell me you don't know who George Stephanopoulos is?" I agree: "I'm not going to tell you." I can't name government officials or recognize new celebrities. I aspire to the banal, dredging up phrases like "How are you today?" and "Looking forward to it" with visible effort. I'm empty. Do Ed and I use death as an excuse to hide? He keeps track of Polly— he is Polly, abducted from his bedroom by Death the Intruder in the plain light of day. He gathers phantoms to his illness.

I want Ed's experience. A portion belongs to me already. It's hard to ask him to tape our conversations, because it means he is going to die. Am I stealing his memories? They already seem derelict, value withdrawn. We were lovers during our twenties so we grew up together, performing toy versions of our parents' marriages. *My face becomes my parents' face when it roars down an argument's Niagara.* I knew how to be badly loved, but not what love entails, so I substituted frantic effort for vulnerability. I didn't want to be understood! Is it a secret if there's no reason to know it? I wish I could convey the feeling, lying in bed together in the late morning, membranes still humming, the big empty day ahead, expectation and anxiety. Ed spent money on his clothes, his dope, his hair, and his art. He grew marijuana ardently on the back porch under the alien pallor of Gro-Lux. The economy of this cottage industry was separate from the one we shared. If Ed's agenda determined page count, marijuana would have a sprawling chapter. I spent money on the house, trips for us, treats. I cleaned and shopped and cooked (my mother). Ed lived for himself and that was fascinating. *I hold up a mirror to your transformations and I watch you, deity of the eyes.* His indifference to my labors made sense. I nursed a resentment that I needed (my mother). Did I labor so hard to avoid giving myself to him? Did I substitute work for feeling? He would not give up his seat to an old man and said in a cold femmy voice, "I paid my quarter." The country was still at war.

Life is an intolerable burden if you have no idea what to do with it. *There is a voice on the inside and outside that says "not this."* I was a writer, but not the writer I needed to be. For that I had to become a different person. *Bye-bye plot line, ACE bandage of my style and heart.* I thought the answer was Ed and maybe it was. He gave me a vantage from which to construct a narrative and an identity. He exploded in rages we did not understand (his mother). His fury struck like dangerous weather, war in all directions, all against all. Lily crawled onto my lap and trembled as he stormed above. Then his rage jumped a level, his features distorted or maybe revealed. "You think you're a god," he shrieked—amazing.

Our work lives were so erratic that weekends and weekdays slid together and we couldn't afford to eat in restaurants or to go on trips unless we hitchhiked. But we had time—only the poor and the rich have time. And I love monotony, I'm the perfect citizen of the village.

Ed worked: for a tuxedo rental company cleaning petrified vomit off bug-ridden formal attire; for Bank of America, justifying accounts on the night shift; as a nude model for the San Francisco Models Guild. Ed's pro bono shrink saved him from the draft in 1971—I was a conscientious objector—and got him SSI in 1977. Did Ed sleep with him? How shocking the list of mental disorders: "Anxiety of psychotic proportions and evidence of schizophrenic thinking patterns emerge from the projective tests." Depression, paranoia, what else? "Currently things at his home are unstable as his roommate is unprepared (and questioningly able) to handle the patient's voicing his thoughts rather than stifling them and playing the role of 'good guy.'" Ouch.

Ed and I belonged together: the pressure of a more coherent self would have been intolerable. Our life: *the tears and skins of an onion*. I am more comfortable portraying Ed's isolation than my own because I give him more credit. My loneliness had a taint of corruption, displaying my deformity like a beggar to gain a penny. His was solitary confinement, pure, stark, without context, without audience, as though pain were certainty. As though having pain were the same as having certainty.

What is the right question to ask about a life? Do I harm Ed by not knowing or by deleting some fact or anecdote? His grandparents lived in a guava grove and spoke no English. After we separated, Ed worked as a waiter at the Rite Spot, on a city road crew (money in the bank, and a beefy body that vanished like a trick when he turned sideways, same flat ass, etc.), and as a gardener at the Conservatory of Flowers in Golden Gate Park. Did his access to dreams create his rapport with plants? I was the mail boy of Philadelphia Life Insurance on Sansome, the entire labor force of Allied Textile on Harrison (along with a benevolent Swedish manager, a snarly bookkeeper who never removed his fedora, and a short distracted Jew who rarely visited his slowly failing business), an English tutor at Golden Gate University, a light carpenter, and the token male in the Feminist House Painting Collective. Then I painted alone. After Ed and I separated, I worked at literary nonprofits and as a teacher. My love for Ed returned as disinterested affection, wanting him to be happy, to succeed.

"Why did we break up?"

"I don't know," he replies, sitting up as though to prove his sincerity.

"I suppose I don't either."

Ed was the genius of the seventies, a god in the clouds. His isolation expressed itself as sex—that's what excited me. The revolution was not exactly a communal blaze, but flame burst from his body in public. *The burningness of sex of loneliness don't touch it touch it it's hot.* Was it lust or rage or the desire to explode? Those who came out in the sixties in the profound night of the suburbs know the meaning of desire that won't be controlled. Know to fear and respect desire: all profundity, all completion, all connection, all configuration. My feelings told me that Ed was the only other person in the world so committed to sex. There were not enough orgasms in the universe to cut through the knot of tension that was Ed. Control at one end, chaos at the other: the long short distance from chance meeting to *exploding at an angle like a fizzed-up Coke.* Ed was the god who satisfied everyone, aroused by the arousal he caused, god of access, courtier of the moon, passed from man to man in Dolores Park in the imperishable night.

On June 21, 1975, Ed found his first glory hole: "Hanging by my hands from the top of the stall, my legs rattled, I came hard in quick explosions. Bob, I collapsed inside from excitement." Sex operated as a kind of middle distance where we recognized ourselves, a kind of realism that let us into the story: "Would you like me to have sex with you or write a sexy poem about you putting all my loving lines together like clouds or sex acts reflected in a teaspoon that measures a medicine of cherries." Earning a living was an exotic activity, domesticity a salute to the past. The shirt and pants and job and chatter only prefaced the nakedness beneath, obscured the home ground of intimate touch, *framed appetite with a keyhole.*

Where was I? Walking Lily, perhaps. Her piss sparkled under the streetlights and raced down the sidewalk, a glittering stream. The streetlights exercised a principle of order, lifted buildings and trees out of darkness into the inky, stately night. I passed a house where a stereo played a love song I knew, conventional lyrics, obvious, a melody climbing predictable changes, and it flooded me with longing. *Ed says a man was embraced and embraced. Bob says new hope to my hands.* The song said, *I found my home I found my home I found my home.*

Has anybody adequately described the sheer boredom of promiscuity? I did not have Ed's patience, although I admired it. Public sex is an answer to many questions—perhaps it's what society needs. Ed waited in bars, waited at the baths, waited in sex clubs, waited in parks, waited at parties, waited for the orgy to begin. *An ordinary citizen who had completely gone over to sex.* Someone's outraged boyfriend burst through the door: the swarming limbs absorbed him but then the bed collapsed, the extra weight a comedy. Gender was only the beginning. "I have an idea," Ed said, patting his erection as though it were a thought. He cantered on a human horse, slapping its reddening flanks. He had an affair with a family. He had a fling with a Macy's rug buyer on a stack of Bokharas in the storeroom, and with an obese man. It tickled him to agitate so much flesh with so small a button. "He came with one little squirt, it sat on his belly, so little and innocent." Put another way, his isolation was a kind of clarity that made nakedness happen—an exertion of will revealing the life of nakedness.

By 1978, our marriage was so open it no longer included me. We broke up in November. *The story begins whoosh! It ends, to go elsewhere with the silverware or remain, eaten and beaten, the victim of a common but rare disease.* Was my reason Ed's reason? He outgrew our relationship. I couldn't adjust to his growth. That's likely. He felt oppressed by a mentor boyfriend—who wouldn't? His rage was his mother's, perhaps class anger gave it shape. He wanted to be on his own. He wanted the next thing. I was always attracted, but that is unusual—he probably stopped wanting me. The city was floored by the Milk and Moscone murders and the Jonestown massacre.

I moved out of Clipper for a few months to give Ed time to organize his departure. I stayed with my friend Denise. It rained constantly. Somehow rain leaked down the electrical cord and over the bare lightbulb and trickled to the floor of my cold, horrid room.

I thought my love was sentimental and fake because I did not think Ed was worthy (what a joke), because I could not love someone who was comically selfish, who had so little irony, who had so little logic. I proceed against Ed. I protest till the void is filled with my bad infinity—and what then? Ed was tender: "Oh my Mimosa," he would say, and he closed his letters "Only Yours." He was exactly what I was looking for. He gave shape to an isolation that was intrinsic. *He shaped it*—an ancient fragment might say—*in a sacred manner*. What did we have in common? Everything! We needed erotic touch to tell us what we were.

I had my affairs and adventures. Ed asked, "Did his body arch?" But I was lonely in San Francisco in the seventies, when all you had to do was glower at some guy at the bus stop across the street or walk a few blocks to the park. I installed a desert in the Land of Milk and Honey. *A language where hunger and man are the same word. The mythology of resentment, its deficient spirit lives in the empty egg.* Oh, one would always be lonely with Ed—so beautiful, so fucked up! Or was I Beauty sleeping through the orgy in my glass coffin, bitterly waiting for the exact kiss.

Question with a Question

We climb low steps—streets and destinations in Mexico City. Two molars change places. My teeth crack into bits when I clamp down. Stairs lead to a dentist as I suggest finding one. In an alley an old man seduces a boy with caramel corn. His kink is force-feeding children to death. I bang on the window to show that I see him. Others warn me that he takes revenge. A nurse seats me—she doesn't know how to treat my mouthful of calcium and metal bits.

(Ed's dream, July 14, 1974)

AS USUAL I lie in Daniel's place, on his pillow, on the heavy indigo blanket, and Ed lies under it. His skin has darkened, the side effect of an MAI drug, and his features are abbreviated, pinched, wasting back to his skull. Between us a tape recorder internally rotates. His memory is the archive of many pages of my experience. I'm afraid of losing the shape of my life, a shape I can't recognize without help. If I step back (grow old enough), will I see it? Is stepping back equal to form? Is form the stepping back? I waited too long to obtain this record. I'm the "he" who hesitates in the proverb. Silent Ed returns and the frantic image-making has come to an end. What replaces this: the way light falls in the sickroom, the mullions' shadows on the curtains. The day will be incomplete. Is this the fulfillment of his silence, or a completely different silence?

Ed begins, "The first thing I think of is our big trip to Mexico and Guatemala. A very magical kind of trip. Very glad to hear other points of view about, I don't know, certain things. To me it is very rewarding to have the ability to do that. Make lists of the past and incorporate them into the present. It happened in a part of my life when I was not very conscious."

I remind Ed that we made love behind a pyramid in Palenque. He says, "I was so terrified, I was just beside myself. A *federale* with a machete came around the corner just as we buttoned up. Two seconds earlier and he would have caught us with our pants down, literally. We were on LSD. When was that? My memory... I remember the wild turkeys—they were blue-gray. Those things on turkeys? Wattles, they had turquoise wattles. I depended on the wattles quite a bit. They were sort of dirty colors. Regular turkeys have orange and red and yellow in their feathers and somehow it all looks great—oh there I go ..." He wears a jangled expression, as though he's hearing bells.

"We were there for my birthday," I remind him, "and for my present Diana sucked one nipple and you sucked the other."

"Oh really? There was that bus trip to Chichicastenango where everyone got sick and a boy vomited into a plastic bag over our heads. I remember that. Just like me currently. I can't go out into the world because I don't feel safe without having extra ammunition. A lot of my fear was garbage from my childhood. I was never proud of that. Not really knowing what I was saying or doing, what the repercussions were going to be. I feel like I was unconscious about everything."

I resist Ed's account of his fucked-up self since it includes his relationship with me. I remember drinking from little bottles in a café, too moved by a song from someone's radio. I conducted my despair, my hands raised in the space hollowed out by intoxication. Hot, stuffy, radio static. Ed's cheek pressed against the window and I reached toward it. *Now it's getting harder to believe I'm being touched.* The memory dims as I reach for it.

"Ed, we were in a café, that little café by the airport in Tikal, and you spotted a dragonfly up in the rafters."

"A spider had captured an iridescent butterfly, big as my hand."

"A butterfly?"

"Cobalt mixed with cerulean mixed with ultramarine. Lampblack edges and silver along the body line. I wonder what the place is like now?"

"It must be built up."

"Built up and I wonder if it's dangerous."

"Yeah, it could be."

"The jungle and all these people carrying automatic and semiautomatic rifles."

"Guatemala was going through terrible years."

"I always thought there was permanent damage but they must have gone through the earthquake."

"Worse than the earthquake. A civil war—it was happening when we were there and long after. They murdered a lot of Indians."

"Jeez—"

"Two hundred thousand."

"Probably the beginning of the one that we have now. Why can't people be nice to each other? Everybody's got an agenda. I find that happens a lot when I have a new attendant. They want this, they want that. Dorothy is the worst, a bright red sweater down to her knees—that red allowed no other nuances of color, never allowing different feelings. Can I have a little taste? Eating is difficult—it's so hard to eat. And then she eats the whole bowl."

We start up again. "What happened that one night? There was something significant that happened one night. Oh remember we walked into a reserve at Tikal. We didn't know that there was a big gate, just a light shining way in the darkness. And we did all our playing and someone shined a flashlight at us and started shooting. Someone in a shack. That was very scary. Any of us could have taken a bullet."

"Hopefully he was shooting into the air."

"I loved Tikal, and Palenque was nice too, because it was different."

"How different?"

"The colors, the butterflies, the clothing, the food. There was that chicken."

"?"

"She spread it open and shoved it in my face. *You want you want?* And I kept saying no no no so there was nothing for me after that."

"No, we ate there, we had mole. She gave us the breasts and they were huge and flavorless. A hen with rows of eggs inside. My mother said that when she was a child the unlaid eggs were a delicacy."

"So they would kill the chicken to get them."

"That hen had been around the block a few times. A big laying hen."

"Yes because I remember the two rows with four eggs on each side starting with marble-sized eggs, getting bigger."

"I was self-absorbed, looking at myself in a new way. I guess not being afraid, because I always was. Remember how paranoid I would be over nothing? So I would change that—what was your question? I liked the spontaneity that we both had. That means a lot to me. So what was your question again?"

"Oh, I was just asking how we were relating during that trip."

"I was relying on what we had between us to get me through each day. What two people say is Time."

"Remember when we had that argument in the middle of nowhere? We were stranded on a highway that went north in a straight line to the horizon, and we were so furious that we slept on opposite sides of the road."

We were a Beckett play for homos, without a shattered tree, one leaf or none. The high desert road, painfully molten moon, troughs of darkness below. *The cold took the form of men pursuing us with guns.* At dawn a battered VW slowed down and we ran with our packs to the car, united once more. Pedro, a civil servant, had crashed his car and then got plastered on a gallon of clear mezcal—he pointed, "from the mountain." Ed and I bent his fender back so the tire stopped scraping. Pedro kept roaring, "Take it easy, baby." We put him to sleep in the back seat and I drove.

"And that pineapple."

"What pineapple?"

"Remember I cut it open on the road."

"Was that part of our fight?"

"Yes but don't repeat it because those were hard times, weren't they? For being young and in our youth, it should have been more fun. But it wasn't really. 'Fun' isn't the word I would use."

"No. We were too fucked up. We did lots of fun things. But that's often true of the young. Older people have more fun. If they're going to have fun at all. Do you mind that I ask you to remember or is it just frustrating?"

"No, I haven't had any uncomfortable thoughts. I like when you sit in a room with me. That means a lot to me. But those were tough days for both of us. I had been in a couple of relationships but I still denied that I was gay."

"Really? I don't remember that."

"Do you remember when we drove cross-country with Elin, and I felt totally left out of your conversation, and we ended up at some truck stop, looking for something to eat, and I was hysterical. I had a pocket full of change, and I went out to the field behind the gas station and threw those coins as far as I could. It was a very big open stretch covered with grasses and small bushes. They were selling sandwiches and snacks. I felt like those pennies were the problem, not me. But as I look back, the problem was HIV. No, wait a minute, I was diagnosed in 1987, and we're talking about something that happened much much earlier. And these aren't even short-term facts, they are facts that have been around awhile.

"There are so many things I want to say, so many things I want to do. Talking is a creative process and I really miss that. And of course I miss all the facts that I can't remember."

I want to tell Ed about Chris, my new boyfriend, but how to fit him in? If Chris turns his head or leans back on his elbows, the gesture occurs inside me gigantically. This day, I want eternity to know I had a great orgasm with Chris, that I'm having sex with someone I love. Instead, I tell Ed about a neighbor on Clipper. "The snarly old biker who shoved his junk mail into our mailbox?" He'd return from the leather bars around two a.m. If I heard a crash, I'd go down to help. At that hour he was drunk and chatty. He'd grown up in that apartment, yet he had a clipped British accent. "He died on the freeway, and they found his windows nailed shut and newspapers and old mail stacked to the ceiling, narrow canyons twisting through."

Ed says, "So his junk mail was a gift."

Ed asks, "When did Lily pass away?"

"About six years ago."

"Eighty-seven?"

"Yes, I think so. Soon after I started seeing Loring. And I started seeing him when I was forty. She passed away—"

"You had a birthday party."

"Yes, you brought me an eighteenth-century sake cup that I keep on my dresser. Lily died the same day Loring returned to New York. He had been with me for two weeks. My downstairs neighbors heard me crying—they thought it was because Loring had left. I was indignant. 'Loring will never make me cry like that.' In a way I was right, since my grief for Lily was unalloyed."

"So you found her?"

"I was with her. It took a long time to get over the minute of her death."

"She died when you were together? Wow, that sounds difficult."

"I made up my mind that she would die at home. And she died quickly, she collapsed in the morning and by evening she was gone. I let her go—I could have dragged her to the vet but she hated that. She was sixteen—a long life for a big dog. Every movement was painful and the medicine completely flattened her. Her body couldn't deal with it anymore."

"Poor Lily."

"Well, lucky Lily. To have a long life, to be completely loved, to die quickly. So, lucky Lily." I buried her under a climbing tea, Gloire de Dijon, beige and apricot like her. Then the rains began—her grave emitted a stench like nothing I'd ever encountered. I called it dog soup. I begged Richard to deal with the problem—I didn't want to run into her. He replaced the soil with fresh dirt and sand. Lily sent no more messages unless you count the roses.

"I told Chris he's Lily come back—he didn't appreciate that." Ed and I laugh. "He's like Lily, you know, a bouncy blond. A bouncy blond who demands to be held at night."

"Lily would jump in anybody's door."

"She gave kisses to all and ran out. Chris is like that. Last night we were spooned together half-asleep and I felt odd little pops. 'Chris, you're farting on my cock!' He said, 'That's impossible'—he had nothing else to throw at the truth." I have the satisfaction of making Ed laugh. He doesn't care about wit for its own sake and only laughs when the joke is accurate or scatological.

"I guess I haven't spent enough time with him. He has a great laugh."

"His whole family does. They have the same laugh. It's amazing to see them together. They amuse each other immensely. They all have big necks and broad faces."

131

The window darkens and Ed slows down. "It sounds like he's got a good support system. When I think about my family, they're so totally dysfunctional."

"They're better than your family and they're better than my family too. But they are a family with their own problems."

Ed's weariness takes me along. I turn off the recorder. My needing to say *I love you* is a problem. I want to protest this requirement. Did we say *I love you* when we lived together? In the absence of the word "love" we live exposed. Old relationships maintain their failings, even as new relationships are conducted with more generosity on firmer ground. Are relationships time capsules? With Ed I get to be my young self even as we age, our interactions retain the Bob that was his lover. We rarely talk about our relationship. Do we both see it as a failure? Do I?—but not our friendship.

Ed snores lightly. I tiptoe around the bed, kiss his forehead, and carefully tuck him in. Then I climb back in, this time under the blanket. Ed slowly gets up, comes around, tucks me in, kisses my forehead, and tiptoes back to his side.

I hear Denny's voice. Ed is already up. It seems Daniel, Ed, and Denny are going to Eliza's, a Chinese restaurant in the neighborhood. Can Ed manage this?—we only visit in his home. I drag myself out of bed. "I suppose Bob is going to invite himself along?" Ed speaks coldly, rolling his eyes as though I constantly annoy him. Daniel and Denny pretend not to notice. As we walk to the restaurant, Ed asks mildly, "Who's the other person with us?" We tell him there is no one else. "Of course there is," he scoffs. I feel a little jealous of the invisible guest that Ed seems to want. At the restaurant, Ed stage whispers to Denny, "Who invited *Bob*?" Out of the corner of his eye he catches sight of the guest who won't take shape.

The Earth Is Full

A HUNDRED TULIP BULBS doze in the soil.

I arrive at Ed's door full of plans and juice, a festal figure, while Ed sleeps and drifts, face averted, one eye open. The world shrinks to the size of a bed. Life blazes on its own, incapable of including its own absence. Now life is a collection of details: fingering a fold in the blanket, turning the head, a bit of cuticle chewed solemnly, the awareness of prickly skin. Ed floats on his back, his breath apparent; his eyelids don't close completely and the whites are yellow and clotted. He feels a new sensation, as though water were pouring into his chest from a great height. As though there were a drain in his chest for heaven's waterfall. It's funny at first, distracting and freeing.

I am preoccupied by a huge new fact: the birth of my son, Reese. I continue to invent as Ed's invention unravels. In Ed's bedroom, strength is like weakness, the ego's frantic arrangements, cartoon fingers wriggling with greed. Ed's face does not have enough flesh to be slack. He's swollen and emaciated. The light in his little bedroom and the stillness it conveys. The translucent window's swaying shadows. To die in beauty.

Daniel puts on Ed's favorite music—Barbra Streisand or something classical?—Daniel? I was the first Jew that Ed encountered.

Streisand was exotic. Ed's possessions take on a sort of emphasis. The indigo blanket, the blue-and-gray kimono. The cornucopia of pills has shrunk to Morphine the Rich, the Gentle. Ed clings to a teddy bear. I always climb into a sickbed because the sight makes me so tired. I can hardly keep my head up, it lolls and small bursts of sleep jolt me awake. I sink into the mattress, he floats on top. It's now or never and because of his dementia it's probably never, but I can't keep the words down. "Ed, I love you." That's the place to start.

Ed slowly lifts his head and props himself on an elbow to look me in the eye. The late-medieval artists painted death—pinched and generalized—excited to see life slipping away. I'm a little afraid of Ed. He's wearing the face of the missing man in the *Chronicle*. The article said he was found naked, killed by blows to the head, yet there he was, in a suit and tie, a three-quarters profile, and I realized that this handsome young man looked odd because his muscles had no tension, his eyes no luster. I felt the full brunt of the phrase "All hope is gone." The back of his head was dented or missing—like Abraham Lincoln's! It's strange how the image persists, this young man pretending to be alive so his corpse can be recognized.

Ed doesn't speak, his face is big with suffering, but he gazes steadily with his muddy eyes. Perhaps his fatigue is greater than his fear. The closer to death he comes, the more apparent the empty structure of finitude. Although he's motionless, he's rushing toward a frontier while I exist in slow motion—ever more a representative of the world he's leaving. Ed's life goes only one way and there is only difference.

We look at each other with the knowledge that dying is happening, beyond recuperation, that we are saying goodbye. I cast about for something that will please him. "I want you to know that you did a great job." At living and dying, but he could take it to mean his art.

He startles me by whispering, "Thank you."

"Can I ask you what you're feeling now?"

After a moment he says, "Yes." It's so typical that I laugh—Ed is restored to me. I haven't been so close to Ed in twenty years. I go to kiss him, and as I embrace him he whispers, "Doggy ears." I wonder if he's addressing Daniel, maybe he's mixing us up. I'm crying, and Ed cries along with me, and rubs my back in sympathy. I whisper, "Are you ready to die?" and he replies, "Is anyone?" The house is silent, perhaps we are alone. The soft weight of Ed's blanket. When I wake up, I roll on my back to savor the rich sleep, I can taste it, and I listen to Ed's breath, one two three four, another breath, one two three four five six, another breath, one two three... *Living* is what I hear. I'm calm, trouble falls away in the dusk. For the moment death is the heavy blanket and the pleasurable buzz in my limbs.

Die with the Living, Live with the Dead

FEBRUARY 13, 1994

DANIEL CALLS ME: Ed has died. Daniel puts feeling into it and that irritates me. I don't know why—Ed's death belongs to Daniel. There's only so much emotion to go around. I sit down for a moment of luxury: something ended and the rest has yet to begin. I look out across the street—somehow Mac is involved. Mac's death goes through an adjustment and so does Lily's. The part of them that involves Ed's presence in the world is destroyed. The day without Ed is entirely unusual. It casts my senses back on themselves: I am wearing sight on the front of my head and the blurry frames of my glasses surround the view. The top of my stomach presses upward —why?

I'm already behind the wheel. I drive to Ed's house as though I'm late, wind buffeting the car, the wind my urgency. As though Ed were carried away by wind. I feel my heart beating through my body, even in my hands and groin—why? Will I relate to a corpse incorrectly? Will I fail as a mourner? I was a little scared when Lily was dying because I thought she might attack me—that is, death made us strangers. She arched on her side, shuddered, and deflated as life

137

passed into the air. I was afraid of Lily's body because all my love for her was turned away, and I sat with her while a few fleas crawled off her corpse sluggishly, as though her cooling blood had slowed them down. I've never touched a human corpse, but how can that brutally general word be applied to Ed? How can I explain it?—his corpse is a falling horizon.

Daniel and I have agreed to wash Ed as a last rite. I remember my mother's story, a story from her mother that occurred long ago in Oradea, a town in Hungary, now Romania, about women washing a corpse on the heavy mahogany dining room table. It was a great-great-aunt, I suppose. Rigor mortis had set in so they cursed the stiffening corpse to shame it into flexibility. Now my mother denies this story, has no recollection of it, though she affirms that those Hungarian ladies could really swear. Yelling to wake the dead a little. Skip in the hospital, twisted back, dead eyes, a Jesus freak shouting in his face as though calling long-distance: Do you believe in *Je*-sus? Do you believe in *Je*-sus?

Ed's house is dark and holding its breath as though the monster were ready to lurch, but after all, what is left to destroy? Like a horror movie victim, though in slow motion over seven years, Ed stared into the face of death, screaming with awareness, and he felt dread and sorrow to the limit. Ed's bedroom appears as I look into it. Ed lies on his side under the blanket, his knees drawn up and his hands gathered to his chest immemorially. I catch a glimpse of his sallow face, the dark eyelids not entirely closed over the muddy custard, his lower teeth visible. I turn away from that. I find Daniel and talk with him almost festively—a raucous companionship, but guilty. My place is with Ed and I am stealing from our relationship, preserving myself from Ed's death through inattention.

Finally I enter the twilight and sit on the bed. Death turns the room into a shrine: darkness is a fact and light is the belief in something else. Curtains hang in the silence, a clock ticks heavily. The light is soft. Silhouettes on the frosted window flail in repetitive frenzy, assaulted by the unheard wind, never tiring, always gesturing for the first time. Somewhere roofers are beating metal. There isn't much to do. I start slow. I draw a simple wish from a life filled with wishes: Ed is not dead. *Just sit up Ed, resume.* Ed is too complicated to die, too loved to die, even the dead body is too alive to die. The body still confers scale instead of the opposite. I put my hand on his forehead—cool, but living foreheads are sometimes cool.

I'm mentally tiptoeing, testing my own reactions, listening for a false note. I was raised and trained on wishes, so I am stymied and oppressed by this finality. Ed lies on his side, he does not struggle for breath. How odd that there are two of us but one breath. He's not a corpse yet, he's just holding his breath. Why not admit that I'm afraid, not because this corpse changes everything (that comes later), but because it pushes me to the border. Ed's body makes Bob's ghost. The room itself is robbed of breath, the corpse stole it out of the air. What is possible in this shut-down world/body/hope? Thwarted possibility is an ache in me as I sit in the quiet bedroom, the failure of systems that will be myself from now on. Or, how to go on from here with Ed if Ed is staying?—a perplexing question since the rest of the day obviously continues without him.

Rather than entirely absent, Ed is slipping into tepid retirement. I sense that he is listening from above, as though mortal gravity pulls ghosts into the room's upper corners. Will death change Ed's personality? Injure it? That's not impossible—the body that lies before me is impossible. Just in case, I say, "Ed, I love you." I want to improve

our relationship, so that I can have been a better friend to him, and
we can have been better lovers, as though now that he's dead he can
go back in time. I would like to protect him, perhaps from myself;
I would like to protect his consciousness.

The room is so lukewarm that my body bloats outward as though
from lack of air pressure. Ed was the first person and now he's dead.
Where is a breeze that will change the present, so hard to inhabit?
If I reject my experience, I disown Ed. He took for granted that we
had not loved each other passionately. Yet wasn't his passion how
our relationship began? In the park in 1979, Ed told me that Skip,
my replacement, was the first person he ever loved. Skip, tall and
blond, invited Ed for a walk. "I felt disbelief and unworthy. We
found a glade and made love. I had what I wanted, the world opened.
Skip took me through his house to his overgrown backyard. He has
insight into the body, he opened himself completely." Ed was moved
to tears by his own feelings. To my expression, he replied, "You loved
me that way?" And I was not sure I did. I'm reporting a conversation
in a novel in which the whole truth is delivered. Instead, our feelings
were hidden in subordinate clauses, passed over in an instant, pieced
together later. With Skip, Ed began to laugh with his hand in front
of his mouth like a Japanese woman. His life was as harsh as any
obsession with any jerk, and now Skip is dead and Ed is destroyed
and here I am growing angry next to his corpse because he is leaving
me yet again.

Ed would have enjoyed being bathed by his two lovers. Daniel and I roll up our sleeves. We try to ease Ed out of his kimono, blue-and-white cotton. We are sending him to the flames in something smarter. No decomposition for Ed, the story of the body ends here—the fragile body that endured cataclysms of pleasure and suffering. Daniel and I unfold him and try to lift out one arm but it won't be guided. It's so like Ed, I have to laugh. Trying to steer him was always a challenge, like pushing a shopping cart with one bad wheel. Now we dig in our heels and yank him around a little—he is putting up resistance, as though he were an error in measurement. His heavy head bounces loosely on the mattress, not at all like my great-great-aunt. His hand is tangled in a ball of threads in the kimono sleeve. I break the threads and free each finger as though it were mine. Daniel and I share glances of mock exasperation. Ed is being awkward on purpose. Not on purpose, he makes knots unintentionally, an anarchic spirit, as a child might "close the universe" in his play. Our amusement at his awkwardness shows how such fun is corpse-making. I cover half my face to hide my grimace.

I hold my face in my hands. It's strange that it fits into them because it feels bloated, ballooning with harsh surprise. Then we roll Ed back and get the other arm out and peel the kimono off. He is dressed in bikini briefs, the silky kind he favored. Daniel and I have sponges, towels, and we operate from a white enamel basin at the foot of the bed. I tackle a leg. The lonely flesh is rather heavy; it splays outward, then his knee falls inward, loose-jointed as a broken umbrella.

We hurry as though Ed might be impatient. Here is the dusky skin, here the straight back, the slightly bowed legs, the narrow waist, the flat ass. AIDS restored the body I lived with long ago, so thin that I watched his heart beating against his chest till my senses bled in marveling tenderness. I'm practical, guiding Daniel or following his suggestions, rolling Ed over to wash his back and to dress him for the undertaker. Daniel and I are rather jaunty, then I collapse abruptly. My almost-tears are fucked-up laughter, the comedy of strings cut, laughing without control. To bracket my misery, I cover my face again, amorphous and doughy. It feels helpless, like I'm full of laughing gas. To cover my face is to say grief is contained.

I get back to work and Daniel has to sit back, head in his hands. Daniel and I are working in the gap between the past and the future, the bitter sorrow of having no future in the present—here it is. Washing Ed is something I can have from Ed's death, something I can take away. We turn Ed onto his back. The urgency, the towering needs of that skinny body. Now there is nothing to wish for so the world is small. If he exists alone in the air, as he might, would he still be Ed? I need to feel there is still something to protect. To protect the creation of reality: Ed's consciousness, furiously making the world, raying out experience and time.

I am thinking about the absence of gore. Daniel pulls down Ed's underwear and milks one bright red drop from Ed's cock. The drop of blood is the only indication of the pandemonium that occurred within this body. Is Nemesis finally dead, or dying, in this red drop? Here to present itself for a bow, Ed's murderous blood. Ed's cock does not look different from the one he wore when we were together.

In 1974, we hitchhiked to Cortes Island in Canada. One night we slept in an old turkey shed. I went inside myself and yet gazed ever more at Ed's tender flesh, sank my face into it, held him with joyful reverence, the vanilla and musk, the swells and shapes that equaled a treasure to gloat over, a buoyant, all-encompassing lust—here's luxury, here's surfeit. How did I go from reading a book, reviewing the day, to *this*? Rigidity was meaning, making him more rigid was making more meaning. It was obvious how reality came to be a god. There was straw on the floor, dead weeds poked through the cracks, and old calendars and newspapers from the Depression were pasted to the gray barn-wood planks. The mountain in the window had the same weak texture as the grain in the wood. Ed went into a trance, serene ecstasy. He luxuriated on his back, occasionally cooing, while my hand grew numb and my arm grew sore performing their seemingly hopeless task. I realized with horror that he was delaying the orgasm I struggled to produce. All my inner necessity drained into boredom and exasperation, so I fed myself his erection. I wanted to cry to heaven at the injustice, to lift my tired hands and face to the highest court. My jaw was growing sore and I felt a tinge of nausea. Ed purred like a cat. I licked his balls as his cock bounced against my eyelids, thinking, Where is my union contract, my forty-hour week, my coffee break? But to view that antique sex properly, subtract my personality and Ed's—let sex be the loneliness of flesh itself, loneliness that does not even struggle toward communion.

The next morning, a bar of light fell across my stomach while a wasp flying tight circles checked out my sperm. I asked Ed to hold me. He climbed into a different position and protested, "How do you expect me to hold you in this position?" *He cut his arms off and said How can I caress you with no hands?*

Later, Ed walked ahead of me on the beach: his long heavy black hair, his broad shoulders and impossible slenderness, his jean jacket and orange corduroys, his elegance, his isolation, the gritty salty wind blowing light off the water, the thump of the surf. The morning light becomes harsh as I resurrect it, holding down the sand dunes in a farce of hilarity and despair. I felt queasy and groggy from a typical huge greasy breakfast. The cook and waitress quarreled in tense voices in the kitchen, then the waitress slapped our plates on the table. Ed's held two eggs burnt to rubber and a huge pile of half-cooked potatoes. Mine held two eggs so runny they covered the plate with salmonella and three chunks of charred potato. "If I was you," she advised, "I wouldn't pay for that."

Oh I remember we ate in silence in the glass-walled café right on the ocean and I felt bitterly estranged from Ed, bored by him, moved by him. At a table across the room, I saw the back of a man whose ears stood out like a fawn's. I urgently wanted to know if he looked like a satyr. I pictured his triangular face and delicious goat eyes. Could a face reveal that temperament?—ready to laugh, excitable? Would that be enough? We are married, he's relaxing on the bed with a knowing smile. Are people how they look? He kissed the woman he was with and jumped out of the restaurant just as a huge aggravated man in a dirty apron—the chef?—blocked my view.

I thought understanding did not exist between Ed and me, but now I wonder what understanding means. By now I mean this minute. Does it mean safety, like an insurance policy to cover the unreality in me? The beach was as boring as a hallway in an office complex, pressured and empty. There were many things to wish for so the world felt huge. I asked the wide blue sky to free me from chance. I was looking for intensity, wonder—but as places to arrive, not points of departure. I was a dead end to myself, banished from the present, and I wanted to find in Ed something to latch on to that was outside my egotism and fear, my stale relation to the world. Ed's innocence conveyed an erotic hope. A leap through Ed into lyric time. Those were my thoughts walking behind Ed at my slower pace, testing and questioning my tenderness for his body and life.

For some reason I regarded his cock as stubborn—a stubborn cock. Ed was going through a period of not wanting to come when we had sex in the morning, as a variation. He liked to be held in my mouth for as long as possible. My tongue moved slightly or just pressed. It was like praying. He did not want to go beyond his self-control. In the turkey shed, after he finally came—an orgasm I knew almost as well as my own—and the jolts of pleasure subsided, he asked, round-eyed, "Are there still turkeys here?" and my exasperation turned to hilarity. This image is so pressing, it can only be an escape from the present. Washing Ed's corpse seems weirdly tamped down. I escape into wind blowing the light off water.

Ed's body looks like proximity to the world because it's so thin. I am taking care of Ed and supporting his beauty as I used to. I want to reach out and give him a helping hand back into life. Washing his forehead, I now realize that Ed declined to come first thing in the morning because in that era he was saving his orgasm for someone else, someone later in the morning. Suddenly it's obvious. Our sex was an act of consideration on his part, or a tribute to my need. I should have put two and two together, but it was not the right time in the story to do that.

Daniel and I dress Ed in better briefs, blue silk. "You can open an underwear museum with the rest," I say ruefully (why rueful?). He stuffs toilet paper into the briefs to absorb any more blood—why? The drop of blood on the tip of Ed's cock—bright, erotic. I feel like deriding it. *Idiot, killing your host. What is the profit if you break the bank of the cosmic casino?* It killed itself through its own reproduction: safe sex. And then we dress Ed in his favorite kimono. Daniel, you describe it.

Daniel calls the mortuary and also Denny. Denny will deal with the mortuary people, sparing Daniel and me the sight of Ed being carted away in a body bag. We act out an old scenario—Bob and Daniel are sensitive (inexperienced, middle class), Denny is comfortable with matters of life and death (experienced, working class). I recognize as a failing that I avoid the sight of Ed's body going out the door, and of course if I had to deal with it, I would. And useless, because now I see it clearly, whereas the memory might have faded?

It's funny, Daniel and I have never been alone, even when we were with Ed's unoccupied body. It's February 13, 1994, midafternoon. The wind has died down. I suppose I'm supplying calmness in the midst of collapse? It's a weird kind of play, someone's death, that pressures the actors. I'm acting like my mother, I speak in her calm voice. I'm terrified by the possibility of breaking down, and behind that I want to reject the interruption of my solitude. The weather is early spring in its extremes: hail battered the plum blossoms this morning, now the sky is blue, the air is soft. I know that Daniel and I are alone, because how can a ghost look at the sun? We walk through the stable neighborhood, skirt the volatile one. Denny's carelessness used to aggravate Daniel and Ed, but it is Denny we call with our most serious problems. Denny's special competence, to honor the moment, to love without demands.

Climbing the hill with Daniel: our exertion. I mistake an ant crawling on my inner arm for a bead of sweat—a black ant, I flick it away. Fear or terrible sadness might appear in our faces, but do not. We don't talk about Ed. That drop of blood is a shocking image. It's weird, we are like two businessmen not wanting to discuss the meeting that just ended. I marvel at my coldness—was Ed one of my life's companions or a time-consuming distraction? My tiny soul kicks the scream beyond this. Daniel and I are too alike, each figuring out a plan that replaces what we might be feeling. Or: What is there to say? What do we know about death? How can we prepare a passport for the wandering spirit? Or: Didn't we both depend on Ed to cry, to rage when the time was right? To feel joy? To break down? Ed had good instincts. I am the frog who must wear the same genial smile even as he disappears down the snake's throat.

Daniel and I avoided the subject of our grand coincidences for so many years, it's as though we'd already dealt with them: why Daniel and I both loved Ed and Denny, why Ed and Denny preoccupied us for so long. We live these coincidences as we live the rest of life. Ed was ill for so long the catastrophe became who he is, and that is the worst I can say. The drop of blood on Ed's tip, as though we could see the virus, there it is, displaying itself in its last moments, exulting like an exorcised demon. Don't get HIV on yourself, I warned myself, while HIV exulted on its throne. Of course the virus is merely chance, only chance, always chance, yet it is hard not to take that drop of blood personally. How much effort that drop of blood cost us!—oh more than effort, it changed everything, every single thing, like some all-powerful impresario taking his final bow in front of the flesh curtain.

Open in All Dimensions

I'm dead in my small wood casket, big brown eyes staring up. Look in—head and feet wedged at top and bottom. I emerge lying down. I tape-measure my growth-spurts—I'm eleven feet. Now I fit in my tiny coffin.

(Ed's dream, July 27, 1991)

ED TOOK UP RESIDENCE in his tomb—I went out to have a look. I see Daniel put a photo of Ed in the niche, adding a human scale that Ed had ruled out. Ed hadn't planned to face outward, but to display his isolation. "Then there is the time needed for the list of projects about my early death—memorial plans, obituary, will. Finish those first, then the sky is before me."

I drove home and ran to my cedar bed to daydream. I couldn't lift my head. I felt pressure in my gut. It would be dispelled, so that wasn't me. Something behind. I wondered, "Is that what a hemorrhoid is? That might be me." Earlier, I'd had an orgasm that rushed into Chris's mouth but strangely reversed itself, as though pleasure pumped emptiness into me. Likewise, some part of me battled against the walls and ceiling of my little room, also me. Also me, the silence in this room. I rode a strain of fragile sadness. Deceptive sadness, not fragile but structural, not something to vanquish or resent. I read a few pages of *The Emigrants*, trying to decide if I liked Sebald's repellent nostalgia. His strange rhetoric supports complexity, his antique prose is a time machine (as a library is a time machine). It marks a change in Holocaust fiction, because the shock of mass death does not overwhelm the complexity of his characters. Was Ed's death a trauma that replaced his life? Was he thrown into the mass grave of HIV? In mass death, recovery occurs in the collective mind over time. It may take a generation to reacquaint ourselves with the dead, for their rich complexity to be apparent once more.

Daniel lent me Ed's dream journals. Ed put a lot into his dreams. The task of reading decades of them returns me to the labors of our relationship, looking after Ed, anticipating Ed, trying to make a career happen for him. I startle when I encounter images that I used in my poetry. I suffer as Sean takes my place. I see it happening. Sean had an iron fleck in his iris that Ed loved. Violence, terror, paranoia, and sex don't surprise me, because that was Ed. I'm not surprised that his mother Alice is a fearful monster. But I didn't know that he hosted a vibrant multiethnic community in his sleep. His friends and lovers were mostly white. That disparity is a blind spot in our relationship. How can I know Ed if I don't know the kind of problem that race was for him? Am I the only one who will read his dreams? Am I writing this *for* him? They go *through* me, place him *inside* me, but that doesn't mean I know him any more than I know myself. What will happen to me? The grief and chaos of illness, his scary mother, the exploding cosmos. I often show up in his dreams. Do I allow him into mine?

Ed started a journal on October 3, 1967. He was seventeen and still
living in Tacoma. He made only three entries at the time. The first
describes a panorama of sky and rock open in all dimensions. "I parked
the car on a low hill overlooking a vast barren plain extending for
miles. A dreamworld one might expect to see in the future, no
humans or buildings, not one object showing that civilization ever
existed, no trees, just dirt and stone and blue sky with huge white
clouds. It could be life after death, infinity, no time or dimension."
That describes the tomb he built twenty-six years later. He continues, "A certain sound I keep hearing (in my thoughts) that one would
hear in a void, or when living after death in the fourth color—a
color all its own—dimensional. It is so beautiful to be in the womb
before the mind and body become organized." Trippy! Ed connects
womb and death through color. Color is a thought, a dimension. A
sound in a void. His floating heroes embody that silence, an elated
silence "from above." So much of our story is threadbare, but not
Ed's silence. Mine, yes. His was *before* language, inviolable, mineral,
complete, living, listening. Perhaps his father threw him out on his
eighteenth birthday, as his journal suggests.

Ed couldn't be distracted. His life occurred in silence despite the
music that was always playing. What led him to a landscape of rock
and sky? He recognized himself in crystals unfolding (acid). He was
a pattern to himself. I was more jealous of those morphing crystals
than of his lovers. Is that true? I knew he would return from his
lovers. Could he return from rock and sky?

Ed's isolation was not antisocial. In fact, Ed asked me to join him in his niche after I die. Now my assessment of his tomb and the conclusions I draw become irreversible. Will I share eternity with Sophie the cat, who is scheduled to move in when she shuffles off this mortal coil, and with Daniel? Then why not invite our dear friend Elin, and Denny too? And I hope you, Reader, will join us in Ed's small exhibition space, in his work about death and the future.

The Moon Is Brighter Than the Sun

The sun has set but the sky is still bright with luminous rain clouds horizon to horizon. All races and casts scramble up the bank, feathered Maya, Chinese, Africans, middle-class housewives. Children, babies, people I recognize, foreigners, my Japanese grandmothers—twins with brown lined faces. They jump up, I pull them over.

(Ed's dream, November 30, 1984)

I LET MY BODY go slack playfully and Chris lugged it over. I'm limp as a corpse, I told myself—and then I was Ed's corpse when I rolled it over. A second of almost-laughter, then I couldn't speak and my eyes widened as Ed's death crashed inside me. Part of me wanted to move around, make the bed creak, make a difference, while another held my breath and pointed my face and toes at the ceiling. I shouldn't have done that, I told myself. I rolled away but couldn't—in such alarm—couldn't blink. That mental gesture became shorthand for my being dead with Ed, the beginning of a faint, falling backward.

The world emptied out. It was weird—the smallness of desire and the smallness of the world. Later, I sped across town to my son's house as though I were late. I was thinking of a public person I hardly knew, the admirable Mark Finch, who jumped off the Golden Gate Bridge. He was the director of the Gay Film Festival in San Francisco. His suicide was shocking, yet it made suicide an option for a while. Ed's sickness gave purpose to my life, or distraction from it, but his death did not.

I slipped out of my moorings. Nothing changed except that I became derelict inside. I was trying to give up. This forbidden thought marked a change. Time had been ticking for too long. Give up what?—pushing the sun across the sky. On one hand, I was teaching, greeting, touring. On the other, I lay on my side, eyes wide open, unable to judge in the shallow horror of the night, feet knocking together. I was perfectly fine. I was a desolate mistake. I cowered under the judgment of fellow writers—actually self-criticism assigned to friends and strangers. A pat on the head could allay my fear, my transparent need, long tongue lolling, imploring eyes cast upward. I was urgent for company but unwilling to waste ten minutes on anyone. How to keep the toxic chain letter going? I had no more ways to respond, nothing to respond with. That is, right there I could have begun my suicide note. It was not prompted by drama— what's more detaining than drama?—but by loss of faith. That's what I would take into death. Faith in what? The house opposite, the street ahead, the collapsing light. Death stole the middle distance, or perhaps it always belonged to death? My suicide note: "This moment of emptiness I want to exploit..." How against fiction it is to die without commitment to my life or a singular attitude toward my death.

For a few days, jumping off the bridge was the source of my existence. Did I maintain my relationship with Ed this way? Ed seemed to grasp his relation to death: *An emptiness that I can't fill.* He was smart about negative space. Ed and Mac were certain of the value of their experience, achieved by valuing the particulars and then changing the scale. Ed planned the menu for his funeral—including those succulent ribs. He wrote, "To create the ambience of who I am and what I was." The mix of tenses amazed me. Imagine writing about yourself in the past tense of your death—*Who I am and what I was.* Ed was loyal to the present, even when it does not include him.

Oh God, I prayed, how is this my life and no other? I was jolted out of inner necessity. There was no more sense and no more nonsense. The world did not appear as I entered it. My *life* was an emptiness I couldn't fill. I had been the weary minimum-wage custodian of an identity that I continuously saved by mixing its feelings into everything it saw. A pain in my chest could have been a siren or a pillow. I slept so lightly that I complained in my dreams that I was still awake, and my bored unconscious did not even bother to shape life into symbols. It was amazing that a day existed without Ed.

It amazed him that it would be so. His mild wonder in his dementia—"This house is so beautiful, the light is so beautiful here—we have to move—I don't know why." Now it was drizzling, sunlight raying below gray clouds, and I allowed this weather to make an instant of joy and sorrow together.

A high drone could have been the city or the engine, but when it blurted in my ear I realized it was a mosquito. How odd to find a mosquito in a car. I was driving to Potrero Hill, Ed's neighborhood. Ed had lived around the corner from Reese and his moms. I was on an errand to fetch a rose. Reese's house: fear and anticipation.

I feared my own impulse to give life away—not live it, but use it up. The drive was tedious and nerve-wracking. In San Francisco the east–west journey is full of obstructions. Cesar Chavez is as beat up as the road to the airport, Eighteenth Street has Castro congestion and then Mission congestion, Sixteenth has the new coffeehouses. I took Seventeenth, feeling some allegiance to its double-parked trucks and its little factories that made doors and windows. Since it was Sunday, most of them were closed.

It was June 19, 1994, Father's Day. My emotional states didn't jibe. I can observe that, but I can't average them out. Reese was ten months old. Ed had been dead for four months. He lived long enough to hold Reese in his arms, but we shared a blunt silence: What could be said about the future in Ed's presence? Reese was not a joy that canceled the pain of Ed's death. Instead, Reese amplified a vibration in my chest, which was feeling itself. I feasted on his expression and eloquent brow, partly mine I suppose. I was in love with my son. "It's intoxicating," I said to my mother. "Now I understand why people have children." Reese and his mothers left for the week. When we celebrated Father's Day that morning, Camille solemnly gave me a celebrity from her garden, a white cabbage rose with a shameless fragrance. In the chaos of our departures I forgot my gift and I did not want them to find it blackened in its vase. What would that say about my paternity?

Taking care of Reese was not so different from taking care of Ed. My job was to protect the inexhaustible reality of a consciousness: Ed and Reese, furiously making the world. A birth may point to the future, but it also opens the door of nonexistence—somehow matter had become sentient. The inevitability of Reese had not yet replaced the strangeness of his being alive. First he moved his arms and legs, still swimming in the amniotic pond. Now he crawled around on his own, somehow isolated as a dragonfly. Life would change us, but how? Demands would be made, but what? The complexity of Ed was temporarily replaced by the fact of his dying. Sentience would become matter. Like Reese, Ed couldn't do much, yet he was the occasion for huge expenditures of energy and feeling. *Is the earth as full as life was full, of them?*

After Ed died, I felt a weird euphoria. Perhaps I desired Ed's death as a way to keep him. The inexplicable burst like a bubble, and I resolved not to degrade ten minutes of my life with bitterness or lack. Then the perilous nights connected me to the grief of other catastrophes—rejection in love, say, or when The Figures rejected a manuscript. I couldn't go to sleep and I couldn't wake up. I was free to change positions, but the right one eluded me. I thought a book from that press would make me the writer I lacked the courage to be on my own. On my own: deep staleness, the pallid feeling of having jacked off. At my job I was sawing wood inside. I was weary after I slept, hungry after I ate, excited after I fucked, grieving after I cried—the present could not take shape.

I kept slapping my forehead as though I were having good ideas. I felt the mosquito's slight breeze. If I really want to die, I reasoned, wouldn't a mosquito be less annoying? I allowed it to land and crushed it against my skull. Broken limbs and a splotch of my own blood on my palm—for an instant I believed the mosquito was Ed. I asked Ed to help me give chance meaning without capitulating by saying chance *is* meaning—that is, by allowing himself to die. If I could find a way to wrest meaning from chance, I might be able to save

Ed's life. I thought, I can't go on, but what did I mean? That Ed carried to the grave my future as well as my past? That I could find Ed by not going on, as he did not? I thought, I can't do this, but what could I not do? Bury Ed in my imagination? Live in the tension of his presence and absence? Writing this does not alter the hope that Ed won't die. Even though he is dead, the hope will not die. How to explain it? A cloud in which Ed is dying and not dying, a flavor in which Ed is dying and not dying, a minute in which Ed is dying and not dying. I couldn't tell people that he died—that would have added to his suffering. Until this chapter Ed occurred in the present tense. The past tense is an affront. It's hammering nails through him.

Even though the reality was far different, I felt I was the widow with ancient rights, a sense possession born of thinking and writing about him all these years. In the shower I loved to drink water off his skin. He was the subject of my poems in 1970 (when the beautiful and arbitrary reigned in the form of Ed), just as he is the subject of this sentence fifty years later. Identifying with Ed, I went to sleep. I couldn't write because writing opens the weave of experience, unlocks the present, and gives it density. Is that why they call it fiction? Even in hotel rooms I slept on the edge of the king-size bed, the ghost stole the blankets and pillows.

The buildings were new on this stretch of Seventeenth, but their image was scratchy. My corneas were dirty screens. The 49 Van Ness passed by, drone of a rolling barrel. A dog barked once like a brick dropped on the sidewalk, a hollow clunk, as though this were a nineteenth-century village with sounds from across the valley. As though inside my eyes was a scream. A line by Frank O'Hara ran through my head—*Is the earth as full as life was full, of them?* I often said it to myself, not really understanding it. Is the earth as vital as it was when Ed was alive? Is there a kind of steady state, so the world will always be that full and no more? Full of life. As Ed was full of *life*, or as *life* was full of *him*? Ed's corpse: a moment of silence in which feelings bled outward. *Is the earth as full as life was full, of them?* The misdirection threw me, from the *earth* being full, to *life* being full, instead of Ed being full of life. Was life *still* full now that Ed has gone and Reese has arrived? Was it always? Was it ever?

Reese was experience before language. In me, through him, experience went through a painful revolution. If language is alienating, that familiar alienation is who I am. Then the state before language alienated me from who I am without offering an alternative. Reese was entering the experience of speech and Ed fell out of words into the experience of dying. I say, "He died, but..." and there is no "but." *But* when I improve a sentence, I'm that much closer to him. To pack death full of words, to force death to speak, to fool death, as though this writing were last words carried *into death*.

Into death. A tidal wave was about to crash. "Oh no," I cried. *Is the earth as full. The earth* does not mean our world, Planet Earth, it means dirt, burial—is *death* as full. *Is death as full as life was full, of Ed?* I had not allowed myself to see that meaning, because I would not take death's point of view. Life may be the fulfillment of itself, but that's not the whole story. Since I could not mourn Ed, I could not recognize his death. I could not acknowledge his *presence* in my life as a dead person. That is, I could not bury him, so I was "maintained" outside of life—self-preservation of the purest form. *As death is full.* I needed to pull over a moment. As though in the full sunlight. Some rain splashed my face—I felt it. It made me want to lift my face and make a vase with my arms. In my mind I lifted my arms into the shape of a vase, another word in the language of Ed's death.

I had to think. *As death is full.* I touched my face. Keeping Ed with me depended on *not* feeling the pain of his absence—as though we could work through this second breakup! I was too tired to lift my head. I climbed over the seat—ugh! I was forty-eight years old. I crawled into the back with the last of my strength. I smelled the sweet dirty upholstery, laid my cheek against it, and my own odor was like a blush. I felt sadness so great that pain shook my chest. Ed was lost to me—overwhelmed by this pain. Losing Ed was all the more painful, and though it seemed impossible, the pain increased because it was driving Ed away. We were breaking up again—the stale misery, lying on my side, eyes open, the pressure behind them.

I had preserved my relation to Ed through inattention, Orpheus to Eurydice. The sound of Ed's voice and the sight of his flesh were still keen but unreachable except through memory, memory not yet accustomed to this chore, life not yet forgotten or rounded off into anecdote, the web of skin between Ed's thumb and forefinger, the flat fingernails, the splayed toes. I counted fingers and toes as though he were a baby, a baby memory.

Suddenly images of Ed were pressing, his laughter behind his palm (like his mother, I imagined), an elbow on a table, a droll smile, his childhood apparent in his round-eyed surprise, his head turning on his long neck when he had long blue hair, his heavy Asian hair, his loopy walk, the sweet odors of his navel and underarms and testicles, his slightly bowed legs, his long, skinny orange corduroys, the red velour shirt I made for him. Images from the past. He's drawing at his drafting table, cross-legged and straight-backed. He's jacking off in the bay window for the entertainment of someone waiting for a bus across the street. His lucid flooded expression as constellations tumble inorganically: Purple Owsley. Remembering him was the same as giving him up, consigning him to the past. Ed's nonbeing called to me, death asked for help. It called for my recognition. I felt so drowsy, I could hardly lift my head. I kept losing consciousness as though pushed down, then waking up with a guilty jolt, opening my eyes to see where I was, as though somehow I had stayed on past closing. I had the weird sense of letting myself down because I was being weak rather than strong. I was weak, my arms and legs, my puffy lolling head.

I retreated in order to recover Bob—but which Bob? I was a file saved in too many versions. The world belonged to Ed because he believed in it. He and Mac had joined the human race. I depended on Ed's tulips, his commitment to a patch of ground. The exact day was not subverted by irony, by loss of scale. Ed forgave the world and meanwhile did not lose the meaning of his apple tree fruiting.

Oddly, I had parked across from the loft on Seventeenth and South Van Ness, where Ed lived after we broke up in 1978. Gone was the mysterious lumberjack statue—a vast ad for what?—whose florid bearded half-averted face formed most of the view from Ed's second-story window. A window from which Ed watched the brothers in the Chicano family across the street jack off together. The street where Ed saw a girl crossing too far behind her mother. The child was struck by a car and tossed high in the air, one shoe sailing in the opposite direction.

I helped Ed paint that loft even though our breakup was full of rancor. We barely spoke while we worked, or we spoke tonelessly as though we were outside our relationship and outside ourselves. We'd been together so long that tackling a big project alone still seemed impossible.

Now I recall last night's dream. I am the one moving out, and there's Ed, helping me paint my huge multistory loft, and also undertaking projects like locating a copper bathtub. Denny is in the dream: he just got a puppy and tries to restrain the unruly dog with his I-know-I'm-in-the-wrong amused expression. I thought I was supporting Ed even to the grave, but the dream tells me that Ed is giving me a hand with this book—this project in which we will separate a third time. In the dream he wears the body I slept with for eight years, except when he was with someone else.

Ed overflowed like a fountain. He was awed by his body, it dazzled him and made him cry out with pleasure. Sensation is the world's thunderous ovation. Then his body betrayed him and became the source of anger and disappointment. Then he felt that his body would see him through the experience of dying as though he had stage fright. It was marvelous—putting his faith in the sinking ship. Is that what O'Hara means?—*Is the earth as full as life was full, of them?* By putting his faith in the process of death, Ed filled it up? The fertility of death. In that amazing reversal, wonder replaces fear. I smiled for sheer pity. Ed's head tilted into the shadows and yellow light lit his chest. His hands were folded like the Man of Sorrows and he radiated clear disinterested sorrow.

Notes for a Novel

NAZIS MURDER my parents. I push their bodies into a mass grave. Is shame recognized by those who live completely in shame? Guiltier than Nazis, I pry off their wedding rings because I need money to get through. Today's headline, GERMANY REUNITED, October 3, 1990. Do Nazis distract from the point of the dream?—to end my parents' marriage?

For the Soul of Ed Has Gone to His World, February 13, 1994. Daniel held Ed's memorial in the Conservatory of Flowers, where Ed had worked. I hadn't cried in public since I was a child. My Humpty-Dumpty head sank into soft shoulders—I was sunk. I was weak in the face of death, arms and legs lolling, the bereaved's deportment. Faces distorted by smiling consolation leaned into view. In the seventies, Ed and I had visited this Victorian greenhouse to swipe coleus cuttings.

We walk up a country road, rutted and stony. Moonlight shines from the ground. I'm eating doughnuts from the Silver Crest Donut Shop on Bayshore. "You can't have one." Ed is aghast—I've denied him life. Death is so close that we think this way. Ed turns into rotting rags, one leg collapsing. We cry strongly and caress each other's face. With posthumous simplicity, Ed says, "If it weren't for my body I could go on forever." Tears for the tender infant who can't take care of himself, then for a skinless decaying horror.

Today I discover a strange thing. Ed's dream journals mostly cover our years together. One journal is lost: years with Skip and the beginning of Daniel (1980–1985?). This is a blow. I want Ed's life to refract through the infinity of his dreams. Can I edit a dream? Can I change a name for the sake of my book? Ed would say yes—does that answer the question? I feel him inside, or the dreams shape an Ed-feeling that was already there. Can he go inside you?—will you be his tomb?

Writing against the idea of the world. Disbelief is something to believe in, but where is Teddy when faith in lack of faith is lost? (Who's Teddy?) This atheism includes faith, so belief exists, floating like clouds. Hence vertigo in the creative act. Faith in emptiness, in a cup on the sill where nonbeing is free to idle: the miracle that commands my belief. Emptiness is a commons producing images. It could be alienation from the self—empty, manufactured—or revenge on the self. Do I believe in pleasure too?—pleasure that occurs in the reader?—a second commons for the faithful.

Ten years after our dinner with Carl's family, my mother confides that she recognized me in a novel. In *The Hours*, a gay boy loves his mother fiercely and singly. Did my parents avoid talking about my childhood to spare us that shame, that failure? Did they simply lack the word? I forgot I was abnormal, but they did not? Poor Mom and Dad! Failing in school, morbidly shy—a wraith in my mother's blue floral housedress. If they noticed.

After making one of my "donations" at the women's clinic, the chatty nurse said I rated excellent in quantity, motility, and freezing. My family used to joke that my mother was cooking for the freezer. I called her up: "Mom, now I'm cooking for the freezer too."

During the eighteenth and nineteenth centuries, childhood replaced death. Freud versus Montaigne—"Teaching people to die is teaching them to live." Death was shunted to Science. Childhood (the theater of the family) became our *Commedia*. Did poets and the clergy willingly release their grip on death? Soft white moths keep this secret, *moriendo, revixi*. Autobiography depicts a battle already lost. Childhood and death are inevitable, but childhood structures the present and imprisons us in the box of psychology. Autobiography happens when childhood replaces the good death, when the truth of experience replaces the truth of right living. Right living: I learned about sex when I was twelve from a guide my mother handed me. Intercourse was like correct grammar minus inner necessity—you do *what*? If the book had depicted two men? What standard should measure the value of experience?

Okay, two sausages are schvitzing in a frying pan. One says, "Whew, it's really getting hot in here!" A joke about language and death. The other says, "Wow, a talking sausage!"

The sausage adds (consuming pain turning to fable), "In 1983 I learned for the first time that a man I had sex with had died—his grave drew me in."

Ed and I Attend a Josef von Sternberg Retrospective in 1972 at a Theater on Eighteenth Street in the Castro That Disappeared Long Ago

FROM THE INTERNET: Adapted from the same Pierre Louÿs novel that spawned Luis Buñuel's *That Obscure Object of Desire,* Josef von Sternberg's *The Devil Is a Woman* (1935) takes place in an intricate studio version of Spain that sets Concha Perez, a cigarette factory girl, in a love triangle with an older military man and a young revolutionary. The desirable and arbitrary reign together in the form of Concha, who tells one of her admirers, "If you really loved me, you would have killed yourself." *Devil* is a farrago of decadent romanticism, thirties left-wing activism, and Sternberg's preoccupation with authoritarianism and freedom.

During the years 1930 to 1935, Sternberg and his discovery Marlene Dietrich were the most successful tandem in Hollywood. They worked together for the last time on this notorious box-office flop. Antonio Galvan (Cesar Romero), a young military officer, meets Concha and falls under her spell. Antonio confesses his love to his friend Don Pasqual (Lionel Atwill), an older, higher-ranking officer. Pasqual is horrified; years ago, he had a disastrous romance with Concha—she repeatedly lured him into her web and drained him of his wealth. The film was thought to be lost until Dietrich provided a print from her collection for a Sternberg retrospective in 1959. John Dos Passos cowrote the screenplay.

CONCHA: Arturo, a cup of coffee.

PASQUAL: My emotions seem to make little impression on you. Aren't you afraid of anything, Concha? Have you no fear of death?

CONCHA: No, not today. I feel too happy. Why do you ask? Are you going to kill me?

PASQUAL: You play with me as if I were a fool. What I gave gladly, you took like a thief.

CONCHA: I thought you would be glad to see me. I'm sorry I sat down.

The Devil Is a Woman was the most controversial film of the 1930s. The Spanish government demanded that Paramount destroy all copies. Paramount withdrew it when the State Department asked. It lost heavily at the box office and careers were damaged. Sternberg did the photography himself. This film was Dietrich's favorite. She is an evil goddess, her beauty on the edge of absurdity.

CONCHA: What did you do?
ANTONIO: Politics. A little bit revolutionary.
CONCHA: Is that all? I thought it was something important.

Now I cry easily, but I need this film for its glycerin tears. If I make the motions, in a minute I'm crying deeply. Possibly I am depressed— but more often I have the pre-tears feeling that comes after reading a Russian novel. How to contain, as one must, the time that has passed, childhoods, adulthoods, and deaths? The way vast historical events impinge on the individual. All the possible outcomes and reversals at every moment gather into an imminence that rides with the story inside each breath, so even the unknown, which is never known, dwells inside the time of the story. That's why these tears belong to the experience of aging. They contain intolerable distance, distance impossible to contain, so while I may be congested with feeling and my body clenched and even wracked, there is also a delicate filigree, a pattern mostly empty, which I enjoy with a kind of recognition, the spatial equivalent of a death's-head but lovely, or rather, harder to endure. It's said that happy people live in the moment, or that we live in the moment as we age, like it or not. Does the awareness of time equal grief? What is mourning? The will bends back, nailing me to the awareness of time. I spend days staring at a bright spot on the wall that moves with the sun, so I become a sundial, the melancholy motto is the self.

PASQUAL: I love you, Concha. Life without you means nothing.
CONCHA: One moment, and I'll give you a kiss.

I cry after movies, not so much in the theater, but at home at my dining room table, even over dessert. After any movie really, because movies compress so much time. I wonder if I am more "in touch" with my feelings, as we used to say. We used to say, "We've got to get ourselves together," and nothing seems more improbable. We never *got* ourselves together—are we likely to now? How will Ed, who is no longer alive and yet fills up most of the screen, get himself together? In that era, the early seventies, we looked for films that supported an overall sexuality and an aesthetic that suppressed the difference between figure and ground.

Pasqual is not cured of his addiction to Concha. When he encounters her with Antonio at a carnival, jealousy overcomes him. The duel occurs in a forest at dawn. Dietrich wears black lace as though already mourning the death she instigates. She raises a black lace parasol. This is what Ed and I took from the film: In order to make the screen dazzle, Sternberg slid beads of glycerin on hundreds or thousands of invisible threads. Slow rain, each drop catches a bit of light and carries it down.

The roar of rain was out of proportion to the slow movement of light, just as the roar of sex was out of proportion to Dietrich's fairy-tale passivity.

The image is somber camp—I flaunt myrtle in my butthole. It was camp the minute it hit the screen in 1935. Why fabricate this ornate moral slapstick for the act of penetration? To support it with so much beauty. To subvert it with so much melodrama. To support it with so much artifice. To activate the pure and impure, saint and whore, love of flesh and horror of flesh, the perpetual binary of hips pumping.

CONCHA: Ha! This is superb! He threatens me! What right have you to tell me what to do? Are you my father? No! Are you my husband? No! Are you my…? Well, I must say, you're content with very little.

Languid decent, slow beauty that Ed and I imported into our hippie lives, slow and anxious. Was Sternberg directing? Slow arousal, slow fear, arousal never completely expelled, fear never facing its source in consummation.

We didn't understand the deep mourning of this image, we could not add mourning to our farrago of decadent romanticism and counterculture politics. Yet obsession is the way I hold on to a world spinning me off.

The acting is no better than a PTA skit. Dietrich is supposed to fascinate but she plays only one note: swagger. She's macho, besting the men with her cunt. But indifference sets her apart, indifference to the costume drama on almost every level: indifference to the story, to Sternberg, to the actors, to the script, to her fate, but not to the gaffer or to the light.

Not sex, but light—Ed painted his way toward it: naked men float to the edge of the canvas and beyond—clouds, sky, light, experiments in empty space and arousal. That's what the glistening drops meant. They were light and they were tears. Not tears for the paper dolls in the film, they were never alive, but tears shed by the blathering oracle whose fragments bring us closer to the dead: something bad is going to happen. A prediction, a command. The opposite of nonsense is nonsense. Something bad is coming our way.

Yes, an oracle. The talkative sun comes around and a canary trills in its cage. Align yourself with light and the knowledge of death, thank the cameraman, the lighting crew, make sure they are on your side.

What confused us?—her makeup is grotesque, the white skull dome, the pencil eyebrows in perpetual surprise, the jaw hollow at the sockets. Like a Mario Bava witch, an Argento witch. Whatever protects the inside of her body against itself has vanished, the tendons snap over bone, the pain flares from her wrists and ankles.

Last night I had this dream: I call to my friends, "Hey look, there's Hitler, let's kill him." They say, "Oh yeah, Hitler, he's looking good." "Guys," I protest, "it's Hitler, c'mon, we've got to kill him." They say, "He's in good shape—yeah, he looks okay." I am Bob and what does Bob know about killing someone? "Hey guys, let's kill Hitler."

Besides, the worst already happened, so what was the point? That was Dietrich's stance, the Weimar expression: the worst already happened. I pick up a rock to throw. It lands a few feet away from me. Hitler isn't even upset. That's what Dietrich's skull-face was saying: universal ruin already occurred. That's why we did not understand her in the early seventies. She brought mourning into the sexual realm which was, it seemed to us, founded on hope. The skull was already laughing.

CONCHA: Good morning! Good morning. Good morning! Good morning. I came to see if you were dead. If you had loved me enough, you would have killed yourself last night. Bad. Not made properly. I make much better chocolate.

Your lover takes a lively interest in your death, since she is dead. You are left with nothing to grasp, nothing to believe, nothing to understand. True sadness does not know what it has lost. Here it is, the real grief!—without self-interest, without story or loyalty or language or scale or measure. Oh Ed, can I find my way to you through this fucked-up image?—the black parasol, the light weeping down a thousand strings? Is finding you my goal?—to make love last forever? You have been gone twenty-five years and I will die before long. To put experience into words is something like love and something like revenge: my unrequited love for the world.

(I break a promise to myself—I promised I would not speak to Ed in the second person, as though language could float me over to him. More resolution than aesthetic protocol. Do I talk to his photo or his image in my mind? Not to the Ed I last saw, but to a younger Ed. Do I mourn my lack of access to his beauty—the glory of my own youth, arousal and glycerin tears? Ed, in life and death, a wall to beat my head against. Sometimes I say, "Oh Ed." If I could "unpack" that sigh. Maybe I am not prepared to talk to Ed in public. I'll make myself naked when company comes, but I am reluctant to talk to Ed in your presence. And how does a corpse speak?—in a voiceover, from the future, about events leading to his death.)

Ed's Things

I race with others up the mountain through the fall pine forest. Flames speed overhead. Somehow I get ahead of the crackling orange light and climb into a tree house. I can't breathe—smoke fills the air. Rooms on different levels open onto thick pine branches. Panic makes me clumsy. Photos take or leave, black bag pack or not. I flee with the others, leaving art and belongings to burn. The sky rages yellow, we run for our lives.

(Ed's dream, November 12, 1978)

ED LEFT INSTRUCTIONS in his will for the disbursement of certain objects and a great deal of art. I spent an afternoon in his studio in June 1993, helping him make these decisions. We were dry-eyed, strangely festive, even though a PICC that went into his arm, past his shoulder, and then a fraction of an inch into a chamber in his heart, was being replaced the next day by an apparatus that entered his chest. He said, "This week the mockingbirds returned. Their song is so pretty, sometimes I hear a robin in it, or a seagull, or a sparrow." We made a game of determining who would like a certain painting or drawing. Ed took for granted that my mother would be given something nice. We chose a female torso that was also an ascending spirit, drawn with light instead of shadow.

We kept ourselves going with tea poured into Ed's spongeware mugs and with a lemon Bundt cake whose recipe he was perfecting, marrying bright tartness to decadent blandness. He told me he wrote to my mother for advice about mixing—he was getting little balls instead of smooth batter. She said the liquid and dry ingredients should be incorporated into the creamed butter in smaller amounts. Even when Ed and I were not speaking, he talked to my mother and she sent him food. He did not want to lose her—"the perfected version of you," he once observed. The blue-and-white mugs called forth a certain intensity. One horrid day Ed carted them off along with the years we spent together. He was not going to break up his current household, where Daniel would continue to live.

Ed's bequest to me was the hardest part. Two paintings from his ghost series have hung above my desk for twenty-nine years, the two ghosts my writing companions. I chose them because Ed and I watched horror films together. Skulls invite thoughts on the brevity of life. This skull ponders the delicate terror of its own naked bones: the loss of flesh is brutal sadness, the gesture of unfurling fingers.

Later, Daniel returned some blue-and-white Imari dishes I gave to Ed on his birthdays during our years together. Daniel also gave me a little *tansu* from the forties that Ed and I had shopped for, which was nice of him, as well as two shirts. I'm wearing one now. The stiff muddy gray cotton is not comfortable; instead of buttons, it has snaps that catch the stubble on my jaw. When that happens I remember that Ed did not have much facial hair. In the mid-seventies, he tried to grow a punky beard to accessorize a tough leather jacket and that failed effect—a few scraggly black hairs—was so ravishing that my attraction to him doubled.

The owner of these objects continues to be dead; the objects continue in a state of dereliction. When will they belong to me? The shirt smells like Ed, sweet: these objects represent his body, his choices, choices I made for him, and our bodies together. I used up all the time in the world deciding on two Imari patterns. I chose a set of eighteenth-century scalloped bowls with a loosely painted blossoming cherry: spring. A sapling grows out of a fat, ragged stump, the impure cobalt burning purple. Discrete episodes of a nineteenth-century landscape decorate the other set: cliff, pine, lake, bridge, boat, and temple. Around the rim a strange stylized wave carries autumn leaves.

I own many things that Ed and I bought together or made when we were a couple. I sleep in the cedar bed we built in 1975 when we moved to Clipper Street. Our sperm hit the headboard, a plain of roiling grain. When we broke up three years later, neither of us relinquished the bedroom so Ed made a pallet on the floor and there we were, sharing our unconscious hours yet too angry to speak or touch, except once—as if we made the jolting discovery of the other's body. Ed whispered in a rush of caresses, "It's a body to fuck and suck." My body was on the market. In 1978 muscles were requisite, in 1970 none had been required. Then we lay together, drifting into bitter thoughts, the connection becoming arbitrary that had over-whelmed us minutes before.

I've slept in our bed for forty-seven years; it will be my deathbed if I'm lucky. Late-medieval meets Danish modern, my taste for gran-deur curtailed by our lack of power tools. You climb into it: the mattress rides almost three feet above the floor. I wanted to give it a roof like the bed in Bosch's *Death and the Miser*. Ed vetoed that, but we made a headboard so high that on either side an angel and a devil already haggle over the *mourant*'s soul.

When Ed's possessions were distributed in February 1994, my own belongings gained potential energy. I could see that everything I owned was ready to travel, to desert. The healthy and the dying don't have the same relation to objects, and I inherited Ed's feelings along with his goods. My white Pyrex cup from 1953 will outlive me, visible on the sill, throbbing between world and nothingness. It came to me from beyond someone's grave. I could see it for what it was. My books came from a corpse's library; my own library will fill alien shelves. My tables and chairs—stripped of their aura of choice and intimate touch—arrived from dead people's living rooms. Someone will take my white glass cup for granted until the knowledge of death returns.

Or perhaps Ed's familiar objects become familiar to me in a different way. I eavesdrop, listening for news from these solid memories. Solid memories that develop amnesia.

One day in July 1994, five months after Ed died, Elin, Daniel, and I faced the hopeless task of putting twenty-four years of art into useful order. Just as I grapple with twenty years of notes for this book! For decades I moved fragments from one journal page to another—pieces of Ed's life and my own experience, decaying haystacks in the computer, events without dialogue, codes breaking down and formats degrading from one platform to the next, scraps spindling on my desk and in my head, gestures that yellow and fall from the branch. Some notes became illegible and others were legible but their context dropped away. I try stitching these decaying rags together—Ed's suffering and my insufficiency—but tension and resentment put me to sleep. Tension: I want to be a good girl but how can I pick up clues without smudging the crime scene with my dirty fingers? That is, truth may exist, but it is stronger away from me. Resentment: yes. Why must love prove each time that it exists on its own without contingencies?

At first sight Ed's studio was ordered to the point of tranquility: clean surfaces, potted plants, and objects isolated by the pressure of placement. Daniel and I stood back, mirrored irresolution. Elin plunged in, dividing our project into tasks. Elin is a small woman, tender and bold, with heavy dark curls and tremendous forward momentum. We looked at the slides—thank God they were dated—and arranged them chronologically in slide sheets of Ed's various series: his clouds and vapor, his ascending heroes, his fish-bone watercolors, his fish-bone sculptures, his ghosts and samurai helmets, his dividing cells, his flower drawings, his suite of illustrations for a children's book about dying. The next step was to make duplicate sheets—but to what end? Over these activities arched the memory of Ed's corpse, helpless, arms and legs akimbo. His lack of presence in his body made grief happen but I can't explain why. It has something to do with the awareness of time, and something to do with my being human *after all*.

In Ed's studio, my own life passed before my eyes. I modeled for Ed in the seventies, so I reviewed the generalized beauty of my young self. My long white face and caved-in posture, my skinny larval body under loose denim and flannel. Those years seem distant because they fly away inside me. And there was Gus in 1974, sucking me in drawings for a new gay magazine. What was it called?—after a few breaths it expired. So many journals died in the crib! Gus, editor-publisher, went to the mat for his publication. He was a stocky Italian with a jovial tooth fetish. He was more attracted to Ed's small translucent teeth than to my robust corrected dentition, which made me wildly jealous for ten minutes. After our sweaty but matter-of-fact afternoon on and off a foam mattress on the floor of Ed's studio under Ed's eye, Gus paid for my time by taking me to a double feature at the Castro. He had obtained free passes as a citizen of the fourth estate.

How easy it is to put myself in his apartment after the forgotten films. In most homes, the thrift store and garage sale ruled, but Gus's apartment was decorated in French provincial, generic as a hotel lobby or grandmother's parlor, complete with clear plastic seat covers. The coherence of his environment felt weird. Was it rented furnished?—or rented furniture? Gus sat forward on the gold brocade settee and asked me to piss in his mouth. Actually I don't recall the upholstery, but I do remember that my horizon of pleasure broadened right then. The plastic cover was sensible. It took concentration to remain soft enough to piss while inside. After finishing, Gus leaned back against the gold fleurs-de-lis and said mildly from the depth of his barrel chest, "I want to kill myself." It was two a.m.—bars were closing across the city. Fatigue is a speedy drug. Gus's nameless roommate entered with a trick and we all piled onto

Nameless's bed. Gus blew the trick while I rubbed against the roommate. He had a haggard, acne-scarred face and a superhero torso
with as little character as the furniture. His features were so big that
I saw a Claymation cyclops when I climbed aboard. I was unpleas-
antly aroused. I wondered how he came by such an unusual body—it
seemed to belong to someone else. That he'd attained it through
exertion in a gym never crossed my mind. It was three or four in the
morning in the mid seventies and clobbering my body with five or
six orgasms was a more familiar diligence.

Ed dreamed that a man in briefs moved in geometric poses across
the sky, watched by a wondering face—which Ed emulated in his
sex and art, somersaulting through the vault. Bodies sailed through
gleaming clouds, heroically foreshortened. Are they the clouds per-
sonified, or rather eroticized? If I assemble the paintings like the
frames of a movie, the god shrinks and drifts off the edge and the
clouds retain his essence. Flesh falls away and what remains is arousal
in mineral heaven. They were experiments in empty space and
arousal. "The power to look death in the face and to perceive in
death the pathway into unknowable and incomprehensible conti-
nuity—that path is the secret of eroticism and eroticism alone can
reveal it." Georges Bataille

I am describing art that Ed made in our second apartment, the
railroad flat on Sixteenth Street between Dolores and Church,
where we moved in 1971. Ed turned the south-facing front parlor
into his studio. I took over the living room by constructing the
People's Wall out of cardboard. We slept in the back parlor and
conducted social life in the spacious kitchen. We painted it bright

avocado and pale lavender—I smile to remember—and it held a sofa covered by a blue chenille spread. A sofa in the kitchen was great. We were surrounded on four sides, mostly by an extended Puerto Rican family. A continuous slab of run-down three-story buildings circled the block. Half-toppled barns from the nineteenth century decomposed in the open rectangle of weedy backyards, and at dawn a rooster crowed. On the drab treeless street, we collected glass from shattered car windows for Ed's sculptures. They were wall pieces, fish bones and glass suspended in polyurethane. Sometimes he covered them with Mylar scales. One horrid night in the dim garage we tried to extract bones by dumping dead fish into a plastic bucket of Drano—a vat of seething gore. Then the hot toxic sludge melted the plastic...

Daniel found a batch of résumés in a drawer and we used them to find and record which pieces had been sold or given away, to cross-check the pieces that remained in Ed's studio, and finally to determine which still needed a slide. A small page from a magazine dropped out of a stack of drawings: a man has lowered his red bikini briefs, his dick sticks out like a lever, foolish, as though his body is switched *on*. A seventies body, a skinny blow-dried blond. We looked at him without comment; he disturbed me because our task was so boring. I wondered if Elin found him arousing.

Order and disorder. If I knew why Ed left his art in disarray and left precise instructions for his memorial service down to recipes for the buffet, I would know something more about Ed. Elin found a silver earring in a clear plastic box in a drawer. "Where's the mate?"—Daniel found it in a tray by the window. Here is a box of crayons, except for gray, green, and magenta. They're in a bowl across the room. What did this combination of order and chaos mean? The serene surface, the welter below? What can you do with the unruly scrawl of a person's life? I started this book two decades ago, so now it has turned into a ritual to prepare for death, and an obsession to put between death and myself. I want a tomb to keep up appearances in the face of death. Will I occupy the tomb I have been building for Ed?

I flee from the screen as I do from my notes. *About Ed* grinds to a halt. If I knew why this novel is falling apart, I would know something more about myself. And yet I'm glad incapacity is accumulating. I'm beset by opposing feelings of failure—I am not equal to the task of writing this book (laziness, ignorance) and I long to be stripped of knowledge and motivation, to be an empty room, or as Ed might put it, an empty sky. I want to conserve experience and I want to throw it out. Making experience *useful* by turning it into a book is repugnant, but what else can I offer? I need this book to be impossible to write, I need to become a different person to write it.

Here's a note from the pile—did Ed bequeath his share of this event? One afternoon I returned home, and Ed's door was closed in such a way as to suggest he was with someone and they were naked, and sure enough I could hear gasps and sighs. I crept to my room, the cardboard wall and curtain-door, and sat disconcerted till naked Ed appeared and without saying a word organized me back down the hall. "Hi," I said to the skinny blond whose name I don't remember, and I put my mouth on his skinny cock with its flange of a head. Tie-dyed curtains filtered light from the bay window. I felt nothing for him: I went to his flat on Prosper Street two or three times, just, *Hi, hey, oh oh, spurt spurt, 'bye.* Anyway he was more interested in Ed. His cock had two mouths and his sperm sort of dribbled. Who was he? Sandy and white, monotone and blasé, orgasms didn't excite him. He had a lover, I now recall.

Daniel, Elin, and I arrived at a master slide sheet. We wanted to make an archive and place Ed's work in galleries and museums. The lack of Ed's presence in his corpse affected a part of me that I had never encountered, caused grief that I can't explain. It didn't affect my speech, which carried on. The past is no longer behind me but in front. My notes don't collect insight and drama—what someone said, how someone moved. Instead of composition, I copy them insanely from notebook to notebook to computer, where they replicate through many files. Why shouldn't they continue as shards hurtling away from each other like the big bang, if that's how Ed exists for me?

Or like Don Bachardy's death drawings of Christopher Isherwood, where the empty space conveys dissolution?

Elin showed Daniel that the plants were stressed from lack of water, then she watered them. Elin had been part of our hippie family— she'd throw an overcoat over her nightgown, drive across town with Eli, her dog, jump into bed with Ed and me, and watch old films. Ed and I were not a counterculture success story—Robert Mapplethorpe and Patti Smith. We never doubted that Ed was an artist, yet he worked alone. Often I was the world—how could I be? Perhaps his lack of success was due to an inability to prolong his forays into the art scene or even the world. He emerged every few years with new work; we carried it to galleries, to an art market remote as a mandarin's inner court. I still want him to be recognized—for justice to be done. Ed's grandest moment occurred in 1991, when he represented San Francisco on Day Without Art. His paintings of samurai helmets based on Japanese woodblocks hung in the Asian Art Museum—they looked great. He'd added his mother's maiden name, Sugai, as he focused on the Japanese part of his life. It seems Ed Aulerich-Sugai dealt with sexuality when we lived together, in the seventies, and with race in the eighties. Mayor Art Agnos congratulated Ed and gave him an antique geisha doll, a gift to Agnos from Kyoto, but the museum didn't buy a piece from the show. Was a sick artist a bad investment?

Catalogs from cheesy outlets like Ah Men and pages ripped from porn mags were tucked into bankbooks, journals, sketchbooks, among résumés, correspondence, and income tax forms. Arousal refracted through every activity. Thongs projected genitals up and out in see-through mesh, Day-Glo Pucci polyester, and chaste white cotton. Bikini briefs dominated. Sometimes a photo conveyed an idea by the way a cock was shaded, held, framed: that a cock can be all reality till it comes. What did Elin make of these Donny Osmonds with boners? Gaggles of hard-ons can look silly and I felt gender embarrassment. Elin and Daniel didn't seem to notice, which heightened my unease. Daniel and I—why not say it?—look alike, soft Jews.

Meanwhile Donny duplicated himself a hundred times in Ed's studio, where he kept his imagination, his dreams, his unconscious. Did Ed want Donny? How did he end up with two fuzzy Jews?—two Jews to care for him endlessly and to uphold his beauty? Did he feel Donny was too good for him?—or was he always fucking Donny anyway?

Then I remembered Skip, Donny times ten, the love of Ed's life. No, that would be Daniel. Skip, Ed's obsession; Skip, my replacement. The damaged goods whose "mother" returned him to the orphanage she had plucked him out of. Skip was a lawyer who moved to San Francisco to reorganize the police department. He arrived on May 21, 1979, the day Dan White's nothing sentence for the murder of Harvey Milk sparked the White Night Riots at City Hall. Skip was having a drink at the Elephant Walk, a Castro bar, when the deranged police charged in riot gear. The organization that had just hired Skip sent him to the hospital with a concussion and three broken ribs. Skip sued and of course he was fired. Later, Skip and Dr. Palmer—their doctor—kept Skip's HIV status secret from Ed. Isn't that fucked up? When Ed told me this, I said, "Dr. Palmer should be arrested—and what about Skip?" Ed offered, "He's dead," as though finding an excuse.

We were drinking tea from the blue-and-white spongeware mugs that Ed brought back from West Virginia. I told Elin and Daniel about it: In 1975, Jock, a much older man, a designer, took Ed to Huntington to work in a Holiday Inn. Ed painted a vast mural in the banquet hall: the Ohio River flowing through the seasons. Before

Ed left, he carefully let our friend Stanley know that he did not want me to be lonely, propelling Stanley and me into an affair. It seemed logical because Ed had a fling with Cliff, Stanley's boyfriend, not long before. Ed was not attracted to Jock (gray sperm) and Jock was passionately in love. I scolded, "If you're selling yourself, at least make your customer happy sometimes." Ed confided that he cheated on Jock with other men. I was making Daniel uncomfortable. Their project went on for months—at one point Jock tried to push Ed off a bridge. What edge did Ed push Jock over? That Halloween our friends observed, "You're going as Ed." His tight orange cords and sheer black shirt displayed a body ready for pleasure. From his vast collection, I chose white bikini briefs that launched my cock and balls. After we separated I took Ed's qualities into myself. A movement of his head, the patience to play with Reese forever. Using his measure, not my measure. And after he died? My hero: fragile, heedless, elegant, determined, bonded to home, masturbatory, dreaming, thinking optically: "The fog drifts quickly. When I let the image fall from the center of my eye, I can't tell the changing gray from the blue—the moving edge, white to blue, a screen of intricate white veins intermingling with soft veins of blue." Then I am Ed.

The day took forever, but a day is not so long to inventory a life and by the end there it was: Ed's life, with its shape and no other. I can't complete the inventory of what he carried into death.

Denny joined us for dinner. He told us this story from 1982, when we first dated. Denny was still living with Daniel—they had been sleeping in separate rooms for some time, but Daniel was still Denny's lover, at least from Daniel's point of view. It's well known that Denny gave me a taste of Daniel's chocolate mousse, and I observed that some brandy would improve it. Denny reported my suggestion to Daniel, launching a mild rivalry that Denny nurtured through the years. I guess it tickled him that our battle was waged on the field of butterfat. Denny now revealed to Daniel and me that for a month or two he'd dated another man, Ted, who thought a few tablespoons of rum would help.

"Ted," I cried, "did you play Elgar's *Variations* for him too?"

"I remember that mousse," Daniel said wonderingly, "and that it kept disappearing."

I drove home alone—where was Elin? With friends in Marin for the night? Evenings are often mild and clear after the four o'clock wind dies down. I was driving west into the sunset so I suppose it was after eight. Perhaps it splashed my face with yellow ochre. When I was a young poet I wrote about death. What did I mean?—some kind of ironic absolute. Later, I used language as a net to trap experience, to pin it down. Now the empty repetitions and amplifications of language give me notice—ten years with luck, fifteen at most. Will this story belong to me after I die? Will I belong to it, as I may already?

I sat on the edge of my cedar bed. It supported so many moments of fullness and emptiness that started with Ed and continue in the present. It has four big drawers and a cabinet, and a hidden compartment where I keep boxes and portfolios of art. The mattress is a Cadillac because Carl had a bad back. The sheets are... I just wanted to sit for a while in the decaying light. I was glad for a moment of emptiness, aspired to it. Led myself to it. Stopped disguising myself from myself with the aid of the emptiness Ed loosed on me, and it's here now, as though he'd rendered me with negative space.

I lay down, arms crossed behind my head. Ed's voice on the phone: it seemed to come from inside me, but that didn't mean I was always glad to hear it. I half listened to his dire sagas—the brutality of one doctor, the indifference of another, nausea caused by a drug or perhaps a different drug. There may be a place where actions are full, where feeling meets event, but I was not there. A slice of Clipper Street through the blinds, my white cup on the sill, the neighbor's dog barking hoarsely below. *Arf. Arf. Arf.* Death was partly a shrug and partly uncontrolled grief. I lived with my generation so I was not looking for the meaning of life, which was obvious: life is the fulfillment of itself. We accepted the infinite—the expanding universe, the World Wide Web, the national debt. The finite had become mysterious, illusive. The opposite of physics, each new version was more disunited. I couldn't find life, as though I'd lost my feelings with my glasses in the folds of the blanket. It struck me that I was somehow responsible for Ed's death. That was consoling. Worse was the thought that it had nothing to do with me.

Then sadness gripped me as though it were fear—wild, focused, and cold. I couldn't catch my breath. I felt a weird buildup: to die is to disobey a rule. I needed to cry for Ed, who could no longer care for himself or obey rules. I began to cry, or rather howl, a sound I'd never heard before. My body could not arch enough to meet the demand. A hook in my throat dragged me through salt water. Sickening tears, because the shape of Ed's life had become apparent. This flat for now, this city for now, this job for now, these friends for now, this lover for now, this art for now—in one stroke he became the life he lived, the irreversible shape. I couldn't change it. Going through twenty-five years of Ed's art, so full of hope, I was filled with Ed yet there was no Ed. I could only express his presence and absence with cries and shouts. I had never known tears so entirely linked to an event. My ribs hurt, I could not arch enough to wriggle off the hook. I didn't cry over his corpse, but over the body of his art. I thought, Oh *please* Ed, I don't want to *be* in this. What did I mean?

I was bursting with Ed—my head rolled as the top of it exploded and my eyes went back. I felt the vibrations of a boxcar moving in the darkness. The dust cleared but there was nothing left, a loss of density. I went beyond self-protection. I became the image on a strip of film—that's how I can explain it—slipping into two dimensions, a photographic negative lit for an instant and then curling downward into darkness. As though I were falling into darkness down a slot. I lay in bed with that pressure behind my eyes and hot skin. Ed had no more life but also no more death. The pain in my chest still blared, a feeling of expectation.

My tears were a starting point. That would be true of any outburst so purely physical. Time began again with a difference. Emotion found its story. I experienced that justice. From threadbare material—Ed, sickness, myself—a full-fledged sorrow had emerged, weirdly impersonal, below my shame, not regardful, gathering strength till I barked out grief like a dog. At least this sorrow could not be assessed, found incomplete. Or did Ed's death allow me to feel what was there all along? We were typical, one who dies and one who escapes infection. I had thought I was surviving Ed. Now in the pathless night I was waiting to join him. It's not something I believe, not something he believed, yet the words convey a feeling. I was not ready to die, though I'd considered it. I was not too young to die, and for centuries I had been trapped in a grueling conversation that only death could interrupt.

I turned over and over to find the position that led to sleep, but consciousness roused itself in defense when sleep approached. I could not draw into myself. Maybe it was a problem of expression: I needed to find a language for Ed's death. My eyes turning away meant the sight of a corpse. My head falling backward meant the empty body. Covering my face meant grief is contained. Arms raised as an urn meant showing ashes to the sky, meant readiness and openness to the sky, and film spooling into darkness, what was that? I pushed down a frantic feeling. Dawn, pale gray. I could not lose myself until I remembered to unclench my fist and lay my hand flat against the sheet as though absorbing the horizontal. I spread my palm as though registering my identity, then pressed against the door. My breathing grew regular and waves of sleep carried me through.

The problem: how and where to place a huge archive of Ed's documents and photography. I take it on, but it must come with some money for preservation and it should go where people have access—scholars and the public. I'm talking on the phone in my funky apartment above Haight Street, where in the dream Ed and I first lived and where out of the dream Steve Abbott lived till he died. The man on the phone complains about the price of the photos he buys, some as much as three thousand dollars. I see one—a man splayed outward, butt toward the camera, and the presence of the man is its value. That is, you are *with* him in a series of close-ups and have access to him, meaty, tender, and gracious. Meanwhile, beef stew boils on the ancient stove. A siren blares, I go down to see what it's about. The street is empty. It's the devolving Des Moines Main Street in *Ubik*. Reality is losing its support. A black car rattles by, a monster, old and makeshift. Then nothing, a siren. I am still alone. Another car, a silver Pierce-Arrow, threads through abandoned vehicles, makes from the twenties and thirties in a state of decay that everyone accepts.

I woke to a half sleep. I was not dreaming, but remembering my dreams, paging through them: the dream above; before that, I suck Kathy's cock in the front seat of my car. Before that, my family and friends have Thanksgiving dinner—*surprise!*—the surprise is that I'm not invited. Mom and Dad are clowns in whiteface. Mom doesn't have a mouth and I sort of run out before nothing is said. Before that, Chris and I are returning home late—I had to miss the episode on TV where Ed and I—what? Our life is a situation comedy. I want to see the rerun. When we break up? Go to Mexico? Make sushi? The fish and Drano? Chris and I pull into the weedy driveway and there's Ed! I'm slightly confused. "Aren't you dead?" Then I allow myself the joy of seeing him. He's relaxed, lanky, glad to see us. He kisses Chris and then comes to kiss me but he is thrown to the side. He looks winded and his eyes widen as he's thrown backward and disappears.

I opened my eyes to see where I was. My senses began with nothing, with consciousness you might say, dissected into birdsong, cool air, an insect bite, hunger, stale flavor, expectation, floaters drifting downward, the foreshortened hairy body, a strange body whereas its inner tingling was myself. I tried to get up, rich sleep, thick feeling, then fell to marveling, I was so comfortable. "I love this city," etc.

Notes for a Novel

MY MOTHER affectionately scolds me in a dream, "Well, if you love *bones*..." She means, *If I love* her, *who will soon be bones and thus* already *bones, I'm bound to suffer.*

Reese: The child sleeps nearby. He is nine when this book ends. I am the son, give me what is already mine.

In 1988, my senses jumped as though something were about to happen when the art writer Robert Atkins said Ed's name. "Ed has AIDS, but I'm sure he won't die." Responding to Robert's expression, I wondered aloud how I could be certain. Robert volunteered, "Denial?" I was highly annoyed—did he wish for Ed's death? This exchange gives me access to a time when I didn't assume Ed would die, though perhaps I withdrew the gravity of my statement out of social anxiety. Was I complicit in the virus by naming it?

In 1982 Denny warns me that one of us must have a good body. Objectification is needed. Does it matter which one?

He calls in 1997: "Quick Bob, turn on the Discovery Channel— they're giving a dog mouth to mouth."

He tells me in 2013 that Skip and Ed were his cocaine connection in the eighties. They were dealing? He scolds a lavish flower at my kitchen table. "Couldn't you have found a pollinator that doesn't need so much attention?" Orchids (my self-dramatizing friends?—my self-dramatizing self?) should get over themselves. Has Denny reversed his position on objectification?

When seven-year-old Reese did not get his way, sometimes he fell to the floor and reverted to an earlier phase. Loss halts our forward momentum unless we achieve mobility through a change of scale—it's what the universe wants, justice wants, the future wants, my country wants, *the reasoning of the eternal voices*. Mourning is the fear of losing Ed combined with the fact of losing Ed. I can't work it out and the problem shackles me. I see why doctors suggest travel, because I can't find a different place inside—intolerable rigidity. I console myself: I never have to accept his death. Do I write to remain in contact?—when I'm finished will he be truly buried?

Ed's stories were drastic, his sex life was heedless, his dreams were volatile, yet he gave advice like a foreign speaker aspiring to the ordinary—statements so simple they were at once false and ringingly true. I don't recall a single one. "Thanks for your stupid good advice," I once said. He mock-strangled me.

Possible Homework: I'd like to change my mind—*from what to what?* What if I'm crying for the wrong reason? What if an error—obvious from a vantage I have not reached—keeps me from the cause of my sorrow, like film spooling into darkness, loss that is structural, a comprehensive grief.

Is neglecting this book the same as harming Ed *inside* our relationship? If he had reason to complain that I used language as a weapon against him, he should be appeased—now it installs him inside me.

Is the body a crime against time? Is it death's trophy? A thought so hard-won it becomes useless during its flash of comprehension. Somehow we live both inside and outside the expanding universe of our systems. Somehow this disconnect causes a free-floating remorse that lacks an object. Is *all* life a distraction? From a condition too simple to believe?

In Edinburgh I see a Titian that I saw fifty years earlier when I studied there, *The Three Ages of Man*. Cupid climbs on top of two babies who sleep in a heap like puppies. The babies become a naked man and a clothed woman about to embrace. The way she holds two flutes suggests arousal. Finally, an old man plays with their skulls. *Plays with skulls? Wait a minute, wait a minute.* Then it strikes me— that's exactly what I'm doing.

Ed reorganized my imagination by dying during the first two weeks of February 1994. It's April 2023, and the greatest difference between us—he's dead and I'm alive—has an expiration date. Reader, allow me to erect a monument *inside* you. Life can't last forever but memory can. Writing that banality does not alter the hope that Ed won't die, will stop being dead. Mourning occurs in the empty wasteland between the crowded past and the crowded present.

I play the interview I taped with Ed thirty years ago. The moment it captured was threadbare, tattered. A sort of Proustian telescope, the beautiful mysterious world was *already* empty. Now our conversation seems full. That measures my distance from Ed. Our conversation is empty compared with his presence and full compared with his absence. The sound of his voice fills it up. *Ed, we're bound to each other by nerve-like cables.* It's odd that our voices are so similar, both gentle voices. Sometimes I am not sure who is speaking. On the phone, our mothers couldn't tell us apart.

False Knowledge

NONIE'S NEIGHBOR Michelle had a daughter living in Coconut Grove, Florida, as Michelle told me on a walk we found ourselves taking together down the block to the corner store. It was a simple afternoon, a few clouds, a breeze. I'd gotten older in the, what, five years since we'd last talked. Now I was in Michelle's age group—I had given up being young. Being "older" was still a novelty, a new condition, something to remark on. I had a new body, still strong but more feminine. For example, I was getting breasts, which shows that all things come to those who wait (and stay alive).

Michelle's daughter had not visited in eight years, so Michelle sent a plane ticket. The daughter did not arrive with the plane. The alarmed mother called her in Florida and the indifferent child offered that she could not find a cat sitter.

I did not know how to respond to the heat in Michelle's grievance, her beautiful ruined voice, and her helplessness. This elegant silvery woman had a banal family problem. She threw out her hands with the fresh surprise of the badly loved. I didn't want to see her point of view because I didn't want to see life that way. Michelle was so likable, she had been a teacher. Was she also a monster? Was her daughter in some way justified? Did Michelle have faith in the connection between us, or was she compelled to tell her story to everyone? I pretended to be different in order to talk to her in a casual way, but at the same time I wanted to be myself.

While I was thinking these thoughts, Michelle was telling me how brave Nonie had been, that her relatives came for her. Had she moved away? I'd been meaning to visit her for, oh, a year or two, and I felt a little sheepish. Michelle was discussing Nonie in the past tense. I began to see—Nonie is dead. She died of emphysema about a year ago. I still waved to her when I left my house. I thought of the portion of eternity Nonie had slowed down with her life, making it crawl like a snail through most of a century. Goodbye Mac and Nonie, I was on my own.

Ten or twelve years earlier, I was wondering where to store the garbage cans. Mac said, "Hey Bob, put them under the stairs." As usual, Nonie stood behind Mac, supplying large gestures. She pointed at my porch, nodding strongly.

"Under the stairs?" I looked at the blank wall.

"June of sixty-three they covered the door with cement board for no good reason." Nonie shook her head solemnly.

I pried off the board and sure enough, there was a door.

"Did Nonie have a funeral?" Relatives in Stockton with a long broom swept her away like an autumn leaf.

Bisexual Pussy-Boy

Six hands fondle me from behind. I'm getting hard. A cat licks my lips and presses his lips against mine. He sucks and pulls back, turning the kiss into a kiss with a smack. The door opens, the cosmos descends, the air is glass, the sky is infinite black, vast space is defined. Each galaxy turns before me. I travel, a motionless comet through the vacuum.

(Ed's dream, May 16, 1980)

I WAS FIFTY-FOUR—I was caught in a Mack Sennett frenzy of manic locomotion toward the cliff. I responded to an ad on Craigslist during one of the periods when Chris left me, October 2001. I report on the men in my life—they are coming and going during the second part of this book, except of course for Reese, the still point in the turning world. I'd deduced in a dumbfounded way that Chris was seeing someone, was introducing him to our friends, could not delay their romance. We have problems, I thought, as if to confirm our success as a couple. Chris turned away—a civilization was founded on that gesture. I took to my bed with a weird confidence, like, *Make way!—I'm going to bed!* I fretted and turned in anger. I thought, I'll know it's over when I can look at him. I longed for the days of typical existence—not romance, but the cup on the sill. But disaster was also compelling, to be impossibly sundered, hands thrown apart. I stood at the sink, saying, "Oh no I won't!"—but what *would* I not do? "That's what you think!" But what *did* he think? Once there are sides, I'm lost. It bored or rather sickened me to be on my own side for long. I prefer wars without sides, all against all. In a desire for novelty or helpless sympathy, I "went over" to Chris's point of view. (Or did I control the conflict by deciding to lose?)

Now where was I? I had not been attracted to his photo on Craigslist: his smock bunches at the chest like a housedress, he wears round glasses and his limp sexless hair is tightly gathered, but he stands next to an energetic painting, a huge grasshopper. After a few email exchanges he wrote, "My experiences with men so far have been pretty anonymous but very thrilling, and it seems like the next step is to find someone I can trust who is educated, interesting and experienced enough to boss me around and make me a masterful cocksucker. Can you do that? I've read a little about you online and it's pretty clear that you possess a sophisticated creativity and gratitude for your life that is unusual. This makes me optimistic."

His response made *me* optimistic. How durable the urges to fuck and to write about it! I felt honored to be initiating Zack into the homo mysteries, although driving to Oakland was making me even angrier at Chris. I hated the psychic drudgery of crossing the bridge and I resented losing so much time to promiscuity. I'd thought I'd be with Chris forever so now forever was relegated to the past. Anyone would be a better mate, I seethed: that guy walking on the sidewalk of the degraded street that leads to the freeway. The day was cold and wet, and beneath these discomforts a greater one: weather as artifice. In the car ahead: the young woman contorted with grief as the young man rehearsed his grievances.

I brought some champagne. I learned that from Kathy. Late one night, she asked me to pull up at a funky corner store. She emerged with a bottle of Veuve Clicquot. Her boyfriend was coming over later, she explained. Thrillingly late. I felt a pang of love for Kathy and her ways that knocked the wind out of me. I applauded her escape from romantic desolation, our native soil, and I looked forward to her report the next day. I needed to take care of Kathy. She called to me through the bathroom door to climb into the tub. But we were most intimate in a motel in 1997, when I massaged her cancer-ridden body. She had entered a magic universe and she was distraught, calling Frank, her astrologer, every twenty minutes. (He passed out business cards at her funeral.) I sent her to the hospital with the lie that they would release her in a day or two. She didn't forgive me for that. She was free not to forgive me and she did not.

I was driving across the bridge in the middle of the afternoon on the way to a stranger's body, driven by bitter lust. I envied those writers for whom meaning is abundant. At that moment they were using favorite pens and drinking cappuccinos in favorite cafés, or they were symbiotic with their laptops at home, basking in the screen of their own mentation. Blasts of wind buffeted my little car. Now Kathy was on my mind, and her mountains of pills. In 1981, I started crying in Safeway. I could not go on and sat on the floor next to the chips and bean dip. I felt relief when I was disgnosed with hepatitis. I could retreat to blankets and sheets, pajamas and soup. Kathy needed a place to stay for part of November, till she left the city, so we had the absurd idea that she would take care of me. Kathy needed to be taken care of always, but that did not amount to a debt in her mind, any more than it would to a child, or to Ed. They'd paid their quarter. What was I living on?—how did I run my classes?

I undoubtedly caught the disease from rimming some guy.

I slowly spiraled through nausea that sharpened my senses as the flat oily stink of Kathy's vitamins and obscure supplements pervaded the house. I could not convince her that I was really sick. She returned at eleven o'clock instead of nine o'clock, with a paper plate of Thanksgiving dinner, just scraps she seemed to want herself. I gobbled them quickly, like a dog. "I have friends who *died* of hepatitis," she scoffed. Liver disease reduces testosterone, and for a year I had no sexual hunger, prepubescent. A roaring clanging was silenced, a wheel of fire slowed down and stopped. Instead of killing me, hepatitis saved my life, since HIV spread through bars and bathhouses at that time. When Kathy walked out the door, she thrust a cheap gray wind-up rabbit into my hands and turned away. She had a menagerie of stuffed animals—did she want to comfort me? Five or six years later, the rabbit reappeared on a closet shelf and I realized at once that she was letting me know I was acting like a baby. Like someone who needed to be taken care of. Best girlfriend.

Zack and I sat on a broken-down mohair sofa next to a space heater in his chilly studio in the industrial section of Oakland. He was trembling and it was an honor to take his fear and excitement into my arms. He was the perfect WASP. No more smock; goodbye ponytail. I exalted as though my pick had struck a fantastic vein with the first swing. I felt the skin under his shirt, his skin was luxury. The parts of a mobile started turning on their own inside my chest. I had been invited as a teacher, the limit of my role. That made sense of the disparities. Zack was twenty-eight; he had a preppy face, bred for centuries to retreat from the arousal it generated. His variation on that theme: he was comfortable alone, he desired to be alone.

He took off for weeks in his four-wheeler, camping in the desert, connecting with the earth. Also, he swam in the bay. Was this like an adolescent taking too many scalding showers to cleanse his raddled spirit?

Zack explained that his girlfriend had encouraged our meeting. "Without her this would have been impossible, because I need a certain balance." His emotional life belonged to her. He wanted to forestall emotion in me so urgently that it amounted to an emotional demand. Despite his appreciation, he did not want me. That is, he wanted my age, my attention, and a hard fuck. It was intolerable that I should feel anything beyond excitement. It was a mistake to think we spoke the same language. He wanted me to shut up. It was a mistake to think I could protect him and guide him. He wanted me to fuck him carelessly. I told him what would make me feel good, but my words carried no force and we both knew they were beside the point.

Zack led me to a mat in the middle of the dark space, and he protested a little when I dragged the space heater with me. He did not want to give our sex an association—not with the sofa, not with the tidy bed against the far wall, which I looked at with longing. He did not even care if I got undressed—it was Age watching Youth, that's what it took to transform his straight ass.

I thought this was something to tell Ed about, but he had been dead for seven years. I was reading and copying out and running away from twenty-four years of his dreams. Are they a condensed version of Ed? Shorthand? Distillation? Is he knowable and unknowable in the same degree sleeping or waking? It was easy to read one dream and also the next and the next, but fatigue set in after ten or fifteen. I waited for my name as though I could find insight in the shifting currents, but it was Daniel, Daniel, Daniel. Sightings of Bob were disappointing to me as to any eavesdropper. Bob the Presence, a sidekick without intensity. I revisited dreams I'd read fifty years ago. It was oddly like visiting my own dreams or hearing my own voice. If Ed goes *inside* me, what then? Will his spirit manifest? Will we *cohabitate*? Can he go *inside* you? Can you go *inside* them, Reader? Lost in his dreams? Hidden in his dreams? They are a kind of heaven—not a heaven that culminates in an image that explains a life, but a heaven of endless narration where image replaces image.

I thought this was something to tell Kathy about, though she had been dead for four years and estranged from me before then. Our friendship had become more unequal the more I tried to right it. Loneliness creates an excess of self, so there was always more to give away. Then I got scared, as though together we proved I was disposable. Then I changed the terms by wanting justice. Kathy's friendships were only as good as the last five minutes and could be terminated or abridged with a misplaced sigh, as ours was. How could this experience be complete—whatever that means—if I couldn't tell her about it? Kathy sometimes called the operator to break into my conversation when she felt like talking, and now I wanted to do the same. I imagined reconciliations, they'd happened before: we fall into each other's arms, I still love her. That was in 1987. I was running the Poetry Center. Her food was utterly erratic, she was eating only potatoes.

Ed and Kathy: they are complete in themselves and have no relation to each other—just to their inner dramas, like Bellini saints. I gave myself to Ed and Kathy and Reese, then I couldn't give any more. In 1997, a group of her friends went shopping on Twenty-Fourth Street for a container for her ashes. I thought a bright floral Mexican box from a gift store would do, but the others fell in love with a large bronze urn dripping with flowers and putti in the over-priced antiques store. Kathy's ashes would inhabit the urn for what —four or five weeks?—before we scattered them at the beach. The urn was a sin against thrift. Reasoning with the others, contorting inside, I realized two things in the same instant: the urn was exactly the sort of excess Kathy loved, and *I* will end up in the stupid box. I saw it with a certainty so resounding it had already occurred. The pure jealousy I felt for Kathy's urn restored her to me more than anything had. I inhabited a resentment that had always been too expensive, slightly out of reach.

I'm supposed to be writing about Ed. Kathy intrudes, unfinished business, if that's what you call a ghost. A new death often enters the stage created by a death. Is the ghost empty because she's making room for me?

Zack had a beautiful stomach, taut and small. He liked to show it off, this prize, this flesh. His pubic tuft, a bit of loose fur. His penis was a detail even to himself. I use the word "penis" because his studio was so cold. I put the hard curlicue in my mouth and lifted my arms to his waist (an urn) but that did not seem to please him. I fell back a little (the empty body). The studio had been an industrial ware-house. The room was vast because I experienced loss. He blew me, lightly keening. Pleasure was a mild shock, a silence that pulled the plug on other sounds and left the high note air makes. That turned day into night. The footlights dimmed and a silver shaft fell on us through a crack in heaven's floor. Zack felt compromised and humiliated, yet his face was held up to the light by the action of our bodies finding each other. That is, Zack's reality took shape in that blow job. His faith scared me because I feared the depth of his loneliness and my own, in this barn, in the heaven of his flesh. Its strict beauty was like a happy sermon, like the peaceable kingdom. Loneliness creates an excess of self, which is hell. How extremely strange to find heaven and hell so mixed up. There on the wall gloated Satan with washboard abs and a forked flame for a prick. And there was the giant grasshopper—God stretching out his hand.

After the blow job my cock was returned—I poked it, the skin slick and cold like the fell on lamb. Zack showed me his asshole and what he liked to do with it, and why not? He achieved what few can claim outside fantasy, the complete transformation of an asshole into a sexual organ. It didn't have a name any longer. Pussy. It was bubblegum pink, so clean it twinkled, and without the suggestion of odor, as though it existed in the imagination or as a photo. His rickety daddy longlegs cantilevered outward so his weightless torso seemed to bounce on them.

I am telling this to Ed and Kathy: Long ago at the baths, an old man gazed slack-jawed into the vortex of a churning butt that belonged to a man who was fucking a man beneath him. The old man's head was tipped back at an odd angle, as though a strong wind blew out of the butt, and now I understood that he was using the bottom correction of his bifocals to keep the ass in focus. My head was tipped back as well in order to read the fine print on Zack's little butt. His fingers were inside it, displaying it, running rings around it. He said, "It's repulsive, right?—what we do."

"Sure." I hate to disagree. Zack needed our sex to be repulsive and repulsion was not automatically vetoed. Did my age disgust him? "Can I have some water?" I asked. And "How about some music?" But Zack didn't want to be sidetracked or ruin a favorite CD by tainting it with our sex. I didn't think it was disgusting—declining to communicate was frustrating. Why did Zack want an old man if not to learn from me, since experience is what I offer? Possible answer: he wanted power over me. Communication upsets every dynamic of power. I was that much more an old fool, he was that much more a young slut. This old fool began to feel pleasure, and pleasure made our sex normal. Does arousal make things strange for some people?

When Zack realizes that his inner life is so disjunct, won't that equal terror? It seemed very 2001: bodies coming apart, sexuality parsed out yet intensely lived. Is living in disjunction a kind of heroism? The front of my body whirred with satisfaction—I had forgotten that whirring greed. I was waking from the sleep of marriage.

Then I fucked him as carelessly as he wanted. I entered him from behind, my strokes were so hard that my thighs spanked him. He was hot inside, at last I entered a well-heated room. His intricate lower back and the jiggling of his thin flesh moved me in surges of tender lust. I was surrounded by O, at once the sound of sex and the shape of the orifice I was pounding. I felt the complexity of exciting a body that excited me, an alphabet of sites clutching, oozing, slurping, spasming, squirming. I plunged and probed like a prospector losing his cool, made frantic by the growing richness of his vein of gold. Then I fell into—what—a spatial fallacy, looking down at our aroused bodies where there was so much interaction, if only along a few inches of skin. Emptiness saw through my eyes. From the point of view of vast empty space, our little bodies expressed timelessness, our two little hard-ons like levers that start the toy engine's senseless rotation: the organic reality of our bodies did not survive the cold darkness. I felt the grief of separation, as though time islands were drifting apart, each foot on a different measure. Covering my face meant grief was contained. And weirdly merry, like Slippage the Clown. Nature made a mistake when it gave us a temporary meeting place of flesh and bone. Why shouldn't life last forever, like a Martian landscape? Like Ed's tomb? Why should the inorganic remain and the living change and perish? Zack's barn of a studio, his huge paintings, his space heater. I thought that one day he would understand his disjunction as grief and kill himself—say, vanish in the desert. Until then he would never come to rest.

I told Zack to touch his toes and then to stand on his toes so his muscles were taut and he relinquished his balance to me. I really gave it to him, fast-forward. Oh!—the cries of penetration, of physical outrage, the outrage of pleasure (or pain). My goodwill counted for nothing. Zack felt compromised and humiliated, his ass took the place of his head. Half of our bodies sizzled in the space heater, half froze like planets without atmosphere. I wanted to delay his orgasm till he was desperate. I grabbed his tiny waist, pulling him up, he wouldn't, I pulled harder, and then his huffing moans told me he was coming. "Why didn't you say so?" I pulled out with the pop of a broken seal.

When someone is really moved, it's not pretty—something went out of Zack and he looked sick. He said that was the first time he was penetrated. I would not have been so rough, but he was glad. Then for my eyes he pulled his asshole open an inch with his fore-fingers. It was time to come but I was distracted by this vaudeville show, the fingers drawing the membrane outward. Sex was not the sheer release of yesteryear. Now I wanted to discombobulate a hand-some man with pleasure. I chose one orgasm and pursued it. I used to dodge them like bullets in a shooting gallery.

When I looked in the mirror in Zack's bathroom, I didn't see the conflict and continual surging that find respite in some man's body. Instead, my dead father examined me with scared eyes that are now mine. Turning away meant the sight of a corpse. "You left the lights on in the family room in 1956, you didn't take the trash out in 1962, you wrecked the car in 1967..." Riddled with cancer, leg amputated, he complained in tears on the phone, "Why can't I die? I've had a good life." I was speechless with shock. Did he really think his life was good? Because he had not murdered anyone, gone to prison? Because he had raised us to the middle class? Because he had worked so hard?

Shouldn't I be home putting finishing touches on, say, a trilogy? Would I be writing more if I had less sex? I push gratification down, and up pops a force that shoves civilization forward. I suppose sub-limation was the last gasp of empire, the Freudian version of repub-lican restraint, the call to Duty. If, as Freud mused, painting is the sublimated desire to smear one's own shit, is my writing not subli-mated enough? My father's death was coming. He knew it and he didn't. How amazing and predictable that I am turning into him. Peering at Zack's butt from a distance of two or three inches, I certainly felt as though I were having a good life. At the same time I wondered what I was doing to myself. A new model: desire, the creator of ghosts. My erection, nature's applause meter, didn't subside. Sex made me teary, as though mixing grief into my excitement made it honest.

I had not allowed myself to put my mouth on Zack's asshole because strictly speaking that is not safe sex, right?—but I wondered if I was harming myself in some other way. First sexual experiences shape one's sexuality because they give expression to all sexual need. What about an encounter that could be the last? Fear gathered around my arousal. Testosterone drips from a faucet that someone forgot to turn off. It's rotting the foundations of the structure. Will I want sex when I can't move or speak? Will I spend my last hour remembering an ass seen through bifocals? A vague tear burns miles deep inside the empty sky of my chest, world too large, delicate terror.

Zack wore an alarmed expression when I kissed him goodbye. That was too personal. I forgot that he saved his kisses for the girlfriend. When I told Denny about this part, he said, "God, I hate when they do that."

I returned home and sat in the backyard with a glass of wine. The day could be grasped and held. I listened to the air and looked at the light with longing, as though for the last time. The greed of vision, expectation of the senses. The sky brightened as the sun sank.

The clouds deepened, lit from behind. The shift to gray conveyed limpid sweetness, like sight in heaven. The loud fragrance of jasmine. A green bug turned to green goo under my thumbnail with the feeling of a crack. Trees became silhouettes that stirred in hushed conversation and then subsided. Their movement was like sound. Suddenly a yellow light overhead, a window. Tremolo of leaves. The buzz of insect wings and a vague roaring. Tears fell on their own as though condolences had been accepted. They flowed simply as though they were part of the sky, the child's toys, the weedy yard, the bulging retaining wall, the bird chatter, the worn-out light falling on pearly gray paint. The wine made my mouth dry and I looked forward to falling backward (the empty body) under the weight of pleasure into sleep.

Inside

Inside

TIME BEGINS AGAIN with a different measure. I search for a way home. In and out of stores, buying sandpaper and supplies for a boss who fades into his tasks. I sit on my knees, Tetsuko trims my nape. I wear pigtails, bangs cover the top of my vision. She kneels behind me and wraps her arms around me. We rise and spin like a top, then slow down and topple onto the floor. My face is drawn-on, black lines for eyes. What to wear? My penis shrinks as Mother appears with her disapproving look. I wrap myself in a black kimono. I yearn and cry inside—I want my body back. The finality hits when I open my eyes and see the tubes. Pain has a way of pushing down and down. An opening door—trillions of wet red spiders spill out on me. My chest bounces, my heart explodes.

Before that graceful gray-coated men are escorted half sexually to long graves. Their brims' shadows hide their faces. Weathered cement troughs end in darkness—vomitoriums, urinals, fern-edged resting places. Dawn fog twines around the buildings. Home around the corner, home safe in Daniel's arms.

Before that the sun's a red streak on the horizon. Two men drive me away not knowing they are going to kill me: *Please oh please oh please.* I throw rocks, hitting one—he falls away as the other falls. I search for home above the windows, over the treetops, over the valley in electric blue-purple. Tall windowless Victorians rattle as the sun sets. A landscape from a previous dream. Electric regurgitations, streaking threads, swirling high-pitched gases. A man dives headfirst one hundred feet, boulders and dirt rushing up. He hits the ground stiff as a board and walks away. Another man lands on his feet in a cloud of dust. They walk away as their clothes burst into flames, reappear and burst into flames. Willed spontaneous combustion. Daniel finds a curtain in the leaves. I push history and ghosts out of the dark room. Down the hill I find a cement foundation, just a corner, casket-sized, gray and white. That's where I rest.

Before that I dreamt that Bob (my ex) is dying. He knew it and he didn't. *January 5, 1992* Years ago, discovering each other's body in a swimming pool, pressing erections together, the zest of youth. Becoming comfortable along the way at a hostel for wayward travelers. One last roll of the inner tube, a game we used to play. But the obstacle course keeps changing and the tire bounces and rolls. Bob and I look at each other—it's a game of chance. And now, saying goodbye. A new life is with me. I finally see a room of trophies— toilets in rows. Mine opens to a running spring through the bottom of a stove box. I eliminate. A fresh young woman does the same across the room. I feel okay, at ease. Toilets overflowed for years, were out of order or stranded in crowded hallways with doors too narrow to enter. I was never relieved.

Before that I return to the Flower Conservatory—walls of hardpan, dry chippy branches on the paths. Daniel beckons, I sit on the grass, cupped in his arms. We talk about distances. Flower beds are islands, plants are people I spray on a hot day. I find a bathroom but pee onto a paper towel on the counter. I shit in my shorts and feel scared. I want to hold on to Daniel. He goes to sleep in shirt and tie in a glass baking dish in the sink. I expand and he shrinks. *WAKE UP WAKE UP* but he flattens into the clear glass. I turn on the tap to scare him. I hold the glass to my ear for heartbeat or breath—*he's dead!* My sadness wakes me as my grandfather watches a ritual: a dog unwraps me, pulling clear placenta off my body. Black lips quiver, it wants the thick gel. Maggots drop from my head. The ritual ends, I need to urinate. A pebble rolls at the bottom of the bowl with the heavy current, but I feel pain. Is this how it will always be?—meeting obstacles and overcoming them? I become a robot, skin and muscle harden as if I were boiled, and I become female. I look down—how can this hard flesh bear a child? I remember Mother and her boyfriend in the bedroom. He has a problem: when sex starts fast it ends with equal speed. Magazines fill a shelf next to the stove—there's a rough biker in a red bikini. Wait, they aren't motorcycle mags. Page after page: dead women in bondage, blue corpses in trenches. I'm not sickened, I accept violence—not against women but against humanity and me. A door shuts. Mother is awake and I feel okay about her snuff magazines. I accept her need for them.

          Walking, running, riding, I travel with my shadow friend in starless night. Getting on and off, not knowing where I came from. Watching lives through bright windows. We pass a steaming volcano. Where is my home? I remember the intimate revelers on the chaotic bus, the man's pig's face, the leather queens and how good they made me feel. I stand on the road between stops as heaven spins. I'm alone, of myself, empty, lit by stars that lead nowhere. I blink. A vacant hallway in a decaying

Victorian. We bought the house and now I have choices to make. All doors on all floors are shut. I walk toward myself in a large mirror. He/I touches my hand, he is warm. The house's ears prickle. It comes to life. I thank him, he is pure reality. Like a mirror-maze, exact replicas step out from behind each door. He/they adjusts a small posing strap though his cock grows out of his chest. Four in the morning, orange slanted light turning yellow, palms beginning shadows. Finally my life is art. Artists work around me. Men in underwear carry books. Women at a table recruit us into the Underwear Club. We enjoy our bodies. I wander in semidarkness and find a semi-bathroom. The sloped floor creates a gap so the door doesn't close. I'm well liked as an artist but I have nothing to show. A toilet one foot high, sides rusted, half-filled with rocks, a broken infant seat submerged in filth. Instead of urine, blue foam spurts. In the back, children laugh like slopping water. What do I have to experience?—because it looks like another frustrating bathroom.

Before that an eight-inch scorpion crawled around my room. I chopped off its tail, it became a furry hand-sized spider that jumped three feet. I hit it with a canister, it became a kitten whose face I'd just smashed in, eyes rolling, convulsed. I struck to end its misery. I lifted the dead hairless rat by its translucent shrimp tail and flushed the pink body down the toilet.

Before that I stick my head out the door—vast flat landscape in faint light. Hawaiian monuments crumble back to sand under a parching sky, remnants of a dying kingdom. We walk up a mountain road. Dull white sky.

Before that I dream we slide across the road. Our ride is a tan rubber envelope. All are me, all translucent except me—I/Daniel keep separating. The rubber capsule enters a warehouse. The floor is mounds and levels of coarse dirt and the ceiling is three stories high. I climb a stepladder to a rack of pots and pans bigger than my body. Scary men enter, busy industrialists. I urge my party to return to the hand-sized rubber. The female essence, Daniel and I squeeze in, the rubber stretching around us. From my hospital bed I see clusters of rockets trailing smoke. They plunge toward the desert floor, then climb skyward. I know it's the end. I apply a special salve and pull the rubber skin over me. I'm despondent. The men talk quick, panicky. They rub salve on themselves and flee into their tubes. Daniel moves around in the stretchy material. His sad face needs my acknowledgment. The rubber tears across my back. The salve curdles. Death is seconds away. I know it and I don't. I wish for a different time and place. I keep stretching it around me, trying to climb back in.

I'm walking through a mint-green hospital corridor, black drapes, blood pressure tests. Unknown doctors know every detail of my life. The setting sun reflects off an orange mountain scraped into existence eons and civilizations ago.

Before that Sylvie Jacobson visits to say "it" will be okay. She died in September 1986.

Before that we rushed downstairs—a cyclone! Cylindrical, not apexed. A section broke off, spinning horizontally through the wall so fast it looked like slow motion. The rounded corners of a glowing TV rectangle framed my vision. A blond head tilted back—her upside-down face. A doctor measured it while we talked. When he pressed near her mouth, I wished what I was seeing was not so. He swiveled her face—he'd sliced her cheeks back to her ears. I looked away as the image became a small square in the corner. He loosened the skin so it was pliable. Her vacant eyes scared me. He twisted the knife back and forth at the bridge of her nose. Clear fluid dripped as the entire face lay separate on the bones. It filled the screen. We flowed through gray light, images streaming past.

I pee red and black. I lie on my back under quilts. *January 7, 1990* A woman drives us through my child-hood landscape, recognizable because my sister as a child runs through it. I dash through the air, bare legs, pointed toes. I turn the corner up Hill Drive. My cat Sophie is defecating, it's her life leaving. She falls into the narrow trough between lawn and sidewalk. I feel chaos and the space between images. I hide in the forest where death lurks as failure behind my thoughts. Dark silhouette—I draw back from a faceless shape. He hauls out an enormous cock. I slide away as he circles me.

Before that *flash—look!* A gray/silver saucer pulses light, jerking on its side *boom boom boom* across the sky. Our car skids over the street. It picks us out and flies closer but doesn't get bigger—just the same half-dollar. A single beam watches me. I yell, "Hold on to me." Daniel and I are back-to-back, then front-to-front as it zips around. A mote like a split pea sticks to my bare chest. A particle shower—my scalp's full. I run inside and undress and shake the specks into a pile on the sheet. Send to a lab? I examine one, weightless, porous. Pulsations start again. Flashes at the window, down the hall, outside our bedroom door. We sit in terror. *Knock knock.* A woman steps in, her voice friendly but dead. Darkness moves her like a pawn. I understand what I felt from the particles— sensors tracking every movement every human makes. I sit on my childhood bed with Daniel. *Knock knock.* I'm shocked—the same woman. I close the curtain but she enters through the back. I refuse her presence. She becomes a blur with her screams. Dresden burns and Jews are starved and incinerated. I resist her as she hands me two protoplasmic balls that contain my visions and control my mind. Daniel screams *"No!"* and stirs the fleshy gooey balls with chopsticks. It's now or never for everything. When he mixes the balls, he's mixing our vision and experience. Already under their control, he becomes partly me as he phases out. The woman stands above, explaining silently: *We are non-sensory beings. We subject you to sensations and feelings as a way to understand. This means that each chapter of history recurs in different bodies and minds. You relive the past so we can know your systems.* I imagine a chair dropping from the sky as that happens. A TV screen captures a fluttering white dove. Particles send every thought back. The TV flickers all the intertitles that happened or will happen, ending with THE VICTIMS.

Tony Russo visits to say he's okay, that it is and will be okay. Tony died in July 1988.

I dread sleeping at my mother's tonight because I must share the space with frozen corpses—part of her business. Open the refrigerator, plastic-bagged corpses stand upright. Against my will it becomes a psych ward. We move in groups. Any struggle leads to this: a standing man hooked to tubes is given injections. His body jerks as it disappears. In its place an electric copy explodes in dire translucent greens. He sparks and wavers—he's led away. I know fear and control, lockstep sleep for the night.

Before that aliens arrive in darkening skies. Our whole

population retreats underground. The rock ceilings are sky-high. We have the essentials, dark walks, platforms, roofs, cyclone fencing. We are sexually free but anguished—hiding for generations from alien insects. They dismantle whole life-forms, vibrating molecular structures collapse. A ship finds us—phosphorescence invades the recesses, drawing people in, alone and in couples. White nebulas burn through our hands and eyelids. This is our death and I face it, joining countless others. I hold my female lover's hand and together we step down. Will it burn, will it hurt?

A knife appears—*stab his chest*. The mutant also has a knife. I push the blade in and twist as I hold him in my arms. *Slit his throat*: I cut his jugular.

Bucky, a shiny Black man, heavyset, grows twice my size. "Carry me," and I do. He folds his legs. I adjust his weight as my finger slips into his asshole. I feel the opening of the muscle. I bounce him like a balloon on the way to the Silver Trailer Café nestled in dark trees.

Before that a young lesbian soars above the trees, then drops through birch and fir that break her fall. She plummets again—small trees break her fall. I run to a clearing where she might land. Her lover and I fall through trees. We look at each other as branches shoot past. Again white birches shoot past. I grasp twigs and leaves, keeping my feet together. I hit the snow, the woman lands too—an open slope, darkness-lit starry sky. Firs are silhouettes. A dark-haired woman floats in the branches. She clutches the feet of a large bat that flaps furiously to get away. Her lover is a presence, like looking through water where fact-ness rhythmically sways.

Before that a woman/man bludgeons

a man on a gurney, ripping his chest open, the edges torn. How can a body so ruined be alive? Soft gray tubes fan out from his lungs. I scream at perfection so close to death. Tubes grow, arch over, pulse dull Venetian red. They meet, blood surges into the heart. The tubes are inhuman—his alienation scares me. The image pops. One of the Creators—shadowy figures above—motions to me, *pure acceptance*. Another nods, *deep control*.

Before that we live in a cavernous grocery store. Our ape sets out to forage and returns too big to fit through the door. It roars, aiming its fury at me, its instinct to kill. I back away from the giant hand reaching through the window. I hide behind shelves, work my way outside, down wooden steps above a cliff. Waves crashing far below vibrate the air like heat waves. They spin up the hill, twisting my vision, a whirling conscious unconscious. I inch up the last step as spinning air hits. A wooden door—I dash into a vast room. Spencer Tracy points at me. I'm nauseated, mortal. His force pushes me across the floor. Eyes centuries old. He smiles—terror in my spine. He draws closer, reaching. I oppose him. A man falls dead in his path. I point at him, *"NO!"* I lie on the wooden floor and dream I'm with Daniel.

Before that I talk to a manwoman (my ideal self) in a dim bar, our faces almost touching. Dark people move foreignly. I feel trapped. Erect men are shadows, moving eclipses, tight macho tension, roving gangs of stuffed jeans. In one darkness by a stool, a Puerto Rican unzips his pants and masturbates. A Black Chicano's stands straight. A mustached youth walks toward me "lost in my eyes." The room spins images—he's slashing men, bleeding bodies reel away, exploding spinning lines, nauseating violence. Exhausted, he rests his head in my lap in a white-shadowed space. A ghostly intelligence looks down on us. I wear black satin shorts. His face turns and his lips cup the satin bulge. The room sways when I put his cock in my mouth. Its shaft rubs my arm from elbow to fingertip. A stubby blade flies through the air.

An advanced race of extinct beetles created this room. Shiny black backs and secretions cover the entire surface, their amazing symmetry a network of tunnels and nests. I climb over the semi-crunch domain. I understand at a gut level: there's an endless line on each side of the narrow shaft. An elderly man lies on his side behind me, trench coat gathered above his waist, one knee raised to his chest. His sloppy old dildo-wearing wife crouches over him, fucking more and more to his taste. *May 5, 1988* The lines move on. "Toss me a rope!" My father leaves in a car. Begging then threatening. "Toss me a rope." He climbs into the car and leaves again and again.

Before that a naked youth pins another and slices him from nipples to crotch, screams as he slides through veins and organs. The dead play touch football in the front yard. Daniel and I stay close because we are yellow, only slightly diseased. The answer is yellow and gray. If we contract a disease that doesn't kill us, but kills our present disease, we will be cured.

Before that I bounce into the open, incredibly high. Massive logs lie between stumps. The soil is soft vermiculite. Daniel dives into water so clear it's invisible. A foot of water covers what I took for dry land. I stand on a fallen trunk. Daniel vanishes in the shadows and emerges smiling with love. His soft lips kiss the air between us. A boy stands on the log, a green garter snake coiling in his mouth. His mouth is a pocket. His father laughs, standing in

224

glassy water. The sun's clarity reveals minute buzzing patterns that make these forms.

Before that my young dad, on all fours, lays his face in my lap, and breathes on my cock. He actually presses against my erection and kisses it.

Before that eight women are murdered and I'm drawing conclusions. "I know the murderer." His head is angular—blond crew cut, deep-set eyes, dark crows. His image bounces around the room. He steps down—I run. He shoots at me on Market Street. I climb over crumbling bricks, a ruined viaduct that supports the ghetto. Black kids scream and play. Families jive. I latch on to the arm of a gold-spangled Black woman. She helps me over broken mounds to a narrow jetty. She digs a small hole in the crumbling brick wall. Someone whispers that she shoved the last white man on earth through that hole. He fell hundreds of feet. I climb through bodies and dark rooms into the cumulous sky.

Flying again above Mother's driveway—I circle, taking ballet and modern-dance poses. My takeoff is stiff but if I push hard enough and hold my arms straight enough—Once I'm up it's easier, though I do feel gravity. I spread my arms to go higher and kick for speed. My father watches me in the birch and black pine through one gray eye, dragging me from the sky with his evil thoughts.

Before that the blade falls— total radiation. Fingertips, lungs, and soles tingle. We are poison. My life will be short; my ashes will be hot forever. Military plastics men arrive. I keep a woman and a child in caskets in an underground storeroom cluttered with dusty boxes. The bodies are drying out. They wait for me, my goal in life, covered in green oilcloth. At the bottom of the steps I open the padlock and swing the dry wooden door. The smell is unbearable. The odor is death—continual waves wash over me. How will they react to my treasure? My corpses are legal. Excitement confuses me, I am sick to my stomach, but the bodies are staying, I'm set on that.

Before that I relax at a Hawaiian resort where Annette Funicello was arrested for sucking cock and dealing coke. I'm high above a small community beach. Where is Daniel?—down in the huge complex. I reach the wide terrace. People are running. Black steam and red lava spew, the ground splits under my feet. There was supposed to be enough time to fly to another island. I run through buildings—hallways forever. In a banquet hall people laugh and cry at white-clothed tables. I meet Elin, we cry, she knows where he is. I run to the right, then right again. I backtrack to another hall and there's Daniel in the war room with tired, frightened men. They are drafted, equipped with spiked gloves and helmets, and sent to the front to fight against the other side, outfitted in the same room. Daniel refuses the uniform and so do I. We're not going to the front to kill. The island breaks apart. "We'll never see the outside again." We're crying, but it's our choice, the only one for us.

Before that a moaning gray-and-brown cat smolders on her side on a mound of coal—Sophie! Gray charring pebbles cast intense heat. Daniel and I take turns shoveling embers on her. Each shovelful makes her hornier, howling in pain/pleasure. I sense pain in the skin of her anus. Flaming fur and smoke, she writhes in midair.

Striated clouds part. The moon is near and small as a house—

an eyehole casts toxic rays. We crouch by an experimental station, Sophie too. One scientist lies on dirt in the open in thin, churning mist. He implodes in smoking flame—fine ash drifts. Sophie dies. Another scientist proves that light makes us immune to the rays. We shine a light on Sophie and the revenant hides in the rubble. Trees explode, houses vaporize. Dust and smoke rise through the trees.

Before that I try on bikinis in a dressing room that is open at the front and back. I don't hide my erection from passing shoppers. Across the aisle a man tries on jock socks. I sample color combinations and marvel at their softness. Twilight. Three middle school friends, still confused, run between magazine racks. A man clutching another's eighteen inches comes to life on a cover—he jerks the flesh pole. "You finally came out!" I don't have to relive the excruciation of recess. Freshmen play at an intersection. Genitals drop below cutoffs. A cock bounces out of a loose bikini. One squats with a hose, aims the white gush up his asshole—ecstasy. I feel sick and inflamed all the way through the darkness, knowing my body is ailing, is damaged.

Fragrant garlands drape from pole to pole on a merry-go-round. It's stationary—the world spins around us. A brightly dressed woman stands at each pole. It's like New York with its hundreds of ethnicities but condensed on the pitch of a hill. Long-haired Haida make pottery by drawing in the air with two fingers of each hand. I lounge in a short robe. The Chicano emcee treats me as a special guest. I shift positions, careless of my genitals. As a woman I see a chain of Hawaiian islands just outside San Francisco Bay—an undulating snake disappearing on the blue horizon.

Before
that I receive a phone message. Daniel caught a fatal disease but a pill arrested it. I caught it and have hours left. *"What, is, the, name, of, the, hospital?"*—so sick I speak like the undead. In half-life I search the city. Here's the ward, I take the pill. Daniel is healthy. A Frankenstein's monster hungers for death. Young men face the center of a dark room, backs against the wall. One blows his neighbor. We open our jeans, poke at erections. They condense into an EKG— bobbing hard-ons are wavy lines. I chatter with laughter. Two men hold an air-climbing man as a third plunges in. My turn. *News flash! The monster is loose.* Daniel and I roll down corridors like little carts on tracks. Death staggers after us. We sprint down huge square steps. Daniel revs our car, *screeeech*, the hospital disappears. Asphalt becomes dirt, car becomes bicycle and companion seat. We pass a trench where Red Chinese machine guns mow down cowering soldiers. White mist escapes from a young soldier's head wound. Afraid, I act normal. The night sun blazes, two-dimensional, floating close to home.

Before that my father hurries my sisters and me. He's sending us away. It has the intensity of death. My sisters finish but my suitcase sits empty. I go to hug him, our sexes touch. His averting eyes create distance—the embrace becomes an arm-hold. He's silent but we can stay. We swim in deep water—there's an alligator twice my length. They swim to safety. I delicately board the reptile. It paddles eternally, its eye turned back at me as I sprawl, huge scale for a handle. I disembark at a party in a tall Victorian. My red cellophane shirt crackles as we go from room to room to room. Few are attracted to my skin. I become long, elegant, Anglo-Saxon. We're white now, running along the shore toward high cliffs. *Gunshots.*

Two friends stand on a platform. I witness (eye of the pistol) their confusion and fear—that death is this way and now. Real or not, they fall dead before me.

Before that I leaf through *Earth, End of the World*, a coffee-table book of photos taken after wars and holocausts: barren cliffs, sun-cracked ocean beds, dusty sterile mountains. *January 18, 1986*

Before that drapes from the unreachable create an indistinct room around a pond. Friends dart, bodies blur. A newt swims toward the bank, becoming a prehistoric fish. Reptiles combine to make a plesiosaur with spatula fins and a long neck, snapping at the blurs. It swims at me, jaws gaping, small teeth inches from my face. Daniel drags me away. Curtains divide a vast room. A slight terror. Japanese file in and hide behind a drape. More Asians behind another drape. We're prisoners. A military guard marches by, pistols in hand. People speak out, then militant groups, but there's no escape, no windows or roof.

Before that I need to urinate. A gas station restroom expands, vast as a tire warehouse. Walls bulge and contract, huge lungs. The floor is a mudflat of defecation. Three guardians or janitors sit in the center on red hardpan. Pipes and faucets angle out of the ground for no reason. Piss and shit saturate even the packed soil beneath my feet. Desperate to reach the center, I sink to my ankles in red soil. I piss awake. People settle at tables in different rooms. Dinner comes with the film *The Hoopahook-Chook Wook Dragon of Chinookla Swamp*. I lounge and the movie begins. A dragon slashes a real man's throat on the bloody ground. We watch in shock. It tears flesh from a woman's thrashing body. Tubes squirt red till her head is chewed off. She was a real person. A commercial:

Everyone rises and moves to a different room. Daniel (my love)
emerges from the hubbub. Blood smacks the lens—a child's throat
ripped open. A red strand of meat holds the open-mouthed head
to the lifeless body and when it breaks, a commercial. People go
from room to room. I lie down by Daniel's older brother. We move
in one direction when the film begins—the feeling of riding on a
train. His hand rests on my thigh. I wrap his palm around my cock
as we speed up.

    Before that I enter a huge shabby room, rotting
Japanese antiques, retired ghosts. I rest my heart in twin strips of
shadow and yellow light. We're in Hawaii. My hanging arms hide
my erection. Daniel kneels and sucks the head only briefly because
the others are telepathically aware of our pleasure. White mist swirls
in his absence. A man and woman fuck, they are gray silhouettes.
The room shrinks, a derelict bunker in a police state. We need
purpose, we need direction, we need a reason to live. We follow
rules and snoop on others. My mind is rigid—people are block
letters.

    Before that I ride a shrinking horse to a shrinking Victorian
hotel that houses a miniature village. Tiny poor artists paint on
aluminum siding at makeshift easels. They paint thick, each cubic
inch holds uncountable colors. I half ride, half walk to my destiny.
The image lingers: intricately laced boots. The pony's brown hide
and my bronze skin shimmer in the dark.

    Daniel and I walk up an
asphalt road. Apple trees and dry pasture, slow shadows on bare
skin. Our dreaming eyes meet. Before that he felt my thighs and
groin. We were both surprised when my essence entered his roving
hands—we gasped at the thought of who I am. On his bed the

feeling of apple trees persists. A Black woman in a long green dress strokes her cock above me. In the half-light, come sprays my pillow. I am the house whore, object of delight, untouched though covered in come.

A low bed, two tall candles. The master drifts in with mist, softly reclining. He blows out his life. Currents carry his free mind upstairs into the long hall. Tapers float on either side of his vapor trail: guardians of night, two puffs and they're smoke, his drifting escape.

Footsteps on the stairs, men breaking down the door. Lily locked it—it was natural. I beg the operator: "Call the police." In fear of the police, I carry my pot plant to the back porch, turn it on its side. Dirt spills, exposing roots. I'm down in the street at dawn. A slight wind. I encourage a little girl to fly. We spread our arms, spiral upward, and fly a half block. We sit in the living room. A blond stud is manipulated, mainly by me. He feels like a prisoner but he wants it. We stand—the first thrust is too fast. He yelps but says, "Okay." I fuck him again, again—we squirm in slippery joy. I kneel above his face. He slurps my deep hanging balls, the only place our bodies touch. The warm suction is incredible. Friends watch from the windows and door.

Before that I was crying hard, I don't know where. Before that I crammed the huge envelope of coke into my back pocket as I entered the police station. A man aimed a pistol at me. I grabbed a .22 and fired from three feet away. It was empty. He stepped forward, I stepped back. I plucked three bullets from the air and shot him in the chest. As he dropped he was Skip, looking at me, distance growing in wide blue eyes, open, close, open, close...

Before

that men cheer as she floats above the dark wood saloon in Victorian San Francisco. Black stockings, dark eyes, frizzy black hair, midair sex poses. We dance *en pointe*. We fly up and reappear above the rails in ultramodern San Francisco. White encrustations south of Market—skyscrapers bend global winds. She wants me but I'm playing a game. Space widens and buildings push back. We slide on thin air below electrical wires. I shed my clothes. Bright monoliths soften to gray. Winds running up and down the coast override our differences. Clouds—shallow pans with tentacle downdrafts. I sigh in their direction.

Before that I tell Skip I'm leaving. "Our relationship has no structure." I feel *immense* pleasure calling him vile, toxic, walking around our apartment—"just exactly why I hate you." Skip continues complaining, casual, oblivious. He's used to being treated this way. We flee for our lives. I become Dean Martin, he Doris Day. I'm the cameraman too, bouncing across rooftops. Doris disappears around a corner. I run, hidden in plain sight from the searching machine gun. Doris jumps over the edge. We cling like bats to thick cement, lowering ourselves brick by brick.

Before that, through a grocery window, I see an aged Chinese man stacking duck eggs in a cardboard carton. He shows his wife how he throws them on the raw wooden floor. He proves their durability by falling like a plank on them, face-first. They're like rubber and never break. Over and over from his open cooler he pulls out eggs and falls on his face. On the floor, a shell peels off. In Mother's kitchen, Skip unbuttons his jeans—I cup his penis without thinking. Embarrassed, he pisses on the refrigerator. "I'm sorry"—I piss too. In a yard from an earlier dream, a medicinal stench leads to a warehouse. Stagnation—rot perceived through the soles of my feet. Skip blows a river of bloody phlegm from each nostril. His ignorant family dines at their polluted dirt table. Club-totin', sperm-spittin' rednecks. I take a door from their outside to mine and whisper "Fools."

The next trick is for someone to lean against vertical metal poles charged to five thousand volts. To my horror Skip volunteers. He must be equally energized so that on contact he feels nothing. He wears a pantsuit with yellow-and-black deckled-edged lining. Dials turn—he reels forward, strapped to a chair, blond hair sizzling into a kinky black crop around his electric face. He becomes electricity, a shrieking distortion. He's carried to the stage on a porcelain platter to be tipped against the poles. I find the ticket counter. "I want my money back." "Why?" With a sick expression, "It wasn't worth it." "Good, see you next fall."

Before that a pasture, thick wet moss, scrub at the border. A haystack, hay in the tines disappears as I lift.

Before that a bulky four-cylinder space station flies no higher than a gull. It's a movie—cerulean sky, puff clouds. Gyroscopes fail, the station plummets in tilted circles, black jets billowing energy. Passengers and crew live an instant of panic and certain death. *This is no movie*—Skip and I run. Buzzing, sharp crackles precede explosions that melt the air in chasing waves. We hit the ground to meet them tailfirst.

Tan, curly, sweaty, incredibly developed Italians flew in a V like swans. A vast wing flapped slowly above—its feathers were tiers of undulating fingers. The ceiling had six clusters of men and wings. A rope connected each wing to its own colossal cock. Flapping pulled it up and down, or the cock throbbed up and down causing the wing to flap. Behind the urinals, two men sat face-to-face, gripping each other. Guys stood around, laughing, waiting for spurts. I walked past and looked back to see them come.

Before that people duck as a middle-aged man in a shiny black suit brandishes a pistol. "What's your name?" It's my right to know. His barrel nuzzles my face. People judge: fat, callous, but he has a right to conceal his identity. I float as pellets strike me in faint spasms. What does the moment of death feel like? We both know my killer is my father and he wants my death badly. His gun loses power—speeding bullets are beams, fainter with each shot.

Before that my junior high art teacher stands before me. "How does a homosexual act before a straight man?" The lonely curving lane becomes a tunnel of twisted black trunks. Dots of light poke through. Dry pine smell. Starry sky.

Before that I sit in a grassy field. Chinese youths race past and dive-fly into the pond. Bouncing cocks, magnets pulled by their opposites. The sky is still blue but sunset casts orange on the buildings. Even the setting sun seems artificial. The grass is luminous, shadowless. I whisper, "Tacoma." The boys turn as one. "San Francisco." They show me their fetish: plaid slacks with matching briefs. At night I sneak into their garden to pick a rose. Its tissue-petals are white with salmon edges, rose-tulip. One long petal catches the wind like a feather. I'm getting dressed, a light turns on, there's no one. Mother walks by, the mirror casts a different reflection. She walks by, different reflection. I wake up screaming.

Before that, modern America surrounds us. My ex-boss and I plan to turn me into the highest-paid killer in the world. Our scheme is secret, though I meet her in a pub of young beer drinkers. Her English accent captivates me. In a dark office, a robot-guard emits vibrations to detect intruders. It's taller than a tall man, dressed like a cop with blank dot eyes and a club covered in rubbery leather. It senses me—it doesn't sense me. I fly up, clutch the ceiling. It swings—a gentle swing would smash my skull. I jump and jam the club against its head. Gears jolt in death spasms. I dash from an ultramodern room to one with spy holes in the rose-vine wallpaper. A robot draws near. I am food and it is hungry. I crash through glass and cling to a ledge as shards fall to the garden far below. I let go—the club just misses. I fall fall—*thud*. Look up at the ice-cube-tray wall. Star City replaces the past. A club appears in my hand. Now good and evil, rich and poor are against me. I take a streamlined catwalk to meet my female colleague. We make plans in a pub. We are equals and have only each other. We hide and kill in Star City. *May 23, 1983*

Before that, in an underground terminal ticket office, an ape rushes from her desk to her child behind me. Her face brushes mine, her chest grazes my side, her nap flips where it meets my skin. Her civilization has advanced beyond speech.

Early dawn, wanting a friend, bathed in fresh orange light in the ridges of a stone column outlined against powder-blue sky. I had this feeling as a child.

Before that men watch a film on the screen above. Smoke patterns the light and a feeling of open space persuades. Men love me, I love them. I direct your pleasure. A horizontal line buzzes on the screen. Nude men run breast to breast. I try fucking/raping young Jerry Lewis in a tiny tent that collapses around us.

Before that I scream as the translucent doctor applies layers of skin to my bloody leg. Skip appears with a video camera and spells out the logic of the accident. The point of the video is to advertise a product, namely art. Fleshy foam swells from the muscles' surface, a healing cocoon. An aged lady hobbles around, drapes of foaming flesh, decomposing shinbone like rows of loose yellow teeth. She adjusts to see my situation.

Mother stood before me in gusting winds. She collapsed in heavy awareness of a lifetime of wrongdoing. She was hospitalized because of a deception: women extract the egg with their fingers every month. Out the window, the Temple of the Moon (Palenque), a huge tombstone in a small cemetery.

Before that the memory of a Victorian mansion in a meadow next to a bay. Blackened by age, it shifts positions to house an aristocratic corpse who keeps his two young sons prisoner. One windy wintry day, Father with his long nose assigns tasks and leaves. The boys struggle and Father drives along the sweeping curve of the coast, evil eye scanning from the corner for the slightest trace of love across the watery distance.

Before that, my father returns wise and kind-hearted. We approach the foothills in a flying saucer, almost not moving, but enough to make this happen. A research center surrounds us as we land. They are counting ballots. My dad is the only one running—he knew he was "it." We lecture on the Second Coming and the tiki gods of Maui with a carousel of slides. Teacher bows to my dad. I'm not Father's equal. I am Father and Son.

Before that, in bed with two friends, cocks like sea slugs—rubbing one, the other grows. A Negro teenager cleans his long teeth with a sliding pink tongue. Turning his head is his expression. A Puerto Rican transports himself into one of us. He's black with pale hands. He's on his belly, ass in the air. The other stands above, erection pointing down, and slowly slowly sinks into penetration. In the doorway three women hold their aprons up, hiding from what they need to see. I glance back, rolling flesh, buttocks pinning the other to the corner, arms tightening. I lie down with my hard-on—white jets across the bed.

Two Black women, wavy black hair, feather fountains from their cleavages, short tight skirts, long legs and platform shoes—the world turns around them. My head spins. An orange-black face watches me, female and innocent.

The air is fabricated, the weave magnified so many times that I pass easily between two bands of shadow, or the sky is littered with hundreds of blackbirds, each traveling shadow distinct. Skip and I hide from a giant bald man, his chaotic spell of dismembering bodies, flesh shards of cut paper, flying photos of intestines wildly spinning. We run for our lives, dodging sunbeams filtered through a mesh of arching roses.

Before that Skip offers his body and gentle encouragement when a figure of both sexes abandons itself to free-swinging axery. I join in, slicing an arm. Flesh parts easily but the humerus doesn't snap. Skip is calm, shy about death. Chopping the muscles in his back, cracking his skull, I circle counterclockwise. He turns clockwise.

I swing with all my strength. I can't break his bones. He lives and I live in frustration. No blood but we have energy.

Before that borders darken to nonexistence, one drop of spit crystallizing the idea of syrup. Open flames and friends, a dark woman spreading spit till she makes clear syrup on the hot plate hearth. Tiny soft white moths are the secret—wingless, their scrambling legs carry them through the air. Skinny trees, indirect light. There's no hot or cold, velvet moss covers the bumpy ground. Ahead, the log cabin ready for virgin fauna, a heaven for procreation. I stand in a cloud that shines into the forest. Under the blanket in Sean's arms, an old friend—he isn't gay but allows this freedom in the dark, the sacks of our balls touching. His face is quickly handsome, then immature. Twisted between his legs, I recall a dream of clear syrup and white moths. His wife enters, pure light untwines our bodies. She becomes Mother, a world of complication.

Before that each person walks toward me, visible veins, blood vessels, liver, and kidneys. Each freezes and dies as an outline, raised neon arms, splayed neon fingers. Multicolored fingers jerk toward me—neon contorts. *Superman.* Telepathy works better. *Superman* gathering inner force *Superman.* Superman places my feet on a carpet, tilts my head back. He spins me and the essence is time lost. Kneeling, he presses my prostate, it swells with my erection. Time dies.

Holding my ass, feeling tight skin and the pressure of compacted waste—I can't stand it, I scream with pleasure. One small, compressed ball pushes past my sphincter: *thud.* Two fingers covered in shit—*Look what you've done.*

Before that a

door pops into view, then a projecting sign: T W O. Male right, female left. Racks of porn mags emerge in the hall—shiny cocks, jeans—then packs of underwear. The wrappers vanish, raw cotton black silky nylon multi-cut, exposing every bare bulge. Translucent men in degrees of nakedness mill around aisles of mesh and cotton. A tan blond stands behind me cupping a mag of helpless desiring mouths and rigid cocks. Outlines suggest searching fingers, ribbed close-ups, sweating flesh, pulsing triangular clothes. In full swing, men climb out of jeans into briefs and bodies. A blond pulls his pale butt apart, but discreetly, lifting it a little. Open face, open to the image, my cock pops out of white bikinis, creases become waves of ribbed cotton triangular codpieces waist strings mesh. Jamaican rum navy-blue exposing jeans uncover black cotton on tight torsos in networks stretched over soft skin pushing through mesh. Lying on hot sand, a jungle clearing, I bake in the sun, loose chartreuse super-mini bikini strings circle my waist. My cock spills out, a secret I promise not to keep. My heart pounds through the air.

With my jubilaic singing, screaming my fancy head off, I sing from a bay window into the golden sunlight, romancing the men in my life, those I love and yearn for.

Before that I need to piss in a crowded multi-stall restroom. The stench of warm urine, toilet seats covered in the relics of crowded bowel movements. Sidewalls don't reach below seat level, expose resting thighs and clenching asses. No toilet paper, streams cross the tile floor. The closer I come to ejaculation. I wake as it trickles between my thighs.

Before that I return to a small porn theater, Skip and I in each other's arms, bored, on the edge of expectation. It's damp and icy, a mother and child watch from the back row. The film has three-dimensional actors: two nude boys watch anxiously as a skinny pale four-foot column emerges through a hole in the wooden floor, their erection. Black chairs and dark floor, we shift positions and dream.

Before that a boy genius is worshipped and treated like a retard. I understand the protocol for the disabled and follow bathing instructions to the letter. His body oil films the surface. I stick a soapy finger up my ass to clean the flesh tube. A young woman parts the air below, revealing a forest. Three youths, aspects of escaping genius, push bundles, paddle, and swim desperately. "They're doing fine," I remark. I prepare to live. Back in the study, I follow instructions, squirming on a soapy finger. A genius is lost in the night.

Before that I'm turning somersaults to stay afloat in a small room with the trappings of home, plus hundreds of people, Black, white, yellow, brown, talking with a forty-piece band. I wander from room to room. Where are the underwear and wrestling mags? A German shepherd chases Lily. A muscular Black man in red hotpants and a black snakeskin wraparound shirt contorts in the silent room, earphones tight. He bends his knees, flexing, *coooo*. Loose white pants don't mask his thighs and bulging crotch, buttocks keeping the beat, delicious. I'm lying on the sofa, turning to watch him drift with the music. He says, "I'm horny," fly open. A girl fondles him—it doesn't grow but hardens. Her lips slide around it, her lips are mine. His cock becomes Lily's nose next to mine. She's in my arms, head on shoulder, fast asleep. The golden haze is gone. I'm trapped in a stark white room. Mac keeps me company. "They hid a flying saucer at a base in South America." Mac is a breeze blowing in opposite directions. He holds what we all want to see, a foot in diameter, platinum/silver. "This is a real flying saucer, though it's also a model." He hands it to me—the power and secret of the universe in my hands. I remove the top. Thin metal layers rest on each other without hinges, screws, joints, or moving parts. Out the window, at a military base, silver jets launch over filthy white-gray barracks, palms in the distance. A spot on the Chilean coast circled in red. I sense what new beings feel, violent amazement. Lunch is a midget zombie with gray jellyfish skin—a long, fat object waiting to be eaten. The wall opens onto a chute stuffed full. I shove him in. Souls in white jackets sit patiently, others pace to kill time. We are intelligent and lost, becoming more and less ourselves as our puppeteers deepen the hue.

Before that Skip and I cross the wide highway. I yell "Run" and clamber up a steep embankment. Turning, I see Skip choosing to lie down, letting cars run over his legs, his torso, his head. He still talks, a flattened wafer. I watch in disbelief but I'm not moved.

Before that the cosmos begins. I'm a voluptuous angel in a black bikini. I drape a diamond shawl over my shoulders and dance midair for the others, spreading my legs, curling like an embryo, a pose for every aspect of life.

Before that we semi-horizontally run-fly, lighthearted, through woods and down a grassy gully to damp sandstone caves, a maze of square arenas tipped at different angles. Animals scurry ahead. We enter a chamber with a sandstone altar. A sandstone priest comes to life and others too—a faceless female essence. They're menacing but I feel their weakness: they're sand. My hand circles my face once, the priest opens his white eyes, the faceless woman smiles, a door opens above, light pours in. A busy dime store engulfs us. We look for Needs under *N*. Smiling pals, Skip and I stroll arm in arm in a busy subway tunnel lined with shelves of Chinese food, deciding between salted and dried, smoked abalone and shrimp, clams and oiled crab. "Do you want two pickled cherries?" I take them from my mouth and watch him eat them. Walls radiate indirect sensibility. I try to hide my erection as we discuss the politics of exposing erections in public. I feel freer to reveal it—the head pokes past my waistband. As we stroll, Skip asks, "Can I see it?" Tight white cotton stretches across soft firm muscle, presses between balls, loose sack skin.

Before that Skip kneels in the tub, fucking the overflow drain under HOT and COLD. Bob and I grasp him to feel contractions—comes! The drain gurgles, white shoots through water, gels, floats. The head of Skip's cock shares the same tiny space as his head. His choking gurgling reminds me that death and orgasm are the same.

The toreador conquers the bull. The frenzied audience rips his chest open and devours his organs—he's in bliss.

Before that eeriness sweats over me. Skip and I are two beetles spinning gently through space.

Before that a pale gray man locks eyes with me—I scramble like a deer. His weight pulls me to his rusty knife. Fallen trees cover low rolling hills, miles of rotting logs, wood chips, and small branches. He circles me, I run for my life. I gasp air that burns. Nothing grows. Clouds pass behemothly, blue Eternal between. The large man evaporates like steam. I'm mounting him, his head between my legs, eyes wide. I slice the corner of his mouth to his ear with an X-Acto knife, white meat, no blood, then the other corner till his jaw drops in an endless scream.

Skip, tall and blond, invites me on a walk. I feel disbelief and unworthy—he has insight into the body. We find a glade and make love. Four straight people make love—two women and two men. The world opens, I have what I want. Picnicking families drive up—our spot becomes public. Skip takes me to and through his house to a wooded hillside. He opens himself completely. Construction workers watch our relationship grow (by the minute). We move to the privacy of his house—entwining, we disappear.

Before that the room has no floor or ceiling, just blue space and billowing white clouds above and below. I kiss dear friends goodbye. The whole world is waiting. I don't want to space-travel, I don't want time to change. A metamorphosing gas shrinks us into glass squares, Chiclet-sized crystals —cabins to the next universe. Fearful, I look out of mine.

Rolling dunes, blue-gray mountains, broad horizon, cool blue above a winding asphalt road. Skip leans out the window of a low gray house, watching breathlessly. White muslin slacks reveal my brown cock, buttons cinch the flaring leg. He feels sexy and I prance my cock. Dim yellow light shadows my face. I point one toe down as I rise ten feet above the road, performing geometric poses. Arm forward, leg stretched behind propels me closer to the house and past it. A mirror appears above the yellow sand. Wood rose and hibiscus cover the ground. Delicately I descend—touching the asphalt sends me higher. I desire his eyes and mouth. I imagine talking to him. The house grows distant, and pale yellow light cleans the air. A winding road—white clouds fill the valley below. At eye level, clouds flicker, soft electrical discharge. Above, faint stars.

My parents come out of the air for a spaghetti dinner.

There are two doors. Behind STRAIGHT, toilets are busy with both sexes. I enter GAY. Friends keep me company. I piss so hard. "A gallon of urine," they joke. I fill the urinals and a large basin. I still have the urge.

Before that, pointing a stiff finger at Mother, I feel my pinpoint pupils. Her nonsense blows my heart hotter. Repulsion, resentment, and love are attractions. Father pulls my hand straight into the air like a magnet. We mingle, skin to skin, crotch to ass. I draw back, I was penetrated. I show disapproval by clinging to his dry, diseased body, pinning leg with leg, arm with arm. He's immersed in sweat and sperm as I prove my point. Waves roar outside and conceal my fear. The room turns slow circles. I sit on a straw mat and friends soap my body.

Before that I gyroscope down a tree-lined road. My passenger is a horse who fucks his lover who changes from cow to mule. The smile on my face says to the smiles on their faces: *It's like playing billiards with rows of Christmas trees.* They crack up. The bus turns a corner, the horse becomes Skip. Maple leaf shadows cross the lawn, the blacktop, the roofs of parked cars, the steps leading to our secret room, but we are not there.

May 15, 1980

Before that Bob and I went to Kathleen Fraser's, though she wasn't the mother. Some cat-creatures mewed on the back porch. They wore snail shells to their shoulders and their motley fur was orange and white. Wire feelers circled their ears and rabbit tails stuck out behind. Kathleen's son David encouraged us to pet them. He had crossbred them, though he was only eleven. I stared in wonder, time slowed down, my cock stuck out at odd angles. The creatures on the porch were the first new life-forms to be invented. I felt the presence of naked men, though I couldn't see them. New life-forms! The feeling of naked companions grew stronger. I confessed to Bob that I felt like crying. He sniffled too. Tears of joy gushed from my eyes.

Before that I stand in a dark revolving room with a circular floor and ceiling. Stainless steel walls creased in rectangles are superb celestial mirrors reflecting piercing rays. My expectation is a shimmering obsidian sphere. I turn slow circles, reach slow conclusions. Dusk blue demeaning purple. My ship arrives on a black lava beach in the valley made by two volcanoes. A new old planet, newly settled, devoid of human life. Millennia of awareness in a land whose natives have no physical form and exist nowhere. A new settlement, entropy and glass rectangles, black-windowed monoliths, protruding encrustations, a grid of empty runways. A whistle behind the silence like wind through high wires. A glass building in the volcano's shadow becomes the private home of a doctor who specializes in rare abdominal diseases. I bend in pain. He feeds me pills as he passionately examines my soul. His tall ceilings and multi-level rooms become my refuge. I love my doctor with sentimental affection.

Before that I pass a loose joint that goes from hand to hand. Two tin pans desperately fry hams in deep fat. Fat fries away, leaving crisp bone meat, burnt yellow and blood salmon. My father is not here but his presence is upstairs, making love to Mom.

Before that

levels move in opposite directions. I'm a weakling who grapples with his hands. Steve's a giant. Arms big as thighs punch a man's face into a pig's fleshy reds. I don't want it to be so. Steve swings loose. I duck and grab him from behind. He shrinks as if we were sitting, his back to my crotch. My palm covers his face, fingers curling into his gullet. I pound his cheeks and eye sockets till skin disappears and a breathing skull remains. Blow after blow, his nasal bone snaps. Blood spreads and drips like pus.

Richard Chamberlain is dead. Twenty-nine years old. It was one week ago. I go to his house, I'm not dreaming. So the interview begins. He talks about his wife and his homosexuality in a low voice. He's been dead a week. I wake up crying. I'm an actress playing Richard's wife, huge breasts and short curly hair, half-Mexican, half-white: sound stage, *action*. Sitting on the floor, crying deeply, terrified acting, honest tears.

Before that I enter my black limousine, Father/Bob by my side. My chauffeur drives up a curving brick road, left arm dangling from the window, discussing family wealth and melancholy sexual appetite. "It's easy to live cheaply"—I forget to mention food stamps. His limp cock folds over his balls. Brick walls line the narrow road. It's noon but I'm twilight inside.

Before that a desperate young woman holds me for information that I powerfully give. Bob and Elin pack and leave. Vampires chase my sisters. A tough Black girl closes in—her fangs are tire irons. The monsters vanish, a distant roar. Brown-and-white goats, wild boar, and hundreds of pigs stampede. A reed hut crammed with Polynesian children surrounds me. Piglets scream, frantic swarms of goats—here they come! A boar with curling tusks dashes in to buck a pig, then rejoins the flow. Dawn seems near but it's just the full moon. Thousands of screeching bats—chaos in the sky. Bugs buzz in my ears, root under my tail. Sweat coats all surfaces with sticky steam. O sun, rise.

Before that I return from a long journey. *November 3, 1978* Bob relaxes in a sunroom. I climb in a window to greet him. Plants surround his writing. I can't hear him. "Where is *our* apartment?" He sits. "Didn't you miss me? Aren't you glad I'm back? Where's Lily?" He murmurs. "Don't you know me? Bob, I love you!" He's a fog, elusive glance and love. I hang in the jamb of a yellow window. "Bob, why are we here?!" He moves away. Trees, a Victorian neighborhood, sunshine and flowers. I wail, I can't hold it in, the memory of *our* apartment unseen down below. He's a mirror turning me back on myself with a glint of sarcasm. "All right, I'll find it alone." The hallway is an escaping boardwalk. A middle-aged woman sits close by. Her name is Giulietta. "I met a director and fell in love"—*Fellini!* A hammered silver cooking pot retreats into memory, Bob's favorite. I blink tears into distance, overwhelmed by loneliness.

Just beyond the city limits a snowy yard rises to become a cliff. I'm an upright fox walking on fox legs covered in fur. I feel the instincts of a dog/fox. I breathe frosty air. Massive peaks. Blue snow, black rocks. Waterfalls, crashing ice.

In North Beach I retreat to a small shack, a home for poor travelers. We sleep under tables. Eating and shitting and sweat and wild sperm are one, everything warm, moist, and delicious. I go back to piss and seven follow—the first to fuck me and each to fuck the next. Walking past old sleeping drunks, long hair and beards, dark gray under the tables, sex is everywhere, stench of old sex, dank breath, dark, sticky walls.

Before that the air moves, lights flicker, the ground shifts six inches into a new realm. Gaining satisfaction through Bob's body indicates weaker energy. Masturbating in briefs, I fly to the backyard and resume my ejaculation with the freedom to stimulate you as I stimulate myself, feeling each cell's meiotic division.

Before that Mother, my sisters, and I were trapped under the sky. Thick smoke drifted over the sun. The moon rose—cracked mud—and glowed next to it. They moved farther and farther away. We took cover, sprinting from hollow to hollow, jumping over radiated pools as the cosmos exploded. The empire was dying—Chaos and Beauty. Down the street, boxy cardboard buildings raged in an inferno. Crowds ran screaming. Elin climbed into her small jet, big cameras around her neck. One by one friends flew to safety—I was never on their manifest. Some of them were shot out of the air. Skyscrapers swayed, broke in two, and tumbled daintily or leaned against other skyscrapers that vibrated or fell piece by piece into the darkness.

I fear the cowboy right-winger I'm attracted to. We perform geometric patterns in the air—sexual wonder. Sky, hill, mown lawns at twilight. His massive arm circles my waist, I tighten against his lunge, the huge round head pushes against my contracting anus. A flash passes through my abdomen, galaxies gushing down a vortex. LSD rips me apart.

Before that I make love with a slender woman—she's dressed in a bikini, I'm dressed. She pivots her sex on my hand. She mounts me, becomes a man, pokes through my fly as I swell into his briefs till my penis lolls, surrounded by his warm hole. He extracts it, oils it, then the bumping begins, superhuman feats of fucking, swinging bodies joined only by erect muscles, luckily lubricated. I lather him in white foam. Air flows around an oval of scarf edges spinning like a top, purple, pink, pale blue. I throw my hands up and spin to match her speed, then slow her down to match mine. She leads me by the hand. Escalators take us to a flat box of synthetic underwear labeled HE-SHE. She heaps pale blue, trans-sheer, and black bikinis before me.

I'm part of the group whereas Bob is a sloppy drunk with a dirty Band-Aid across his sweaty forehead. He dances wildly till he vomits from dizzy exhaustion. He's imperfect and detached from me. The pale smoothness of his back shows through his white gauze shirt. The lines of his bending shoulders travel through the night as he fades. He asks maliciously what I've been doing, "Peroxing your hair?" I numbly stab his kitchen table with a pen and yell (though it's muffled), "Why do you want more distance and hate?" *February 17, 1978* He runs upstairs and slams the door, breaking our deal that he won't retreat if I don't smash something. "Okay!" I shatter a cobalt-glass measuring cup on the floor.

Before that grotesque candelabras, Greek statues, and glittering stars overpopulate each block. My eyes sweep panoramas horizontally, a broom pushing chaos away. Candelabras simplify and vanish, Greek youths condense, vast avenues close in on themselves and shrink into clear space. My eyes sweep back and forth. The room becomes lighter till a three-dimensional line runs through the center (the space eight blocks create in a cube), which becomes a slender youth, free of clothing, shrinking till all that remains is a panorama open in all dimensions.

Before that Bob takes his cock and balls off, walks away, and still feels me massaging them. He points to places in the pile of flesh where he's throbbing—balls, skin, blood, flesh, liquid alive in my hands as he stands apart in ecstasy.

Before that I bounce gently from wall to wall, float down corridors and stairs, move with currents. I enter the basement arching backward, reclining midair. Then I clamber up, brown-sugar dirt under my feet. I piss in a small latrine. An adolescent waits his turn, his tough masculinity glittering from a bracelet of grade school scissors. Peddling, Elin requires my company. Her father's death lingers. Her mother, Joan Tower, is quick. She orders us to love her always. The garden path disappears in tall grass and stagnant water. Elin pirouettes across the sky. Skull: pink and orange tropical petals bloom on its bone brow and surround an upside-down children's chorus, *knick knack paddy whack*. Dark ocean clouds line the horizon.

Just then I remember I'm in the carnival regatta. Drag queens abound, even their boats have frills, twills, thrills. A floating stage, faggots screaming, an old blond waiter-friend picks up a French roll, his little ass sticks up, he puckers his lips, a breeze ruffles his tutu. I roll with laughter. Run, scream, red tights bulge, see-through nipples, padded bras hang from wide shoulders, gaudy feather headdresses, whiskers and mascara, thigh-high fishnet stockings exposing organs, fluttering bodies. Flaming glories baring satin chests forever. The race is over. I witness a miracle: two dolphins in drag swim gracefully by. And into the jaws of a shark—needle fangs close on the couple. I feel the moment. Red dirt through clear water. My turn—run, jump, leap to land.

Before that I choose a mesh bikini that ties twice on each side, otherwise is open to the wind. Dunes, ocean coming up, five of us pile into the back seat. Sliding in nude, I lie across naked laps once more. Ocean pounds, fast cloud shadows. We speed past gas stations and drive-ins, open fields, dead dirt roads, racing as though experience were one long tunnel, yearning to see what's ahead.

Before that a stranger at the door asked for a lid. Paranoia!—I uprooted my weed, twisted it into a ball, and buried it in the garbage. Lying on a round bed with some couples, two trays of nail polish, four blues. I proceeded with lime-chartreuse, painting my nails as they grew, as the couple next to me grew aroused, nail polish smudging skin and hair. My face was by her cunt, I held him tight, I tried to caress but ended up goosing her as she arched as he came, one hard thrust. His cock became his face as he receded from the warm shaft.

Before that I stand on a rise at my grade school—it fluctuates with the Art Institute. Diamond lights glide horizontally in the gray sky. An orange line shoots out of the murk, a flattened disc, distant but huge. *This is no dream!* Other beings have finally arrived but the vibe isn't friendly. Three orange lights pulse through the gray. Have they taken the shape of my fellow artists? Then I know—news from nowhere—round-headed robots disembark as more ships land in shallow water. I board a trolley that becomes a round seat guided by my swinging hands. I look between my knees at the tracks. Robots trudge to shore. The sun sets. My seat falters and I float on my own through swinging doors into the dark, each turn a chapter in the chain of events. The world condenses into a seaside village. Ruling individuals—vast connected beings—tell the story and act their parts, from the funky thrift store to standing on hilltops shorter than my knees to seeing the bus arrive down by the water, clear, black, blue. Riding the air, I coast from dream to dream, up the lonely curving path, trying to see events before they happen. I take the next turn, vast distance sharp as a close-up. Bob stands behind me, we arch, my rectal muscles stretch and tear. My body throbs tightly, baring my chest bravely as Bob fills every part of the sucking hole. The fucked wavers and fades as his fucker becomes too real.

Yellow overcast morning. The street is six feet below my bedroom window. Jewish mothers in dark overcoats stroll with their scattering children in the ochre shadows of trees growing through cement in the Mission.

Before that San Francisco appears on a small table. Miniaturize and conquer. I become that thought and fan out. The city is real in the far future. Tiny pyramid clusters of steel and glass fill San Francisco's valleys, reaching three hundred feet over the water, skyways, freeways, flying vehicles.

Before that we round the bend into sunlight, a small bay, yellow daffodils everywhere. The city is half-size. I'm gigantic. I climb into a sports car and open Marty's jeans. He swerves, we're laughing, midair erections. Bright elaborate Victorians whiz by, international spy music and car chases. *December 20, 1976* Purple-pink wandering Jews, single-petal magenta roses, rosemary spilling over retaining walls. I see what is actual today—that is, through new eyes. Yes I am good and no dead star pulls me faceless into the black hole where universes spin.

Before that
shadows hide men roaming the halls and stairs of the hospital courtyard. Jewels shear the night with thin rays. My dress drags on the
steps, my pumps balance me. People surge into this exclusive hospital-
hotel. The blazing sun turns writhing bodies into white foam. I walk
down a clean white corridor. The psychiatric ward is open, but
I must qualify. I explain my crisis to Mac and Nonie. I trail behind,
out of breath, whistling for Lily. They are distracted, climbing the
lonely curved road toward the hospital. Lily appears and talks to
me, my only joy.

Before that a middle-aged woman in pedal pushers
and spike heels kisses her teenage son. She wriggles in circles, little
feet kicking the air. He thrusts his tongue into her mouth, in-out,
and pushes his long fingers into her. She vibrates like a peacock's
tail. I try to shut the attic door to turn the darkness off. An iceberg
slowly revolves at night—a helpless man in dark clothes clings to
his melting island while sharks and killer whales nervously circle
below.

Before that Bob and I enter a vast amphitheater—tier after
tier. He is an invisible viewpoint. Water cascades down steps into
pools and elaborate fountains. His answers become the shallow
water we wade across. We climb to the top and take in the beauty.
Bob fills two pie pans with salt water to melt gelatin. A woman next
to me—the closer she comes, the older she gets. She has pale blue
eyes with thin cataracts. Gray face close to mine, she explains that the
house is haunted because the former tenant was vain. I push but she
hugs tighter, wrinkled and laughing. I fade as she enters. I'm dying—
this old woman becomes me!! I scream awake and continue screaming, waking Bob.

The sun is setting as I walk up the curving path. A giant time-structure crashes gently in slow motion behind the sleeping houses, sliding to the ground without a sound.

Bearberries and thick horse chestnuts surround a vast shallow pond of clear salt water. A human-faced rat big as a car rolled on its back, barking phrases and biting the air. A black dog-cat with razor teeth growls, snaps. Satan's pupil-less eyes. I push him away but the sun sets and he becomes decaying metal cans, wounding me with a bite. Trees contort with blight. Mother hands me pointed sticks. "Kill the vultures in these trees." Everything sways, twisting with evil, black is alive with escaping birds. Mother skins and places them in rows, ready for beheading. They gape, pointed teeth, bulging eyes. I sever necks with my teeth, whole head in my mouth, horror, *horror*.

Before that a young woman hangs by her blond hair, thick entanglement, vast space beneath. I float up in a white gown and Ray-Bans to rescue her. I greet four friends from my past, climb the stairs, show them my erection. They grab my balls. We ascend in pleasure to a classroom where our floor is a bed. I lead the instruction floating on my back. I press my head, shoulders, waist, thighs, knees, and feet. I explain the next act as we perform it, twisting and posing midair. Bob rubs himself, arousing me. I'm in white briefs, his pubic hair is big as a pot roast. We hang on to the bed for dear life, banking curves, tearing down the freeway like a shooting star.

Before that a transparent gold sphere hovers above Jock's bed, emitting rays in all directions, wealth for its own sake. Blue briefs glitter inside. A silver sphere hovers above my bed. White briefs glitter inside. Long threads suspend me. I rock three notches forward to see the silver sphere, three notches backward to see the gold.

Before that a celadon tidal wave swells above my head. It crashes as I struggle upward to pierce the deadly sheet. The ocean's rule is submit to its strength. It recedes instantly and I am high and dry, a white Holiday Inn towel wrapped loosely around my waist and 125 feet of air below my feet. Down down—the towel cushions the impact. My friends sunbathe and watch me crawl, Esther Williams, not wetting my hair. Black rocks below are sharks but I gracefully sidestroke—the social stroke, because I can also talk.

Before that one section of a huge auditorium has rows of produce, another has maestros and barbershop quartets, another has cheap small-town acting—all separated by vast floors covered in flattened fruit and slippery mashed vegetables. I climb up and down stairs, rehearsing my part. Mac and three jolly fat men rehearse their barber-pole throats. Elin's in tight pants—her tiny silver spike heels flutter like bee wings. She squeezes my penis and the Marx Brothers feeling begins, Polly-pecking parrots and yakking mynahs. Tom is a werewolf and Jeannie is Natasha, green parakeets and yellow canaries. Drifting white threads drape everywhere. Tom smiles through his continuous stare. Walls move, reconstruct, earth contorts as it realizes we're escaping. The bridge was washed out, the land sinks. A few quick strides and my shadow-three ford the widening river. On the far bank the Three Stooges gather big tin cans at the speed of light. They jerk a time-face-can-ambulance into existence and their wide mouths emit sirens as they drive quick and lurching. Parrots squawk, the land moves, the big open day lights the river spaces.

Before that I wander in a dark hangar behind Communist lines, long dark ropes, dots of sun filter through gaps above. *April 30, 1975* My assignment is to cover rows of squatting Vietnamese refugees with plastic to airlift them out. No one can soothe my anxiety.

Three self-portraits from when I loved my teacher: I was him or his wife, Diane LeMoine, or she was me or he was both. In one painting I appear four times, two identical smiles and two identical expressions of loneliness. I wander into a sex house where sweating couples sit on upright chairs in a dingy room. A woman is intensely fucked from below. I climb on top—I slide in with the other and she writhes. The highlight is when two men love each other. I wake in jail—outside my barred window, a tree-covered pond. Water deepens near the trunks and water lilies hide in the sandy bottom. A soft Lauren Bacall at my cell door, my freedom in her smile: a sports car for two winds through a village on cobblestone streets.

Before that an unseen moon casts long shadows. Aliens exist as gas in the air we breathe. They twist gravity, but Bob and I cling like lizards to the white grass. My eyes light my path—no life exists but mine.

The stairs lead nowhere. I push the riser between the bottom steps and slide over to the next flight where the same dilemma waits. Rock in rock out. I stop form, then light. I wake up screaming.

Before that the art teacher leads me to a private room for nude models. He offers oranges and fish, which I accept. He asks for my sex, which is difficult to give. I pull a navy-blue skant over my thighs, sliding over dangling balls, catching my cock—I adjust it downward for comfort. It joins my balls as I bounce to set their places. Intense pleasure spreads from my sack. Now I rub myself, stretching deep blue nylon so the teacher can feel danger from my erection. He jumps down, mouth wide. Mother walks in—I throw a tantrum. "Can't I develop my masculinity?! Where *is* myself?!"

Huson Drive curves up the small hill of my childhood home. I walk up with Elin, Bob, and Bruce. A boy follows us, a childhood memory, a framework for remembering. Rolling together, his small body against me, I kiss his tiny lips. He's naked, arching back as I smooth milk-white skin downward. His spasms grow till *pump pump* splatters in rapid jerks, splatters more and more.

Before that Bob and Elin are the Center of Attention, I'm next. Round faces, smiles, white teeth. Bob spits white come onto a gelatinous mound. Elin's fluttering orgasm brings *ah*s and faces gather like the five teeth of a starfish. My come backs up into angry tears, drops fall from my chin.

My invitation to the party is still good and someone has to keep the woman's beauty going, so I put on her jewels and dress exactly the same. There's a Japan Town in Tacoma—narrow halls connect pantry-sized stores. I'm *still* lonely. At dusk I pass a store without walls but with an enclosed feeling. The little owner, ready to help, stands between racks of fishnet bikinis and super-brief bikinis. He also sells comics and pornography. My heart pounds madly when I find four close-ups of white mesh underwear. The last has a shredded hole in the center. Bob tries on boots, convincing me to buy a pair and settle the difference later in our bouncing bank account. The owner's penis hangs out. It's painful to see a penis so fat attached to a body so small. His wife tries to sell me transparent Bermudas, papery muslin. I hide behind a door as she stretches to see my testicles. She's disappointed that I don't buy them, I buy them. *November 4, 1974* The store becomes their living room. I'm babysitting. On my knees I bend to suck the baby's penis but I'm scared. I move to the little girl, who grows one that becomes erect. I caress it with my mouth, my tongue, she squirms. Shocked, I stop. I'm corrupting innocence. The room becomes a BART car slowly rocking on the tracks in bright sunlight—back and forth, making me sick.

Before that a girl laughs, feeling acute pleasure, grabbing the fenders of passing trucks that pull her down the street, legs draggling. Sean and I split from everything for a month. I feel like I'm leaving Bob forever. We check in to a mansion hotel. Spirit hands travel over our bodies for hours as we gesture in slow motion. Curtains billow. I lift a stranger, torn side bleeding from a bullet wound, sometimes hurting him as he hangs loosely. We're in line, waiting our turn. The nurse pulls a baby out of a box in the wall—his red rib cage empty. Doctor and nurse work intently, lungs, heart, liver, moist and separate, the color is real. The doctor transplants them with great speed. He unhooks a tube from a machine-computer and squeezes the abdomen together as rich blood pumps in. Warm blood splashes my face, it's real. They shove the baby back in storage and turn to the next patient. My stranger stirs, the blood on his wound is drying. He gains awareness till he's standing in my arms. I embrace him, he hardens against me, sporadic movements—comes against me and we kiss. Walking home, I'm spellbound—street life and clothes from the turn of the century. The buildings are new but the images are scratchy, my retinas screening an old movie. Sounds reflect off different surfaces, trolleys roll by. I board one—San Francisco is new, less developed, my eyes wide open.

Clear slow midnight, trees and dirt path. The sequence repeats—it's noon, the forest aware of its beauty, lit with shimmering glass. Gray-and-white gorillas dance in unison beneath the clothesline in the backyard. A troupe of soft-tufted gorillas surrounds our house, a gentle ballet. I wash my hair with pink shampoo and the perfect man inside the gorilla pats it dry. I return to the kitchen, the toilet reappears, green defecation. Out the window, fading gray-and-white gorillas fill the ether. Five black gorillas recline voluptuously, their raised right arms dangle long black fingers.

At the Art Institute I learn on the phone that my sisters were raped wildly. Now they live in a different city and time, weeping forever. I travel on water systems past tiny future-city replicas. Climbing the curving path to my studio, I stop for a soda, Sean by my side. We share ideas and studio space. His paintings are woven: yards of transparent glazes surround a square inch of silk thread. He leads me to a teacher and stylish people. Underwear galore! Stars explode on the crotch!—*biiiii-kiiiii-niiiii*. Light fades, orange shadows. Sometimes underwear is more beautiful than flesh. Colorful clutter, chaos, *extravaganza*! The courtyard, the tiled pool, faded Mexican elegance. I close my eyes and drift. Sean flexes his arms, a lightweight pose. Blue lanterns, Sean's image shifts downward, vision distorts, my penis full of blood. He lets me hug him but flinches.

Before that two packs of scraggly dogs surround me,

one good, one bad, gray, black, and wiry. Bad dogs killed the good ones—soon they are all dead. I the observer skim the surface of bodies ripped open, warm steam rising. The dogs' heads are half-human, *horror*. An old Asian peasant, brown mosquito face and hands, sits in the field of half-human meat. She stuffs her mouth with decaying flesh and dangling yellow fat as she tosses arms and heads over her shoulder. All is black and warm. I'm the woman walking away, in my mouth a taste like never before.

The Symbionese Liberation Army calls for poetic knowledge in public life. The secret soldiers are well-mannered and good-looking. Clear light everywhere, environments clean and orderly. A seven-headed cobra—the SLA insignia—floats before my eyes.

Before that we follow a dirt path as the canal widens into a trough that rises thirty feet in long steps, a water slide. Bright sun, clear sky. Bob becomes two Texans, blond and brunet. I slide naked down a torrent pouring from the lips and clitoris of wet dream-wood. My lover is a shadow becoming me, Bob, and herself in soft fluttering waves. At the water's edge, water-people. We talk intimately and leave with the Texans, gliding above a dirt road along the shore. On water skis, my friends give me the kite line. I see the bottom through huge waves for a bay so small-brown and yellow in long ripples. The sun pounds clarity, transistor radio blasting. Bob is my father, he calls me out. I swim to shore, strip with my friends, the white-haired youth's long white penis. They become Bob, change into others, and even appear as no one.

Before that I followed childhood paths through webs and thick tropical bushes. Mother revealed my past (I think). I was dressing with my father.

My genitals were two vines of split-leaf rhododendron. I went to the free clinic. Before that I subdued a Japanese boy in a world of steps and running water where people lived playful emotional lives. It felt like roses had just bloomed. I tricked him into letting me suck him. After a struggle he lay still and came in my mouth. He was me—we paddled on a surfboard. The waves were rough (Hawaii). We paddled to calm water and white sun. Everything slowed. In the distance, antelope leapt across the white ocean. *Attention*—I *see* them.

Before that I slide horizontally, keenly through the air from hall to bedroom, nude and erect. "Where is Sean?" Bob and Elin in unison, wind sweeping through. "Don't know." Sean lies next to me, prepares his mind for the day. I say, "The Victorian houses were painted to match the pastel flowers surrounding them. They symbolize how we learn from what's around us." Opalescence. Sean's hand falls softly on my rump, our bent arms interlock, he passes to me through the fluid of his eyes.

Under nut and spice trees in the dirty shade, India. I climb into my Thunderbird. An exotic young man and I are drivers and our passenger is a pretty young woman. A tall hotel takes shape around us, a white room. The dark exotic man, I, the pretty girl, I, and I. I'm wearing taps and dance the time step over and over, amazing new skill. Time passes slowly, quickly. Killdeer chatter frantically and monkeys cavort. Sean squeezes my hard-on at the base. My chest chasms, yearning to pull him into the dark sucking below.

A dark room was once a restaurant. A man fucks me as we converse, trying to look dignified. We amuse Dan, watching in the dark. A man enters Dan, who makes no attempt to hide his feelings. I'm embarrassed for him but that fades as I fuck the stranger fucking him. The stranger's friends pass by: long hair, hip nostalgic-futuristic dress and attitude with the feeling of tables and served patrons. I return to find Dan on the floor on the stranger, legs high around Dan. The stranger's hole is big and wet, but I decline when Dan offers it. I walk up the curving road, plainclothesmen at my door. Their questions enclose me. Cops everywhere, I'm theirs forever. I remember Lily frozen in time and space at the back door. Memory lifts me to a mountain forest with black bears and Oregon grapes—my melancholy escape.

What does Mother say after visiting Bob and me? *"What did you say?"* "Bob's very slow to respond." I'm peeved but try to see what she sees. Then she says, "He's bullshit." I demand an apology. I feel my asshole, matted and filthy. I know Mother wiped my ass, though I don't recall when. I do it better. I fly up the Twelfth Street hill to Huson Drive, doing the breaststroke, but this time my feet stay together and I float better.

Before that a slow bus drops me on a corner haunted by solitude. I pound on the window. Bob sees me but doesn't get off. I'm escaping with my suffering comrades in an old convertible. Cold takes the form of men pursuing us with guns. When I miss my turnoff, reality crumbles. I'm looking for a childhood friend and find him but I am a whirlwind in his mind. I show him how to fly. We are excursioning through time. I indicate points of interest. A bramble swings in my path, cherry blossoms in my face. A robin chirps, a wasp *zzzs*. My arms stretch out, stabilizers or gyroscopes. To go right, I lift my right arm, my left arm lengthened behind. I swing slow and graceful, almost horizontal, returning to the vertical or semi-vertical.

Before
that moonlight splatters a tree-lined swamp. I stand alone in balmy
light. Sloping Tacoma on Sunday, when nothing moves except to
change positions. Junior high and Art Institute classes unite and
shadows of each create snowflake patterns that change as the dream
reveals itself: a Mafia prisoner chance art student. We look through
clear layers of air, emerald-green shadows and blue sky. Ed's new and
highly respected. They all watch him from busy loft levels. He squats
over a two-by-twenty-foot emerald page, painting diagonals. Reclining, he's a woman on a modeling platform. Two youths descend. Ed,
descending, becomes male and female: a membrane hole urgent to
be filled, a flesh pole frantic to plunge inside. Behind him, *in front
of my back*, Ed grasps two hard-soft muscles sliding against each other,
sticky and slick. Sun pours through the arched window, onto the
dusty floor, students and janitors leaving. Ed lowers himself over the
woman. *I recline in the yellow dust, open to the body descending.*
The
world appears as I enter it. Through the window, above the treetops,
over the valley, the sun sets in electric blue-purple. Either way I fall
I go up to darkness, to the other self.
Before that the center of a sea-
shell's twisting becomes the crisscross pattern of our mesh bikinis.
My erection is Bob sleeping next to me. I'm amazed by how close
he can be. Strangers sleep on scattered beds in the white room. Dawn
has not yet come, pale gray, mist white. I talk to a blond priest in a
black cassock. He strips to his bikini briefs, exposing a pink body.
I pull them down, face in his crotch, up-down once. Semen erupts,
bright red, hanging in slow swags from the white of everything, his
face serene ecstasy.

Before that the huge white house stood in clear darkness surrounded by wildflowers and bushes darker than the sky. The old woman, a giant witch, kept Bob captive. I circled the house—a magic ax appeared in my hands. I chopped at the roses, trying to get closer. I killed the white picket fence and more roses. I chopped at the door and killed it. I killed the wall and the house crumbled and there she was, emitting light. Bob sat on her shoulder—she had shrunk him. I chopped her toes and feet. I sliced her legs. Meat fell in layers and she laughed and cried. I sliced the only spot of pain on her knee. I chopped her fingers but she caught the ax and pulled me in. It was dark, the covers were dark. I jumped because the witch was in front of me. I woke to her realness. I got up with Bob to see what was happening to me.

Before that I look out the window. In the bay two huge rocks—bright orange deepening to rust—emit jaggedness like mist, clouds boiling above. The rocks come from the clouds and vice versa. The still water is turquoise as the sky. I follow the reflection of turning clouds, a tornado on its side. The tide rushes over turquoise sand. A sea slug with a walrus head, ten or twelve feet long, propels itself by erecting and relaxing. Bob, my friend the poet, swims behind it, past my window.

Before that I'm in a forest with two couples on a sex rendezvous. We're nine years old. I look out the boy's eyes as we walk. Then I'm the girl seeing him ahead. The cobalt sky wears phosphorescent pink-orange. The reds are lush like liquid, purple and twilight blue. The sky brightens as the sun sinks. The clouds deepen, lit from behind. They are lips, dead violet, fangs dripping crimson. The sensation is keen. She slides down unbuttoning my pants, sliding them past my balls, my penis a blossom. Her lips—hot oil spilling over sharp nerves *oh how good* the explosion of pain and pleasure is color. I step into space and drift through flakes of gold.

Before that time begins again with a different measure. *December 17, 1970* I call Information. I try pulling my jeans on but they tangle in the cord so I sit talking in bikini briefs while everything whirls. I'm in a car still talking to the operator. I stop where she tells me to. Between blank spaces I'm naked and walking through overgrown brush. Rain clouds move quickly as the sun sets, off, on, a slow strobe. I find myself on an iron bed in a rotting barn with weeds and grasses growing through the floor. Leslie throws back the covers and flirts with my cock. Above me, she becomes erect. Leslie is a girl with a standing ovation. "Where do you want me to fuck you? Your mouth, your ass, your ear?" "Whoa," I say. We walk up dark stairs to an attic bedroom where young men and women in briefs or nude like Leslie recline on mattresses and the floor. Bob and I sit face forward on a small bus. I touch him every chance I get. Our fingers curl, their tips meet, we are doing a secret thing. We zoom with incredible speed over hills and valleys as lightning flashes and rain pours but at the same time all this motion is solitude. We park on a hill overlooking a barren plain, a panorama open in all directions. The sky is blue with white puffy clouds in the distance, the air is powdery and soft. I step down and shove off. I float a stride slowing through the air, landing on my other foot, shoving off and floating a stride for miles gliding long and slow. The light is from nowhere. I spread my arms to catch the wind as I swing upward.

Acknowledgments

ABOUT ED was written over the course of decades. I am deeply grateful to friends who have helped me along the way as readers. You are too many to name, because the list includes almost every friend I have. Likewise, my apologies if I have neglected to include a journal or book in the list below.

"About Ed." *The Paris Review* 240 (Summer 2022).
"Announcement" (an early version of "Middle Child"). In *Children, Youth & City*. Edited by Molly Hankwitz. San Francisco: Lure Art Books, 1993.
"Bisexual Pussy Boy." In *Between Men*. Edited by Richard Canning. New York: Carroll & Graff Publishers, 2007.
"A Dream Journal of the HIV/AIDS Crisis." *Frieze* 210 (April 14, 2020).
"Ed and the Movies." *Harrington Gay Men's Fiction Quarterly* 1, no. 1 (1999).
"Ed and the Movies." In *Pathetic Literature*. Edited by Eileen Myles. New York: Grove Press, 2022.
"Ed and the Movies" and "The Moon Is Brighter Than the Sun." *The Bella Donna Elders Series* no. 2 (2008).
"Ed's Dreams." *Three Fold* 3 (Summer 2021).

"Ed's First Sexual Experience," In *Sluts*. Edited by Michelle Tea, Los Angeles: Dopamine/Semiotext(e), 2023.

"Ed's First Sexual Experience." *The Swans Rag* 2 (2010).

"Ed's Tomb." In *Communal Nude: Collected Essays* (South Pasadena, CA: Semiotex(e), 2016).

"Everyman." In *Men on Men 4*. Edited by George Stambolian. New York: New American Library, 1992.

"A False Step." In *Flesh and the Word 4*. Edited by Michael Lowenthal. New York: Plume, 1997.

"A False Step." *Oberon* 3 (2017).

"La femme et le pantin (1935)." *Vacarme* no. 52 (Summer 2010).

"Final Nest" (an early version of "Ed's Tomb"). *Nest: A Quarterly of Interiors* no. 4 (Spring 1999).

"Nonie in Excelsis." *Your Impossible Voice* 27 (Fall 2022).

"The Opening of Center for the Arts" (an early version of "Ed's Tomb"). In *In Out of the Cold*. San Francisco: Center for the Arts at Yerba Buena Gardens, 1993.

"SECA 2012: Robert Glück on the Neptune Society Columbarium." *Openspace* (blog). San Francisco Museum of Modern Art, 2012.

ROBERT GLÜCK is a poet, fiction writer, critic, and editor. In the late 1970s, he and Bruce Boone founded New Narrative, a literary movement of self-reflexive storytelling that combines essay, lyric, and autobiography in one work. Glück is the author of the story collections *Elements* and *Denny Smith*; the novels *Jack the Modernist*, *Margery Kempe*, and *About Ed*; and a volume of collected essays, *Communal Nude*. His books of poetry include *La Fontaine* with Bruce Boone, *Reader*, *In Commemoration of the Visit* with Kathleen Fraser, and *I, Boombox*. He made a film, *Aliengnosis*, with Dean Smith; an artist book, *Parables*, with Jose Angel Toirac and Meira Marrero Díaz; and provided the preface for *Between Life and Death*, a book of paintings by Frank Moore. With Camille Roy, Mary Berger, and Gail Scott, he edited the anthology *Biting the Error: Writers Explore Narrative*. Glück was a co-director of Small Press Traffic and an associate editor at Lapis Press. He served as the director of the Poetry Center at San Francisco State University, where he is an emeritus professor. Glück is a potter as well as a writer, and has shown his ceramics in the United States and Europe. He lives "high on a hill" in San Francisco.